THE
HONEYMOON

BOOKS BY RONA HALSALL

Keep You Safe
Love You Gone

THE HONEYMOON

RONA HALSALL

bookouture

Published by Bookouture in 2019

An imprint of StoryFire Ltd.

Carmelite House
50 Victoria Embankment
London EC4Y 0DZ

www.bookouture.com

Copyright © Rona Halsall, 2019

Rona Halsall has asserted her right to be identified
as the author of this work.

All rights reserved. No part of this publication may be reproduced,
stored in any retrieval system, or transmitted, in any form or by
any means, electronic, mechanical, photocopying, recording or
otherwise, without the prior written permission of the publishers.

ISBN: 978-1-78681-951-2
eBook ISBN: 978-1-78681-950-5

This book is a work of fiction. Names, characters, businesses,
organizations, places and events other than those clearly in the
public domain, are either the product of the author's imagination
or are used fictitiously. Any resemblance to actual persons, living or
dead, events or locales is entirely coincidental.

For my daughter, Amy – a tiger dressed as a kitten.

CHAPTER ONE

Now

Dan's hand clasped Chloe's a little harder as they hurried through the departure terminal at Gatwick Airport. It had been a mad rush after their wedding reception: saying goodbye to their guests, getting changed, making sure all the arrangements were in place for the care of Chloe's gran while she was away. Even now, as she trotted to keep up with Dan's enormous strides, she was scanning her to-do list in her mind, making sure she would be able to close the door on her responsibilities in Brighton and relax while they were away. Thank goodness she didn't need to concentrate on where they were going, which signs they were following, whether they had their passports and boarding passes – Dan had taken charge of travel arrangements, and how nice was that? He'd even sent her off to buy a new book and some magazines for the flight while he checked in their suitcase.

Someone looking after me for a change.

She smiled.

My husband.

Those two words had a magic effect, expanding her smile so wide it made her cheeks ache. She looked across at him, at the set of his jaw, his serious frown, perspiration beading on his brow. He'd shaved off his bushy black beard for the wedding and he looked so different, it was like being married to a new man. A particularly handsome man at that, with his hair now neatly trimmed at the sides and combed back from his face, in a style favoured by South American footballers. Stylish and suave. She wondered how long it would stay like that, thought she would enjoy messing it up later when they were finally alone in their romantic little beach hut. Just the idea of it sent a thrill sparking through her.

He caught her staring at him and his caramel-brown eyes crinkled at the corners, his lopsided smile more visible now without his beard and cuter than ever. She could feel her insides melting, couldn't wait for their honeymoon to start. She squeezed his hand and grinned at him, giddy with excitement.

'I really didn't think about this too well,' he said. His face settled back into an anxious frown as he checked his watch while they hurried onwards down interminable corridors. 'Should have factored in the traffic getting away from the restaurant. My God, it was mad, wasn't it?'

'Well, you can't anticipate accidents, can you? At least the taxi driver knew a different way round all the mayhem. And we're here, aren't we?'

Chloe's heart swelled with love for him, and she wondered how long it would take to get used to being looked after, having someone else to share the stress and pressures of life. After all those years dedicated to caring for other people, this was the start of something new. Something better.

He'd insisted that he sort out the honeymoon, wouldn't let her get involved – and given that he was paying for it, she had no choice but to give him full control. She'd been insistent on the destination, though, as it had been a dream of hers for a very long time: the Maldives.

The hotel he'd booked was the most perfect place: small but exclusive, right next to a white sandy beach lined with palm trees, a turquoise sea lapping at the shore, hammocks strung between the palm trees. Each guest had their own little bungalow, discreetly positioned to give them privacy. All-inclusive and nothing to do all day but enjoy the scenery. And each other. Yes, she was looking forward to that bit. At last her life had started to go in the right direction. And about time too. At the age of thirty, she'd worried that she was stuck in a rut so deep that she'd be unable to claw her way out of it.

He was getting ahead of her now, pulling at her hand, and she had to jog to keep up. Dan had the longest legs she'd ever seen on a man, and she'd seen quite a few in her job as a physiotherapist. He was also one of the biggest men she'd ever encountered, at six feet six, towering above her not-insignificant five feet nine inches. She caught sight of their reflection in the wall of glass that edged the concourse and started to giggle.

'What?' He turned and grinned.

'I feel like a little girl being dragged along by my dad. Do we have to go quite this fast? I'm getting a stitch.'

'Yes, we do, if we're going to get to the gate in time. And less of the "dad" if you don't mind.' His voice was mock stern, hiding a laugh. 'That's no way to talk to your husband, is it?'

Husband. There it was again. That word. She'd acquired a husband. Her stomach fizzed and not just with the glass of bubbly she'd consumed. If only she could bottle this feeling and keep it forever. She caught her reflection in the glass again, her face flushed and glowing. Yes, she was positively radiating happiness, visible in her posture, her expression, the spring in her step. Her hair shone like a new coin, the bronze-to-gold colouring working so much better than she'd thought it might. It had been her wedding present to herself – a spa day and full makeover, including hair and nails – so that she was buffed, plucked and preened to perfection for her man. She would have to admit, after years of settling for a nondescript ponytail and little in the way of make-up, this gorgeous woman in her reflection still came as a surprise to her. Yes, getting married had a lot to recommend it.

He slowed a little so she could speed-walk rather than jog.

'Are we really in that much of a hurry?' She glanced up at one of the electronic boards displaying flight times and tried to pull him to a halt. 'Why don't we just check? It may be delayed anyway.'

He shook his head, pulled her forwards. 'I've already checked and we're cutting it fine.' He started to speed up again. 'Come on, Mrs Marsden, better get a move on.'

Mrs Marsden. Didn't that sound properly grown-up? She belonged to somebody. She was someone's wife. This man loved her so much he'd wanted to marry her and be with her for the rest of his life. *Isn't that the most amazing thing?*

Until this point in her life, relationships had never worked out how Chloe had imagined they would. But she wasn't a quitter, didn't expect perfection and she'd doggedly worked towards her aim, giving her former boyfriends plenty of time to get their heads round the idea of settling down. Because that was all she'd wanted – a husband and a family.

When she was younger, she'd loved being part of a family, and now that hers was all but gone, she missed that sense of belonging, the noisy messiness of family life. She wanted it back more than anything in the world, but the only way that was going to happen now was if she made her own family. *Obviously, I'll still work*, she thought as she jogged beside her husband, her mind busy planning her future, not taking any notice of her surroundings. *Maybe just keep up the voluntary work at the hospice while the children are little.*

Yes, that had been her dream, but finding a man who wanted the same thing had proved near impossible. After a few disasters, she had finally settled with her long-term boyfriend, Spencer… until he lost his job and seemed reluctant to get another. While she was looking after the flat, the housework and the finances, he was off enjoying other things – including, she found out later, dubious substances, lots of alcohol and betting machines. When he started stealing from her purse, she had to accept the relationship was over and threw him out. He wasn't well pleased, and she'd had to move to a new apartment and change all her social media accounts and her phone number before she finally got rid of him. It had been an exhausting and humiliating process that she hadn't wanted to repeat in a hurry.

Chloe had realised she was doing something wrong and decided to have a time out from relationships for a while to work out exactly what it was. Two years later, she still had no appetite for dating. Then Dan had walked into her life.

Now he stopped and joined the end of a queue of people who were filing through a boarding gate, pulling her alongside him and circling her with a protective arm while he kissed the top of her head. 'This is us. Phew, just in time.'

Chloe wrapped her arms around his waist, enjoying the heat of him, the musky smell, as she pressed her cheek against his chest. His heart was thudding, a slow but solid beat, which was probably quite quick for him, given that he had played rugby for years and was as fit a specimen as Chloe had ever met. She would have to admit to being slightly in awe of him: his bigness, the bulk of his muscles. He was foreign and familiar at the same time, so different from her, but similar in many ways.

Dan pulled their carry-on bag next to him as they inched forwards.

The people ahead of them moved through the gate, and that's when she saw the sign giving details of the flight number and destination.

Menorca?

She read it again and frowned, her heart giving a little skip of panic. *Wait a minute! That's a Spanish island. Nowhere close to the Maldives.*

She tugged at Dan's shirt. 'Dan, we're in the wrong place. This is for Menorca.'

Ignoring her, he grasped her hand and pulled her forwards, smiling at the hostess on the gate while he handed over the passports and paperwork.

Chloe tried to pull away, but he held her tight, his arm clamped round her, and the hostess waved them through. For the first time, she understood the strength of him, and a new emotion stirred in her belly, one that made her feel queasy.

'Menorca?' She turned to him, her voice a harsh whisper. 'We're going to the Maldives. That's where we've booked. What are you doing?' People were turning to look, and she lowered her voice, her cheeks burning. 'What's going on?'

He smiled at her, but his eyes held a determined glint. 'I'll tell you on the plane. A little change of plan.' He squeezed her hand, his voice laced with forced excitement. 'Wait till you see where we're going. You'll love it. Honestly, you'll have to trust me.'

Trust him?

Rather than calming her, his words had the opposite effect, and her mind started working faster, wondering what was going on, what was really happening. Why on earth would he change their holiday destination when he knew what this honeymoon meant to her? They'd had long conversations about it when she'd opened up about past relationships, the disappointments, the longing to be special to somebody. And the fact that Dan had been keen to organise the perfect honeymoon for her had demonstrated that he'd understood. But did this last-minute change of plans, without any discussion with her whatsoever, mean she'd got him all wrong?

The thought made her shudder and she refused to consider the question further.

Chloe had been brought up to never make a scene in public. It was something her mother and gran were both very keen on. Theirs was a family of things unsaid and silence being a virtue. An 'if you can't say anything nice, don't say anything' sort of philosophy. So ingrained was this behaviour that she clamped her mouth shut for fear that her anger would come bursting out and she'd create a shameful scene in front of a planeload of people. *This is not the time to discuss changed travel arrangements or shattered dreams*, she told herself while her jaw worked backwards and forwards, her teeth grinding.

Later, she would realise that she should have refused to board the plane until she'd had an explanation.

Much later, she would dream of going back to that point in time and making a different decision. One that would have saved her from what was to come.

CHAPTER TWO

Two months ago

Chloe eased out her back and did some stretches against the wall of the office, giving herself a few moments before she called in her next patient. It was four o'clock in the afternoon and she'd been on her feet all day, kneading and pulling and pushing and lifting and demonstrating a whole myriad of different exercises for her patients. They fell into two camps in general: there were those with chronic problems, mostly elderly, who were basically wearing out and needed help to keep going; and then there were the acute patients, who'd had accidents or were recovering from operations. She had her regulars, but the acute patients were usually only with her for a few weeks until they were well on the way to recovery. Some were sent down from A & E, some from orthopaedics and some from the wards before they were discharged. A constant stream of battered and creaking humanity, which made every day interesting, the workload unpredictable and not without its challenges.

She took a sip of her lukewarm tea and went out into the waiting room, which should have been almost empty by now but was still half-full. That's when she saw him, leaning against the wall, wearing long shorts and a T-shirt that stretched tight across his chest. Shaggy black hair fell over his forehead and ears. She did a double-take. Their eyes met and something weird happened that she couldn't explain. Heat flashed up her neck and into her cheeks, making her break away from his gaze and look instead at the piece of paper in her hand: a referral from orthopaedics. *Is he my patient?* The idea was exhilarating and horrifying in equal measure, but when she read the name of her next client, she felt a little disappointed. It wasn't him.

'Alma Watson, please!'

She looked around, unable to see a female patient anywhere, but the man responded to her call, pushed himself off the wall and grinned at her, his teeth very white against the black of his beard.

'That's us.'

Once he'd moved, Chloe noticed the wheelchair that had been hidden by the bulk of his body, saw the sliver of a woman sitting in it, her long black hair striped with grey, and large, deep-set eyes. Exotic and beautiful, she gave Chloe a warm smile. *Mother and son*, Chloe thought, judging by the eyes and the shape of the face. *How on earth did this tiny woman produce such a great big chunk of a man?*

Chloe was endlessly curious about her patients and how the human body could reproduce in such an infinite array of variations. Nobody was the same as anybody else and that was a challenge she enjoyed. Each case was a new puzzle to solve, a new solution required to help a person get better, or ease their pain, or give them a wider range of movement. She could honestly say she loved her job, and after the wrongs of her past, it gave her comfort to be able to ease people's suffering and improve their lives.

The man wheeled Alma into Chloe's office for an initial consultation, to establish the exact nature of her problems and her treatment needs before they went into the exercise room to sort out a programme of activities. Chloe smiled at them both and cleared her throat, focusing her gaze on Alma. She felt unpleasantly hot in the presence of this man who, she knew without looking at him, was still staring at her. 'So, I'm Chloe and I'll be looking after you while we get you sorted out.'

The man stepped forwards and held out his shovel of a hand. 'I'm Dan. Alma's son.' Chloe looked up and smiled at him while she shook his hand, which was the size of both of hers put together. His clasp was warm and gentle, not overtly alpha male or sweaty. Just perfect. She couldn't look at him, didn't dare catch his gaze again. She gave herself a mental shake, told herself there was work to be done and she needed to concentrate on her patient.

'Okay, Alma, how can I help you?'

Alma laughed and leant forwards, flapping a hand. 'Well, I did a really stupid thing. I was cleaning the windows in my bedroom, stood on the windowsill I was, so I could reach the top. The doorbell rang and I'd just caught a glimpse of the postman walking up the drive. So, I went to go and answer the door.' Her eyes widened. 'Stepped backwards, didn't I? Completely forgot I was three feet off the ground.' She shook her head, her mouth twisted in a rueful smile. 'Anyway, I managed to land all funny and hit the dressing table on my way down. Broke my right ankle and tore all the ligaments in my shoulder.'

Chloe winced. 'Nasty.'

'You're telling me. Bruises all up my arm. My God, it hurt. And the worst thing was I didn't have my phone on me, so I couldn't call for help. Luckily, I've got a landline extension in my bedroom and I managed to drag myself across the floor and ring an ambulance.'

Chloe nodded as Alma was giving the details, mentally assessing her work. The shoulder would need stretches and strengthening, and the ankle would need to be mobilised. Yes, it was going to take a few weeks to sort this lady out. She wondered if Dan would always come with her, thinking that would be something to look forward to, then reminded herself about her pledge to stay away from relationships. *Get on with your work!*

'Okay, Alma, can I have a little look at your ankle, then? How long ago was this?' Chloe took Alma's foot and gently felt around the joint, assessing the injury.

Alma winced.

'Sorry. Still tender?'

'Six weeks since I did it. I've just had the plaster off today. They've given me one of those boot things to wear as well, but they want me to do exercises to get some strength back in the muscles.'

'Yes, I can see we've got a bit of work to do.' Chloe stood and walked towards the office door, pulling it open to let Alma through. 'Right, let's go to the gym, shall we, and see what you can manage? It's just an initial assessment today, then once we've got a starting point, we can work out an exercise programme, okay?'

'Dan will be able to help, won't you, love?' Alma looked up at her son. 'He used to play a lot of rugby, didn't you? Had all sorts of injuries.'

Chloe could hear the pride in Alma's voice, and when she glanced at Dan, their eyes met again. Her stomach gave a peculiar lurch, the office suddenly claustrophobic. She was glad to move into the exercise room where she led them to a bay containing a narrow treatment bed and a range of equipment used for stretching and building muscles.

'This way, Alma. If you could just get up on the bed...' She was about to go round and support Alma while she got out of her wheelchair, but Dan was there before her, lifting his mother like she weighed no more than a bag of sugar and placing her carefully on the treatment table.

'There you go, Mum.'

Alma patted him on the arm. 'Thanks, son.'

Something in that show of strength, that primitive display of masculinity, made Chloe's legs feel a little weak. She started to massage Alma's foot and ankle, warming all the muscles, feeling for damage in tendons and ligaments, which could be harder to heal than bones. 'So, how are you managing at home, Alma?'

'Oh, well, Dan's looking after me. Honestly, I couldn't have managed without him.'

Chloe glanced up to find Dan was still gazing at her. She swallowed and turned back to her massage. 'Oh, that's good. Must have been hard with your ankle and arm out of action.'

'I'm not going to lie, it has been a bit of a struggle, but Dan's been marvellous. Can you believe he gave up his job to come home and take care of me?'

Chloe hid a smile. *What a lovely thing to do. Will I ever have a son who will do that for me?* she wondered. *Oh God, I hope so.*

Alma glowed with pride when she talked about Dan. How wonderful to feel an emotion like that.

'Couldn't leave you on your own, Mum, now could I?' Dan said, his voice like molten chocolate, all smooth and deep. The sort of voice used for voiceovers, one that you'd never get tired of listening to. 'Anyway, it was end of term, so the timing was perfect.'

'Oh, you're a teacher?' Chloe put the ankle down and stood up, Dan's presence seeming bigger in the confines of the curtained cubicle. She could feel herself blushing, sure that his eyes were following her every move.

'I trained as an infant teacher, but I did languages at uni before I did my teacher training. I've been working in Spain for the last few years, teaching English as a foreign language.'

'Oh, nice. So, this is just a short-term thing, then?' She caught his eye and found she couldn't look away, her insides melting. It was the strangest and most wonderful sensation.

Then he smiled, and she melted a little more. 'That depends.'

Chloe swallowed and told herself to get a grip. This was so unprofessional, flirting with a guy instead of looking after her patient. She ran her tongue round dry lips, her legs all shaky for reasons that she didn't want to consider.

'Right, I'll um… just go and get a walking frame and we can see how you manage, okay?'

She left the cubicle, fanning her hot face with her hand, glad to have a few minutes to compose herself. *You're being ridiculous!*

Then she smiled as she chose a suitable piece of equipment. *Wow, though. Bloody wow.* She straightened her face and returned to the cubicle, keeping her eyes on her patient.

'Okay, Alma, now that all your muscles are warmed up, let's see if you can manage a few steps.'

Alma shuffled off the bed and gamely tried to walk.

Dan beamed at his mother. 'You're doing great, Mum. Really great. Isn't she, Chloe?'

He said my name.

And he'd said it so slowly, with such care, like it was something precious. He caught her eye again and she wondered if there really was something in the concept of love at first sight. Her heart seemed to think so, the way it was pounding in her chest, her body hot, her hands itching to touch him.

For the rest of the session, she functioned on autopilot, putting Alma through her paces and working out an exercise plan, which she jotted down as they went along; meanwhile, her mind planned her wedding, chose her honeymoon destination and named their three children.

'Right, Alma, I think we'll call it a day for now. Better to not do too much too soon. You can take the walker and practise using that. And don't forget the shoulder exercises using the rubber bands.' She showed her the list. 'I've made a note of everything here, but if you have any problems, this is my number – please don't hesitate to give me a ring, okay? Just remember, it's going to feel a little sore for a while, but don't let that stop you doing things.'

Alma gave her a grateful smile. 'Thank you, Chloe. I feel better now I know I can put weight on it. No pain, no gain – that's right, isn't it?'

Chloe laughed. 'Unfortunately, yes. It's bound to hurt a bit, and not all pain is bad. Just don't push it too much. Let's make an appointment for next week, shall we? I'll just go and get my diary.'

She walked into her office and was aware of Dan following her. She turned, and he stood in the doorway, almost filling the space. Her heart flipped.

'I was just wondering if…' He stopped and jammed his hands in his pockets. She noticed he was blushing and hid a smile, silently egging him on. *Do it, go on, do it, please!* He took a step towards her and she picked up her diary, held it to her chest. 'I was wondering if you fancied dinner later? If you're free, that is.' His words rushed out, like a train coming out of a tunnel. 'Or another day. It doesn't matter. You know, just some time.' He chewed his bottom lip, gazing at her.

Oh my days, he's bloody gorgeous.

Her face relaxed into the biggest smile, her heart leaping for joy. 'That would be lovely. Yes, dinner tonight. Lovely.'

'Can I pick you up? What time?'

He wants to pick me up! How wonderful. Nobody else had ever bothered with that. It was all 'meet you at such and such a place' and leaving her to make her own way home. *A gentleman!* Excitement flooded her veins, whooshed in her ears, and she had to lean against the desk for support.

'How about seven?' she said, trying to sound casual, wondering if she'd managed to hide her eagerness. 'If you give me your number, I'll send you the address?' She looked away, unable to handle the intensity of his gaze. 'Now, I better get your mum booked in.'

She walked out of the office, Dan trailing in her wake, and once they'd sorted out a new appointment, she watched them disappear through the double doors, out of the department.

That's when she noticed the man behind her. He was standing in the corridor and she was very aware that she'd taken way too much time with Alma. It was almost five o'clock and her heart sank when she realised she still had one more person to see. She sighed. It was going to be an almighty rush now to get finished and ready for her date with Dan.

She pasted a smile on her face. 'I'm sorry to have kept you. I'm Chloe Black, one of the physios. Do you have an appointment?' She hoped that he'd say it was with one of her colleagues, although there didn't seem to be anyone else around. It was possible they had finished for the day, given the time, which meant she'd have to deal with this man herself.

His mouth twitched and he looked a bit distracted, glancing down the corridor, a frown creasing his forehead into waves. *Oh dear*, she thought, *he's angry I've kept him waiting.* But before she could apologise again, he started to speak.

'No, I haven't got an appointment. A & E sent me down.' He looked at his watch and grimaced, clearly annoyed. 'Thing is, I have to go. Got a bus to catch.'

Before she could respond and suggest an appointment date, he hurried off down the corridor, his gait marked by a pronounced limp, leaving her feeling bad for running out of time to treat him. All because she was flirting with a client's son. She cringed, annoyed with herself. Then a horrible thought struck her: *Oh God. Maybe he's going to complain!* He must have seen her talking to Dan, maybe even overheard them arranging a date. *That's going to be a telling off, for sure.* She knew time-keeping was a weak area of her work, and she'd experienced several rebukes in recent weeks about not keeping to her schedule.

She worried about it all the way home, berating herself for being so unprofessional. *Stop with the guilt trips,* she told herself as she turned up her road and speed-walked towards her flat. *Physios are always running late, it's the nature of the job,* although she would have to acknowledge that it happened to her way more than it did to her colleagues.

Her thoughts continued to snip at her, making her twitchy and anxious, feelings she was so familiar with, they'd become part of who she was. There was always something she could find to feed her guilt, always something in her day to make her feel bad, make her chastise herself with a whole bundle of should-haves and why-didn't-Is. It was a habit so ingrained now, after nine years of practice, that she knew it was unlikely to change. She deserved to feel guilty, didn't she? Deserved that constant unease, the tightness in her chest, the nagging thoughts, reminding her of the past. Of what she'd done.

A heaviness settled on her shoulders as she hurried down the steps and let herself into her flat. Once she'd had a quick coffee, she went round to sort out her gran's tea before dashing back home with very little time to get herself ready. She'd almost convinced herself not to bother and had only managed to pull on a clean pair of jeans and a jumper – not got round to make-up or sorting out her hair – when the doorbell startled her. *Christ, he's early!* That was it, she was in no shape for a date, she'd have to send him away. She opened the door, all hot and flustered, but he spoke before she could get her words organised.

'Oh, you look beautiful,' he said, and she knew from the expression on his face, the look in his eyes, that he meant every word.

That was the moment she fell in love, something she had no control over, something that absorbed her into a chain of events that would change her life forever.

CHAPTER THREE

Now

'How could you do this without telling me?' The anger finally burst out of Chloe in a harsh whisper once they had taken off and were at cruising altitude. 'The Maldives, that's what we booked. You showed me the hotel and everything. How can we be on a plane to Menorca?'

Dan took her hand and carefully interlaced his fingers with hers. She looked down and saw their wedding rings side by side, glowing with the golden promise of a new future. It made her take a breath before she said something she might regret. It couldn't be going wrong. Not yet. Not even a day into married life. But what on earth was going on?

He sighed, and when he spoke, his voice was gentle, patient. 'Look, I know you had your heart set on the Maldives, and I know we paid a deposit and it looked great. But just last week I heard that there'd been a spate of crimes against tourists in that area and it sort of spooked me. So, I did a bit more research and apparently the place isn't as idyllic as it looks.'

Chloe regarded him, eyes narrowed. *Is he telling the truth?* He wasn't looking at her but was stroking the back of her hand with his thumb. A strangely erotic action that was definitely distracting.

'Show me,' she said, getting her iPad out of her bag before remembering that they were on a plane and internet access was not readily available.

He frowned at her. 'What, you think I'm making it up?'

She gazed at him for a moment while she thought. *Do I?* She'd never had him down as a liar, always considered him to be completely honest. Could she have misread him so badly? *Does he look like he's lying?* Her eyes flickered over his face, studying his expression, searching for little tells that would give him away, but she couldn't see any. All she saw was the beseeching look in his eyes. Her resolve wavered.

'And the weather in September can be really iffy,' he continued. 'Seemed a lot of expense to sit in the rain, and I want our honeymoon to be perfect.' He squeezed her hand to emphasise his point.

She glared at him, still unsure. 'And Menorca is going to be better?'

He nodded. 'I found the most perfect place. I wanted it to be a surprise, but we're staying in a villa outside a little village with a big sheltered bay and shallow water perfect for swimming and snorkelling. We can go kayaking, there's a nature reserve, we can go on a ferry to a little island with lots of private coves.'

His eyes gleamed with hope. She looked away. It was like arguing with a puppy and she was struggling to keep her thoughts on track. But apart from the fact that she'd never yearned to go to Menorca, there was an important point to be made. If she didn't make it now, then she was setting herself up to be a doormat, and that was something she was determined not to be. Not if her future was to be different from her past.

She took a deep breath. 'The point is… it wasn't your decision to make. We're a team now, a partnership. And ever since I was little, I've wanted to go to the Maldives for my honeymoon.' She sounded like her ten-year-old self, watching a holiday show and deciding that's what was going to happen. That would be her fairytale marriage. *Is that what I'm unhappy about? A stupid childhood dream? Or is it something else?*

He leant across and stroked her face with the back of his fingers. 'Don't be cross with me, babe. Please don't be cross. I thought I was doing the right thing. I didn't want you to be frightened of being robbed or mugged or something. Not on our honeymoon.' His voice was hypnotic, his words smoothing away her anger. 'I don't want anything to bother us and I thought this place I found would be better.'

She started to relent, telling herself she was being petulant. *Who cares where we're going? What matters is that this man is my husband.* She looked into his eyes and believed he was telling the truth; in a way, she could understand his reasoning. *He's just being protective. Which is nice, isn't it?* This was about him wanting to look after her, and more to the point, if she couldn't trust her husband less than a day into their marriage, then she was in trouble.

She tried a smile, but it faded as disappointment pulled it from her lips. She looked down at her hands, at their wedding rings, the symbol of their union. *Who am I trying to kid?* At the very least, he should have told her his concerns, should have let her play a part in any decision.

'I'm sorry I got it wrong.' He picked up her hand and kissed it. 'Forgive me?' He gave her that puppy-dog look again, and her iciness melted. She didn't want to argue, didn't want to sulk. What she wanted was to enjoy the fact that she'd just got married to a lovely bloke who had her best interests at heart. She smiled at him. *I need to cut him a bit of slack*, she decided. *Give him the benefit of the doubt.*

'It's okay,' she said, trying to sound like she meant it. 'Just a bit of a shock. You know how much I loved that place we booked. The idea of those white beaches and the little huts on stilts. And the colour of the ocean. I've always wanted to swim in water like that.'

'I'll make it up to you. And I promise, we'll go another year, when it's the dry season.' He leant over and kissed her. The most gentle, loving kiss, and she decided that maybe where they went didn't matter. It was who she was with that was important.

Chloe had always been good at forgiving and forgetting. She had a habit of blowing up, saying her piece and then it was over. But this time, it was a struggle to let go of such a cherished dream. Dismissed by Dan for practical reasons, she was sure, but she had an emotional attachment to that dream. It meant something to her, and now it would never happen, because she was only going to have one honeymoon. And it was going to be spent in bloody Menorca, which was a bit more humdrum than she'd hoped for. Images of a modern resort lined with rabbit hutch apartments, funny-shaped pools and beaches littered with row upon row of sunloungers filled her mind. She bit her lip. No matter what she told herself, it all felt a bit ordinary, when she'd hoped for something special.

Dan leant over and kissed her again, his embrace so tender, the warmth of his fingers on her flesh radiating desire through her body. She had no control over the effect he had on her and she felt herself respond. A primitive urge stirred in her belly and she kissed him harder.

'Get a room!' someone shouted from across the aisle, amidst raucous laughter, and they pulled apart, her cheeks burning.

Dan leant his head against hers and whispered, 'I'm sorry if you're disappointed, really I am, but I think you'll love this place we're going to. It's a little gem, and a few years ago, the *Daily Telegraph* listed it as one of the best unsung beach holiday resorts in Europe. So, it can't be that bad, can it?'

A tangle of emotions clogged her throat, preventing her from responding.

He picked up his phone. 'I downloaded some pictures. Let me show you, then you might feel better about it.' A few taps and swipes later and they were looking at images of a little fishing village, Es Grau, all whitewashed buildings with a handful of bars and restaurants, nestled on the edge of a large bay. Behind it was pine woodland and a lake, part of a large nature reserve that stretched down to the capital city of Mahón, which, according to Dan, was only six miles away. Rocky headlands curved out from the beach into the sea, and there was Colom Island, sitting like a stopper in the mouth of the bay.

Curiosity got the better of her, and in spite of herself, she started to relax. It wasn't as bad as she'd imagined. In fact, it really did look quite lovely and unspoilt. Not a hotel in sight, or sunbeds, just a few lines of boats bobbing in the natural harbour created by the bay.

'And this is where we'll be staying.' An image of a rustic villa popped up on the screen, with a large patio looking out over the sea. 'It's just a bit out of the village. About a mile, I think it said, so it'll be a leisurely stroll in and there's nobody to disturb us. No other holidaymakers for miles and miles.' He showed her a screenshot from the Google Earth satellite map, so she could see the geography of the place. Her smile broadened, and despite her initial disappointment, she felt a little buzz of excitement. It did look like a romantic hideaway. *And isn't that all you need on a honeymoon?*

She turned and looked at him. 'Self-catering? You're not going to make me cook, are you?'

'We can live on bread and cheese. I might even take you out a couple of nights.' He was teasing her now and she leant into him, looking through more of the pictures. The beaches did look quite white and the sea was almost turquoise. It was close enough, wasn't it? A romantic hideaway with nobody to bother them. A little world of their own for a week. Exactly what they needed to cement their marriage.

She snuggled closer, breathing in the scent of him, enjoying the warmth of his body next to hers, listening to his steady breaths. He was going to be with her for the rest of her life. Plenty of time to get to the Maldives. Plenty of time for a whole myriad of adventures.

Once she'd accepted the change of plans, convinced herself that it didn't matter, she felt the exhaustion of the day creep through her body. She fell asleep, only waking when the flight attendant gave them a gentle nudge and asked them to prepare for landing.

It was dusk now and a gorgeous sunset burned orange in the western sky, laying a streamer of molten gold across the surface of the sea, the island below them glowing like a gemstone. Her stomach flipped as the plane banked, and the world tilted, excitement flaring in her chest. *It's going to be wonderful,* she told herself, almost convinced that she didn't mind the change of plans, but a bead of hurt still rolled around her mind.

Once they had finally claimed their luggage, Dan pulled her close, his eyes scanning the bustle of people snaking out of the terminal. Wide awake now, she was starving and imagined a cosy restaurant, or a tapas bar, her mouth watering at the thought. She liked nothing better than to eat out. Given the amount of time she spent preparing meals for her gran, she loved trying dishes she would never make at home.

'What about finding somewhere to eat while we're in town?' she asked, but Dan was hurrying again, making her jog alongside to keep up. He didn't reply until they were outside and he'd opened the door of a waiting taxi.

'Phew, got there first. Sometimes you have to wait ages.' He beckoned for her to get in and then slid in next to her, talking to the taxi driver in Spanish before he addressed her question. 'I thought we could get to the village, have something there.'

Chloe frowned, looking back at the airport. 'We're not hiring a car, then?'

'Plenty of time to do that. Let's just get to the villa, shall we? I don't know about you, but I'm pretty whacked after all that excitement.'

Visions of a leisurely dinner in a romantic restaurant evaporated, but she held her tongue while the taxi navigated out of the capital and into the darkness of the nature reserve that lay between the town and the village. It was bordered on the right by farmland. Olive groves by the looks of things, but on the left, it was all pine woodland, and a black wilderness enveloped them now the sun had gone down.

When they reached the village, Dan had a quick conversation with the driver in Spanish before turning to her. 'I'm just going to grab some food from the shop, then the driver will take us up to the house. I thought a romantic night in would be just the job. Won't be a tick.'

He was gone before she could say anything, leaving her feeling like a child, left in the car while their parent dashed off to do a mysterious job, never told exactly why they couldn't go along too.

Chloe bristled and shuffled in her seat, but she decided that he was a man with a plan and it was probably best to leave him to get on with it. Who knew what goodies he would buy, what meal he planned to prepare. It was all part of his surprise, his desire to please her. *Yes*, she reassured herself. *Nothing to get uptight about.*

It was strange to hear him speak Spanish so fluently and it reminded her how little she knew about her new husband. In fact, whole swathes of his life were still a mystery to her, which should have thrilled her – the idea that there was so much of him to get to know; instead, new worries hatched in her mind, pecking away at all the good things she knew about him and leaving a trail of concern in their wake.

Her heart started to race as all the what-ifs started to make themselves known, all the terrible, horrible possibilities that might come from marrying someone you'd only met two months ago. She could hear herself hyperventilating, started feeling light-headed until her train of thought was broken by the taxi driver, who turned in his seat, concern in his eyes.

'You okay?'

She took a deep breath and forced a smile, nodding because her voice would surely betray her. Instead, she trained her eyes on the shop. She could see Dan at the till, packing things into carrier bags. He was smiling and chatting, and she could see the shop assistant laughing at something he'd said. How could she have even one negative thought about this lovely man? *What's wrong with me?* Well, there was no simple answer to that one. For once in her life, she'd followed her instincts and taken a risk. She had a lifetime to find out all about him, and how exciting would that be? All those little surprises, and she was sure that most of them would be good.

He'd definitely surprised her today, with the way he'd taken control. He'd never shown that side of himself before and, in fact, had tended towards the opposite, letting her make decisions, especially where the wedding was concerned. Today had been quite different, though. Today, her opinion didn't seem to count, and a little knot formed in her stomach, hard and uncomfortable. She reminded herself that he was just trying to make amends for changing the honeymoon without telling her, wanting to let her relax while he looked after her. She settled back in the seat as he walked towards the car. *Yes, that's what's happening.* He was being a gentleman, taking charge of everything so she didn't have to worry.

It was something she had yearned for, wasn't it? Someone to take control so she could have a break. So why had she been on the brink of a panic attack? What was really bothering her?

CHAPTER FOUR

Five weeks ago

Chloe smiled at herself in the mirror as she caught her reflection. *My goodness, what a change.* Her skin was glowing, her eyes sparkling, even her hair looked different. She laughed at herself. *Look at you, you loved-up idiot. Take that stupid grin off your face.* But it was a permanent fixture these days, now that she and Dan were a couple.

To say their relationship was intense would be an understatement. She had never talked to another human being so much in her entire life. Not even her best friends. There was so much to discuss, so much to share, to laugh about. She could say absolutely anything to him without fear of embarrassment, and it felt so liberating she could hardly contain her excitement. It was like she'd been living in black and white and the world had just burst into colour.

Love.

She was definitely in love.

At last she understood what it felt like and knew with certainty that she'd never experienced it before. Her past relationships were nothing more than going through the motions compared to this. Dan was both the same as her and the opposite all rolled into one. His strengths were her weaknesses and vice versa, but they shared the same sense of humour, liked to do the same things. He was an exercise enthusiast, just like her, and in the three weeks they'd been together, they'd been out running, hillwalking, swimming and cycling. They were even considering training for a triathlon – a new challenge for them both and something they could accomplish together.

She checked her watch and jogged round the corner to where her gran lived, aware that she'd have to get a move on if she was going to be back in time for Dan. She let herself in and bounced down the hallway.

'Hi, Gran!'

'I'm in here.'

Chloe popped her head round the lounge door to see her gran in her usual place at the end of the sofa, watching an early evening quiz programme, her knitting needles clacking at a steady rate. She looked up and smiled, her eyes still alert, even if her body was letting her down these days. She had a chronic chest complaint and Chloe came to do physio with her every morning before work, then returned in the evening and sorted out food for the following day. She had it down to an efficient routine, and the freezer was stuffed with meals she would make at the weekend, in batches, when she had more time.

'You off out again tonight?' her gran asked, studying Chloe's new jeans and the floaty top she had bought at lunchtime. She'd never been bothered with clothes in recent years, usually sticking to the stretchy gym clothes she wore for work, but now Dan had come into her life, she'd realised what a drab wardrobe she had and decided it was time to brighten herself up. There was nobody to tell her what to wear anymore – her previous boyfriend had been very particular and had liked to choose her clothes for her; now she had the freedom to create her own style, which felt rather weird. Whatever she wore, Dan seemed to approve, and every time he commented on how gorgeous she looked. That was another thing about him – he always knew what to say to make her feel good about herself.

'We're going to an Ethiopian restaurant tonight.' She watched her gran's frown deepen. 'Never been before so I'm looking forward to it.'

'Very nice,' her gran said, her tone holding a note of disapproval. 'That's every night this week, isn't it? In fact, if I'm not mistaken, you've seen that man every night since you met him.'

Chloe couldn't hide her smile. Her gran made it sound like a bad thing, but it made Chloe sparkle inside to think that, for Dan, being with her was his favourite thing. It had never happened before. With her exes, there had always been nights for the boys, or for footie, or weekends playing golf. Or going off on stag dos. Or times when her man had just needed some time to chill on his own.

'Do you know what, Gran? I think he might be "the one".'

Her gran flicked her a glance and carried on with her knitting. 'The one?' She gave a dismissive *humph*. 'You youngsters. I don't know what's in your heads these days. It's all a load of romantic twaddle. Relationships take work and patience and a great big dollop of forgiveness.'

'Wow, Gran. Sell it, why don't you?' Chloe's lips twisted with annoyance and her patience started to fray. 'I don't know why you can't just be happy for me for once.' She heard her gran tutting and knew she was still intent on punishing her for the past. Goodness knows, Chloe had tried to make amends, but it had never been enough. *You can't make up for someone dying, really, can you?* Especially when it was all her fault. The guilt crept back, tightening the skin on her scalp, stinging her eyes, and she turned for the door before her gran could see. 'I'll just get your tea started. Sorry it's a quick in and out tonight for me. But I'll pop round tomorrow morning and we can have a proper catch-up.'

'Oh no, you don't need to bother yourself tomorrow.' Her gran's reedy voice quivered. 'I'm sure you'd rather be with that boyfriend of yours. I know I'm second best these days.' Chloe took a breath and turned to protest but her gran carried on speaking. 'Anyway, I've got visitors. They're taking me out for the day.'

Chloe frowned, surprised. *Gran never has visitors. Maybe she's making it up?* She knew her gran wasn't always completely honest with her, always looking for a vulnerable spot where she could place a verbal barb. Chloe called her bluff. 'Oh, that's nice. Anyone I know?'

Her gran gazed at her, mouth opening and shutting as though she was working out what to say. 'Lucy and Mark. They're both coming, but I thought it best if we went out on our own. After last time.' Chloe bit her lip. Her gran looked down at her knitting, fiddling with the stitches on her needle, smoothing them into a neat, evenly spaced line. 'I haven't seen them for a while so I'm really looking forward to it. We've got a lot to discuss.'

Lucy and Mark. Chloe's sister and brother. She hadn't seen them for a couple of years and had no wish to bump into them anytime soon. Not after their behaviour last time they'd met.

It had been their gran's eightieth birthday and the three siblings had agreed that the day was about her and they should put their differences aside, for which Chloe was supremely grateful. Lucy had always been bossy, being the eldest, with Chloe in the middle and Mark a couple of years younger. Now that their mother had passed away, Lucy had decided to take on the role of family matriarch, and Mark had made his place in her shadow, always willing to follow her lead and back her up.

Two against one.

Her mind travelled back to their last meeting and she gave an involuntary shudder.

The day had started off better than Chloe could have hoped, and they managed a trip out to the pier without a cross word or a snide comment. Chloe had even thought they could be reconciled, could all be a family again. Unfortunately, after a couple of glasses of wine at dinner that evening, her sister's demeanour changed. She waited until the end of the meal, when their gran had gone to the loo, to say what was really on her mind.

'Don't think we haven't noticed what your game is.' She leant across the table, eyes narrowed.

Mark sat back in his seat and nodded, his hands playing with his napkin on the table.

Chloe tensed and frowned at her sister. 'I'm not sure what you mean, Lucy.'

Lucy nodded towards the toilet. 'When the old girl pops her clogs, that house is worth a mint. We know why you're round there all the time, never leaving her alone.'

Chloe bristled, and her voice got a little louder, shrill with indignation. 'Wait a minute. I'm her carer. She'd struggle without me. In fact, she'd have to pay someone to look after her.'

Lucy nodded, a disbelieving smile on her face. 'Oh, right. She seems pretty capable to me. Very sprightly for her age.'

'Because I look after her.' Chloe tapped her chest. 'I keep her mobile, keep her chest clear and free from infections. That's why she's doing so well.'

'Nothing to do with trying to get her to leave everything to you, then?'

Chloe stood up so quickly, her chair fell backwards. 'Don't be ridiculous! I won't have you saying such horrible things to me.'

Lucy's eyes widened, like she was the injured party. 'Gran says it gets very claustrophobic with you lurking there all the time. I don't think she likes it.'

Chloe glared at her sister.

Lucy glared back. 'I think she'd be better with a *real* carer. Wouldn't be so upsetting.'

Mark piped up then. 'You remind her too much of what happened. We don't think it's good for her. We think you're making her unhappy.' He looked her straight in the eye. 'Maybe it's time to just leave her in peace.'

Lucy nodded, an edge to her voice now that cut through the sounds of the other diners. 'You might as well. She told us today that she can't bring herself to leave you anything in her will after what you did. It's all going to be shared between me and Mark.'

Her words stabbed at Chloe's heart. She wasn't caring for her gran to earn her inheritance. She was trying to make amends. *Why can't they see that?* At this point, Chloe realised that the restaurant had fallen into a hushed silence and several people were looking at them. She watched her gran weave her way back through the tables, her expression making it clear that she knew some sort of ruckus was going on and she wasn't pleased about it.

Chloe's blouse stuck to her skin. She glared at her brother and sister, wondering how they had become so bitter and resentful. But she knew. In her heart, she knew, and a part of her really couldn't blame them.

A waiter appeared at her elbow before she could formulate a fitting response.

'Is everything okay?' the waiter said as he looked between the three of them.

Chloe dug in her handbag, got out her purse and slapped a couple of banknotes on the table. 'That's for my share,' she said, between gritted teeth. 'I know when I'm not wanted. I'll leave you all to it. Then I can't be upsetting you, can I?'

And with that she stormed out of the restaurant, several pairs of eyes following her.

Chloe's eyes dropped to the floor, her cheeks burning, the memory of her last encounter with her siblings almost as mortifying as the actual event. She hurried out of the room, leaving thoughts of her fractured family behind as she focused on getting her gran's food ready. Of course, she hadn't left her gran to cope on her own. She knew she couldn't. And although their relationship could never be described as close, Chloe had felt she did a better job of looking after her than anyone else. Nothing more had been said on the matter, and she hadn't seen her siblings since.

She sighed as she put the pasta on to boil, got the tub of Bolognese sauce out of the fridge and started grating cheese into a bowl. She conjured up images of Dan's smiling face and let thoughts of him drag her out of the fog of despondency that her family always managed to create in her head. But a niggling question persisted. Why were her brother and sister coming? And both at the same time?

They're going to cause trouble for me.

That was her first thought, before she told herself not to be so paranoid, but a feeling of unease persisted. She was being excluded. They had things to discuss. *What are they up to now?*

She left her gran tucking into her meal, a cup of tea by her side, and practically ran home. It felt like she was being released from jail, and in some ways, she supposed meeting Dan had helped her to believe that there was a possibility of a different future. A way to escape her family and her past and be with someone who actually wanted her.

Later that evening, they were in the restaurant eating their meal when Dan's phone pinged with a message.

'I'd better get that. It might be Mum. I'm always nervous about leaving her in case she has a fall.'

Chloe smiled and took a sip of her water. 'Of course, go ahead.' She would have liked a bit of wine, but Dan didn't drink and somehow it didn't feel right to be drinking when he wasn't. On their first date, she'd had a drink before she knew he was teetotal, and it had felt really awkward. She'd decided to make do with sparkling water, and, to be honest, she felt her health had improved now she wasn't drinking. Still, it didn't stop her fancying a glass of wine every now and again. Maybe in time she'd relax about it, but for now she was happy to follow Dan's lead.

She watched him look at the screen, saw his eyes narrow.

'Bad news?' Chloe's pulse quickened. 'Your mum's all right, isn't she?'

He didn't answer for a moment, his lips pressed into a thin line. He looked really angry and the transformation in his face was a shock. She'd never seen him look anything but cheerful. He was that sort of a guy. Nothing seemed to bother him. But clearly, she'd been wrong. Something was definitely bothering him now. He rose from his chair.

'I'm just going to make a call.'

'Yes, yes, that's fine, you go ahead.'

He looked at the door, then back at her. 'Bit noisy in here. I'll go outside. Won't be a minute.'

But he wasn't a minute. He was almost a quarter of an hour, and she was wondering if he was going to come back at all when he finally returned to their table. He looked hot and flustered, not like he'd been stood outside talking on the phone. Unease stirred in her belly. *What on earth has he been doing?*

'I'm so sorry,' he said as he sat down, taking her hand. 'Some sort of prank, I think.'

She squeezed his hand, relieved that he'd come back but concerned by the look in his eyes. 'What's going on?'

'It was a message saying my car was going to be towed away if I didn't pay a fine and move it. But when I got there—' he threw up his hands '—just bloody great scratches all over the bodywork and all the tyres slashed.'

Chloe's hand flew to her mouth. 'Christ! That's horrible. But how did they get your number?'

He shrugged. 'Who knows?'

Chloe frowned, unsure why he was being so philosophical. It was going to cost him hundreds of pounds to put right the damage.

'Shouldn't you call the police? Even if it's just for the insurance?'

He shook his head. 'Oh, I don't think I need to bother them. I don't want to make a fuss. I've had to call out a recovery vehicle. It'll be here soon.' He checked his watch. 'Let me get you a cab, then I'll stay and sort it out.'

Not calling the police seemed a bit of an odd decision to her. Why wouldn't he want them to investigate? Or even just log the crime so his insurance company would pay? *Maybe he isn't insured.* It seemed the only explanation, but out of character. He was the most honest, law-abiding person she'd ever met.

'I'll stay with you. I don't mind,' she said, thinking she wanted to see for herself what had happened. *Maybe it's an excuse. Maybe he was doing something else. Met somebody.* Her mind galloped off along a path she had trodden several times before: always thinking the best of people and then being proved wrong when their deception became painfully clear. Had she made the same mistake again? All she knew was that something felt off and she wanted to get to the bottom of it.

He shook his head. 'No, it's okay. You get off home. I know you've got an early start.'

Chloe opened her mouth to argue, but there was something about his tone which told her not to. She could see a vein pulsing in his neck, could feel the anger radiating from him, and his body language was unmistakable. He wanted to be left alone. He had something to sort out and it was going to happen when she wasn't there.

For the first time since they'd met, he didn't want to have her by his side, and she felt the slap of rejection. She wondered then whether this was the point in their relationship where everything changed, the tipping point from which they wouldn't recover, the slow slide into a break-up. But before her thoughts could gather steam and propel her into the depths of despair, he squeezed her hand. His thumb caressed her knuckles, and when she looked up at him, there was something in his eyes that made her heart flip.

'Oh, Chloe.' He sighed, and she couldn't look away. 'You're the best thing that's ever happened to me, you know that?'

Her lips parted to speak, to tell him she felt the same, but the words gathered in her throat, her heart jumping like a gymnast doing a floor routine. *Did he really just say that?* She couldn't quite trust herself to believe it, didn't want to make an idiot of herself by responding to something she may have made up in her head.

He gave her a sheepish smile. 'I love you. I really do.'

Her eyes prickled with tears, her heart thumping so hard she could feel her body shaking. 'I love you too,' she squeaked before she clamped her mouth shut, chin trembling as she battled to hold in the tears.

He loves me. He loves me. He loves me.

He leant across the table and kissed her tenderly on the lips, a kiss that seeped through her whole body, right the way down to her toes.

He loves me.

He pulled away, and when she gazed at him, she could see the emotion in his eyes. He meant it. He really did.

'My timing is so wrong, isn't it? Honestly, I'm such an idiot.'

She gave him a wobbly smile as a tear snaked down her cheek. 'No, your timing is perfect. Honestly. I thought when you wanted to send me home that you were starting to get tired of me.'

'What? You have no idea how—' His phone rang, and he glanced at the screen. 'Crap! It's the recovery vehicle. I'm so sorry, I'm going to have to answer this.'

'You take it, it's fine. Honestly, it's fine.' She pulled her phone from her bag. 'I'll call a cab.' She flapped a hand in his direction. 'You go and get it sorted.'

He picked up his phone, and when his attention moved from her, she felt an emptiness that she hadn't recognised before. In a few short weeks, he had become a part of her, filled all the gaps that had been making her life less than she'd wanted it to be.

But can you trust him? Is he playing you like all the others?

Her jaw clamped shut and she willed the voice to go away, to stop putting doubts in her head, ruining her perfect moment of happiness.

CHAPTER FIVE

Love.

It's as old as time, an integral part of what it is to be human. It's what we crave from the minute we're born, isn't it?

But it also makes people really, really stupid.

She's an intelligent woman.

She has a degree.

Has been a physiotherapist for nine years now.

But just look at the state of her!

As malleable as a piece of putty.

Life has a habit of throwing up happy coincidences. We meet the people we need to meet to achieve our ambitions.

I take it as a sign that right is on my side. Because, from the looks of things, this is going to be really easy.

CHAPTER SIX

Now

Chloe watched from the back of the taxi as Dan came out of the shop, loaded down with a couple of carrier bags. Her jaw tightened, her body heavy with disappointment. *I am not cooking on my wedding night*, she told herself. *I am not.*

Dan grinned as he got in beside her, heaving the bags onto the floor. 'That should keep us going for a couple of days. And I'll rustle up something tonight.' He grabbed her hand while he leant forwards and spoke in Spanish to the driver, who nodded before turning the car round and heading out of the village.

They drove back the way they had come for a little while before turning off onto a dirt road that wound up into the trees, the darkness forming a solid tunnel around them as the headlights picked out the stony track ahead.

Chloe shivered. She'd never been a fan of forests, not after Lucy and Mark had scared her half to death when she was younger. They'd been on holiday in the New Forest with their parents, and the three of them had gone exploring. She was probably ten at the time and Lucy would have been almost twelve.

'We're playing hide-and-seek,' Lucy had announced after a whispered conversation with eight-year-old Mark. 'And you're it.'

'But it's getting dark,' Chloe had said, nervously glancing around at the lengthening shadows, noticing the gloom that was settling between the trees.

Lucy had been in charge of the adventure, as usual, and they'd scampered down a footpath that led from behind their holiday cottage into the forest. Their mother had warned them to stay close, but this had been forgotten as Lucy led them this way and that until Chloe hadn't a clue where they were. She had no idea how to get back to the cottage and had no desire to be 'it'. 'Mum said to be back before dark. You know she did.'

'God, you're such a wimp, Chloe.' Lucy glared at her, hands on her hips, chin jutting forwards. 'We won't play with you ever again, will we, Mark? You just spoil all the fun.'

'Spoilsport, spoilsport, spoilsport,' Mark sang, pointing his finger at her.

Chloe tried not to cry. Ever since Lucy had started at secondary school, things between them had been different. Before that, they'd been close. All of them. But now Chloe avoided being with Lucy, hurt by the meanness of her constant jibes and the practical jokes, which were never funny when you were the one they were played on.

'I don't want Mum and Dad to worry,' Chloe said.

'Okay, well, let's all have one turn. Then we'll go back.'

Chloe couldn't believe she'd almost won an argument with her sister and nodded. It was the best she could hope for and she knew not to push her luck.

'You stand by this tree then, Chloe. And count to a hundred.'

She shook her head. You could go a long way in a hundred seconds.

'Ten,' she said, stepping gingerly towards the designated counting place. 'Or there won't be time for us all to have a go.'

Lucy gazed at her for a moment, then smiled. 'Okay, count to fifty then.'

Chloe turned her back, intending to count to twenty and no more. Even so, when she opened her eyes, there was no sign of either sibling. She listened, and her ears filled with the sighing of the wind in the trees, the squeaking of branches rubbing together, the sudden flap of wings. Her heart pounded. She ran in a circle, not knowing which way to go, the trees so huge, the gloom so thick in the undergrowth.

A scream rang through the air, shrill and ear-splitting. Her heart nearly jumped out of her chest and she ran in the opposite direction, branches scratching her arms, brambles tugging at her jeans, hidden logs making her stumble until she slipped on a patch of mud and tumbled to the ground. She could feel someone behind her but didn't dare to look, staying curled in a foetal position, hoping she wouldn't be seen.

Night came quickly, then it really was pitch-black, clouds obscuring the moon, and a light drizzle started to fall. The darkness crept into her mind, noises setting off her vivid imagination until she was terrified, her chest so tight with fear, she thought she might die.

Some time later, her father found her, cold and shivering, still curled up where she'd fallen.

Her siblings had received a telling-off for playing a mean trick on her, but that didn't put things right. Thinking about it now, she decided that was probably when their relationship had started to come unstuck, her trust in both of them broken in a way that could never be repaired. They knew she hated the dark, knew she was a scaredy-cat. But it was all good sport to Lucy, and Mark followed her lead. He was too young to know any better, she told herself, but even when he was older, she was always the odd one out, the one they both picked on and the one they always blamed when things went wrong. Their father died in a cycling accident when Chloe was twelve, and that had changed the dynamic again, made Lucy even worse.

Way back in her memories, there were the good old days when she'd had a father, a mother, a brother and a sister, who all loved her, and life felt secure. A tight family unit, when they were all alive and spoke to each other. It seemed like another life and she'd been a different person then, ridiculously carefree with no idea how difficult life could be – how actions had reactions that could chop you down like a felled tree and never let you get back up again.

And sometimes… sometimes you only had yourself to blame.

She sighed as she looked out of the window, the darkness reflecting her face back at her, a face that was clouded with sadness and regret. They were travelling uphill now, going slowly over the potholed ground, the lumps and bumps making the car roll from side to side as if they were out at sea. She felt queasy and willed the journey to end. Gradually, the trees thinned until she was looking out over the bay, at the twinkling lights of the village behind them, the shimmer of moonlight catching the ripples on the surface of the sea, sparkling like a million stars.

'Wow, isn't that something?' Dan said, sounding excited as he leant forwards to take in the view. 'Not far now. Should be just up here.'

Chloe felt overwhelmed by weariness, heavy with disappointment. Yes, it was a nice view, but where were the palm trees, the warm Indian Ocean, the… luxury? That's what was missing. For one special week, she'd wanted to be pampered and cosseted and not have to think about making meals or looking after anyone else. But here she was, on a self-catering honeymoon. She caught her train of thought and pulled it to a halt, desperate to shake off her negative frame of mind.

Life is not a Disney fairy tale. When are you going to understand that?

She chewed her lip, her mind refusing to listen to her pep talk. Life did work out for some people, though. She'd seen the pictures: work colleagues, old friends she still followed on social media. They'd had the fairy-tale wedding, been wined and dined, gone to exotic locations, no expense too great. *Why can't it be like that for me?* It's what he'd promised and then he'd whisked it out from under her, like one of those magic tricks where the cloth is pulled from the table and everything lands back in place. Except she didn't feel she *had* landed back in place. Ever since she'd realised Dan had changed their plans without telling her, something had shifted, putting her mood out of alignment.

He's not the man I thought he was.

There it was, an embryo of worry being fed by a stream of little incidents that she had chosen to ignore at the time. Now they demanded she take notice, and her concerns grew until they filled her head.

You're going to spoil this, she told herself. *This is supposed to be the happiest day of your life. It will be an adventure, staying up here at the top of the cliffs, looking out at that view, nobody interfering.* But another voice in her head answered back, petulant. *Yes, nobody to do the cooking or wash the clothes or change the bed or do the shopping. What sort of honeymoon is that? A cheap one.*

A new thought sidled into her head.

Maybe he's got money problems.

It hadn't occurred to her before, but now she realised it could be the answer. And if it was, she wouldn't feel so bad about the change of plans. It was the idea that he could afford it but had chosen not to treat her that was hurtful. Like she wasn't worth it. But this new explanation got her mind racing.

Has he got debts? Is that what the damage to the car was about?

She started sifting through all the reasons why someone might owe money. *Drugs. Gambling. Chancer. Con man.*

Oh God! What have I got myself into? She glanced at Dan, saw the smile had dropped from his face, replaced by a look of steely determination. The sort of expression that said you were worried, or running away from something. Or hiding from someone.

Her heart thudded in her chest, her hands clammy as the possibilities mounted up, all of them far removed from the man she thought she knew.

Christ, will you get a grip! She wiped her hands on her jeans. *Talk about fanciful. Why are you doing this to yourself?*

She took a deep breath and did her best to recalibrate. Her mind had filled with melodramatic nonsense and she was feeling headachy as the worries grew at an exponential rate. *You're exaggerating everything out of all proportion. This is Dan we're talking about. Lovely, kind, considerate Dan.* She glanced at him, saw that he was chewing a nail. Something she'd never seen him do before.

Definitely something bothering him.

You're going to have to quiz him if you're to get to the bottom of things, she told herself, deciding that's exactly what she'd do once they'd settled in and the time was right. But in the meantime, if this honeymoon was going to be special, she needed to get with the programme, give it a chance.

Look at what's real, not what your bloody imagination is fabricating.

She reached for his hand and was rewarded with the flash of a smile. He leant towards her and kissed her cheek, whispered in her ear, 'Don't worry. I promise you, this is going to be a honeymoon to remember. I promise.'

She leant into him, concentrating on the feel of his body against hers, and a few minutes later, the car pulled to a halt.

The villa was relatively small, but the rooms were of generous proportions. There were two large bedrooms on the first floor, each with an en-suite, and downstairs was completely open-plan. It had been recently renovated, and although from the front it looked like a traditional *finca* – with the curved slates on the roof and small windows, suggesting it might be dark and gloomy – it was a different story once you got inside. It had been gutted and reinvented into a modern holiday home with all the facilities she could have wished for. One wall, facing out to sea, was all glass with folding doors that opened out onto a wide, tiled patio, a low wall surrounding it, planted with flowers that were still blooming, even though it was the middle of September. A large leather suite filled the lounge area, positioned to look out at the view, an abstract patterned rug in red and gold on the tiled floor in front of it. Behind the sofa was the kitchen area, and to the left were a large wooden dining table and chairs.

Dan got straight on with the cooking while Chloe busied herself with putting their clothes away and generally getting to know the place. She found herself humming as she tidied their bits and pieces into the wardrobes and cupboards, put toothbrushes and toiletries in the bathroom. Now this was much better; this place was something special, which meant Dan thought she was too.

With her equilibrium restored, Chloe decided that she had to learn to trust him, not be so suspicious and insecure. Of course he loved her.

'Food's up!' Dan called.

She hurried down the stairs, which ran up from the square entrance hall, not sure if she was hungry at all now, or if the feeling had been and gone hours ago.

The smell of garlic and onions and tomatoes filled the air as she stepped into the kitchen, her smile widening when she saw the large bowl of pasta sitting in the middle of the table, flanked by garlic bread and salad. He'd even lit a candle and dimmed the lights.

'Oh, Dan, this is wonderful,' she said as he pulled out a chair for her and went to sit at the other side of the table.

'Anything for you, my love. Got to keep your strength up.' He winked at her and gave his eyebrows a suggestive wiggle, making her laugh.

'It's a gorgeous place, isn't it?' She started eating, her appetite returned now her worries had proved to be groundless.

'Oh, just wait until the morning when you see the view and we start exploring around the villa. Honestly, it's gobsmacking.'

She stopped eating, her fork halfway to her mouth as a question burst into her mind. 'It's dark, Dan. How would you know?' She wondered then whether he'd been here before, with somebody else maybe. She glared at him, waiting for a reply that was taking an awful long time to appear.

'I've a brilliant imagination,' he said as he helped himself to more pasta. 'And Google Earth.' But his eyes didn't meet hers, and eventually she looked away.

He's been here with someone else. He has. That's why he wouldn't look at her. Her pulse quickened as the question formed on her tongue, spoken before she could stop and think. 'So, this is the first time you've been here, then?'

'To Es Grau?' He concentrated on his food, shovelling great forkfuls into his mouth.

She thought it might be a delaying tactic and stared pointedly at him until he'd finished chewing, making sure he didn't change the conversation.

'No, I was here a few years ago. When I was working in Spain.'

'On your own?' She bit into her garlic bread, tearing at it with her teeth as if she were ripping muscle from bone.

'No, there was a group of us.'

'Oh, a group. Nice.' She put her bread down, the need to talk more urgent than the need to eat. 'Couples, was it? You haven't mentioned a girlfriend. Did you come here with another woman?'

He sighed, his fork rattling in his dish as he let go of it, a hard expression on his face. 'Come on, Chloe. You've had boyfriends that you lived with. Let's not get into this now. I brought you here because it's a fantastic place. We won't be disturbed and can really enjoy just being together. You and me. Husband and wife. Let's concentrate on that, can we?'

He leant back in his chair, and for the first time since she'd met him, she saw a glint of something she didn't like in his eyes. Something that made her want to back down.

'Sorry, Dan. I'm just… well, I'm tired and I do get a bit…' She had to stop as tears stung her eyes, emotions clogging her throat.

His face softened then. 'I know, babe. I know it's been a long day. Let's finish this then have an early night, shall we?'

They ate in silence, Chloe picking at her meal, her appetite deserting her. She'd disappointed him; she could feel it in his silence, in the distance that now stretched between them, leaving her feeling alone and strangely vulnerable.

CHAPTER SEVEN

Four weeks ago

Chloe sang to herself as she massaged her gran's back, thumping it in time to a drumbeat in her head. The massage helped to loosen the phlegm, reduced the chance of infection and was an essential part of their morning routine. Even this wasn't enough to stop the occasional chest infection though, and it was clear that her gran's health was starting to fail, an undeniable fact that preyed on Chloe's mind. When her gran went, she would be completely alone, and that was something she couldn't bear to think about. Floating in this mass of humanity, unattached, nothing and nobody to root her to life. If she was completely honest with herself, being alone was probably the thing she feared most in the world.

'Will you stop that infernal noise?' her gran hissed. 'I can't stand it! If you're going to sing, at least make it something with sensible lyrics. That's just tripe.'

'Sorry, Gran. I didn't even realise I was singing.' She hid a smile and stopped what she was doing. 'Right, if you shuffle over, I'll do the other side.'

Her gran started to move but was hit with a sudden coughing fit that had her struggling to draw breath, her hands grasping at the duvet as if her life depended on it. Chloe's heart leapt in her chest, paralysing her for a moment until she grabbed her gran's inhaler and passed it to her.

She got her gran sitting up and helped her put the inhaler to her mouth, her arm round her bony shoulders to keep her steady. 'Deep breath, Gran. Deep breath. One, two, three, go!' Chloe's heartbeat seemed to fill her whole body. These coughing fits were getting worse, and goodness knows how many times they happened in the day when Chloe was at work. 'I'm going to see if the doctor will come and check you over, Gran. This has happened every morning this week, hasn't it?'

Her gran's breathing started to steady, and she slumped against Chloe, her body shaking. Chloe pulled her close, listening to her breathing as it started to settle and become more regular. 'Let's get you into bed. I don't think you're too well, are you?'

'I'm fine, Chloe. It's my fault. I shouldn't talk while you're doing the slapping thing. That's what it was. I'm fine.'

'Oh, Gran, you're not. You know you're not.'

Her gran sat up, pushing Chloe's arm away. 'Don't you tell me what I am and what I'm not. It's my body, isn't it? If you didn't insist on singing that infernal claptrap, then I wouldn't have had to speak, and I wouldn't have started coughing.'

My fault. Chloe nodded, lips clamped together. *Always my fault. Will she ever forgive me?*

She stood and checked her watch. 'Look, I'm going to have to dash, Gran, or I'll be late. I've put some soup in the fridge for lunch and I'll be back at six to make tea, okay? But if you start coughing again, I want you to promise me you'll ring the doctor.'

Her gran huffed.

'Please? You know I worry after what happened to—'

'Yes, yes,' her gran interrupted, her voice snappy. 'We both know exactly what happened. Now stop your fussing and go away.'

Chloe sighed and got up. *Why does she have to make it so bloody difficult?*

'See you later, then,' Chloe called as she left the bedroom and made her way down the stairs. The maddening woman just wanted to make her feel guilty the whole bloody time, wanted to see it eating away at her, chewing through her self-worth like a maggot chewing through an apple, leaving holes that could never be filled.

Her phone pinged with a message just as she was about to open the front door.

Morning, gorgeous. Can't wait to see you later. I've booked Giovanni's at 8 for a little celebration. Our anniversary. One month today! Love you so much xxx

Chloe smiled, and her mood lifted a little. *Thank God for Dan.* And how wonderful that he wanted to celebrate their first month together. She'd never met a man like him before, someone who took notice of the little details, who wanted to make her feel happy and loved. Unlike her gran, who seemed to enjoy doing the opposite. Not to mention Lucy and Mark. She sighed, knowing that she'd never be able to make amends, however much she tried. And my goodness how she'd tried over the last nine years.

Dan's a new start, and he doesn't need to know – will never need to know – what I've done. That was her cross to bear, her burden, and it was in the past, gone, over with. A mistake she would never make again. She could be different, more careful. Dan only needed to see the unblemished side of her. He didn't need to see the scars that her past had scratched through her very core.

'You don't have to ring me every hour,' her gran said when Chloe called at lunchtime. 'I'm not a child. I can look after myself perfectly well, and if I feel the need, I will ring the doctor. Stop fussing. It's irritating.' She rang off just as Chloe was about to apologise.

'She really isn't feeling well,' Chloe said to her computer screen, shaking her head as she put her phone down and started writing up notes for the last couple of patients.

Her gran hadn't always been like this, of course. When Chloe had been younger, she was sure she'd been her gran's favourite of the three of them, her brother and sister not sharing Chloe's love of crafts and gardening that were her gran's two great passions. Maybe that's what had made things worse? That Chloe had been her favourite and had then proved to be such a disappointment. She shook her head, trying to shake her negative thoughts away and focus on the positive. She had her evening with Dan to look forward to and she still had an afternoon full of patients to treat.

Later, she needed to work out what to wear. Eventually, she went for her little black dress – you couldn't go wrong with that, could you? – complemented with her red shoes and bag and her big red beads round her neck. She did a twirl in front of her mirror and had to say she was delighted with the result. After a month of no drinking, she could see that she'd lost a little bit of weight and her complexion was better, less puffy, her hair more sleek and shiny. She nodded to herself. Dan was a good thing, a very good thing, whatever her gran might say. And what was wrong with spending all her free time with him anyway?

She's jealous.

The thought made Chloe stop and sit down on the edge of her bed. Was that it? Her gran was feeling left out after being at the centre of Chloe's world since she'd broken up with Spencer a couple of years ago. She'd needed her gran then, had even lived with her for a little while until her gran told her it wasn't working, and she'd be better off finding a place of her own. Chloe knew what the problem was: having her around was too much of a reminder of what her gran had lost. And why.

Maybe she doesn't think I deserve to be happy?

The ring of her doorbell startled her back to the moment. That would be Dan. She took a deep breath and stood up. Why shouldn't she have a chance at happiness? She'd done penance, she'd done everything she could to make amends. People had committed murder and served shorter prison sentences. Yes, it must be time for her to think of herself for once. *Isn't that what Mum would have wanted?* She strode into the hallway and flung open the door, a smile pinned to her face. She was going out with Dan and she was going to bloody well enjoy herself.

Her eyes widened when she saw the bouquet of red roses that Dan held out to her.

'For the most beautiful woman in the world,' he said with a smile.

Her hand went to her chest, lost for words for a moment, her mouth wide with delight. Nobody had ever bought her roses. 'Oh my God, Dan, they're gorgeous! Come in, come in, I'll put them in some water before we go.'

He followed her into her kitchen as she fussed about getting her one and only vase from under the sink, hoping that it would be big enough. 'I'll stick them in here for now and sort them out when I get back.' She turned and hugged him, then tilted her face for a kiss. 'I don't think I've ever had such beautiful flowers before. It's always been carnations from the supermarket.'

'Yeah, well. A special lady deserves special flowers.'

She shook her head at him, laughing. 'You've got all the lines, haven't you? Smooth talker or what?'

He grinned and took her hand. 'Come on, I've got a cab waiting outside. You're costing me a fortune!'

'Yeah, but I'm worth it.' It was a glib response, said without thinking. She'd like to think it was true, but as for believing it… well, that was another matter entirely.

Dan held her in his arms and smoothed her hair away from her face, quiet for a moment before he murmured, 'Yes, you are. You definitely are.'

She tried to push away, but he held her tight. 'I thought you said we needed to get going?'

He nodded, his eyes locked onto hers, and her heart thumped a bit harder. Oh, she loved him. How she loved him. The words filled her mind, every little corner, until there was no room for her worries, no room for anything but love for this man.

'I was going to wait,' he said, releasing her from his embrace. 'But I can't. I can't wait a moment longer.' He pulled a little box out of his pocket, flicking the lid open to reveal a solitaire diamond ring.

Her hands flew to her mouth, eyes wide. *An engagement ring? No. No, this can't be happening.*

He dropped onto one knee. 'Chloe, would you do me the honour of becoming my wife? Please say you'll marry me. Since I met you… I've never known happiness like this and I don't ever want it to stop.'

He held up the little box, waiting for her response, eyes gleaming.

Marry him? He wants me to marry him!

'Yes,' she gasped before she'd had a chance to think about it. 'Oh my God, yes.'

And that was how, only a month after meeting Dan, without giving the matter any real consideration, without wondering how well she really knew him, she made a promise to be his wife.

But then, to be fair, he didn't know her either.

CHAPTER EIGHT

Commitment.

Isn't that what we expect from a relationship? Absolute commitment. But not everyone can do it, can they? You only have to look at the divorce statistics to see that.

Some people just aren't made of the right stuff. Can't put the needs of another person before their own. Can't live by the unspoken set of rules that govern every relationship. Some people can't give themselves completely.

But Chloe… well, she has heroic levels of commitment. Just look at the way she tends to the needs of others. How considerate she is of each and every patient, how strong her desire to make people better.

Funny when a virtue becomes a weakness.

I like that.

Yes, Chloe gets an A* for commitment.

And that's what makes this coupling so perfect.

CHAPTER NINE

Now

They didn't make love on their wedding night, no consummation of their marriage, which was another disappointment to add to the stack of things already bothering Chloe. In fact, the whole thing turned into a bit of a disaster. Dan got all paranoid about checking locks, going round the whole house a couple of times before he was satisfied that every window and door was secure. And he wouldn't let her have the window open, so they had a bit of a row about that, because by then she was overtired and stroppy as a two-year-old.

'I need fresh air,' she whined, trying to wrestle him away from the window catch and ease it open. 'Look, just a little crack. Where's the harm in that?'

'But it's not even that warm,' he said, evenly. 'And it'll just let bugs in. You want to wake up covered in bites? Because I certainly don't, and they itch like hell, and you'll go home looking like you've got chicken pox, and nobody will want to come near you and—'

She screamed in frustration and tried to push past him, but he imprisoned her in an embrace, putting his body between her and the window. He was trying to make her laugh, make light of it, but she was about to combust with an irrational fury that was burning inside her.

Of course, he was right, but that just made her more stroppy because when you're tired there's nothing worse than losing an argument. Eventually, she burst into frustrated tears and pushed his arms away before flopping onto the bed. He came to comfort her, caressing her hair in long, soothing strokes, just like her mother had when she was a child, and within minutes she was asleep.

The next morning, she woke to find that he was already up. Another disappointment. She swallowed the lump in her throat and listened. He was singing in the kitchen below and she lay there for a while, trying to get her equilibrium back on track.

Remembering her pathetic behaviour the night before made her cringe. *Christ, I was petulant. And needy. And whiny.* All the things she hated. It wasn't who she wanted to be but the smashing of her carefully constructed dream of her wedding day had completely thrown her. It seemed to be the story of her life. Reality never lived up to her fantasies and maybe that's where she was going wrong. After all, there was no way she was perfect, so why should she expect her husband to be?

If she was to salvage this honeymoon, it was time for a big dollop of realism. *You love him, don't you?* She smiled to herself. Oh yes, she loved him more than she'd ever loved anyone. She loved him so much that the thought of not having him in her life physically hurt.

Today is going to be different, she decided. *We're going to wipe the slate and start again.*

Slivers of sunlight shone through the shutters, flickering on the white walls of the bedroom. It was hypnotic and soothing, and she found herself relaxing, letting her anxieties ebb away. She was watching the shifting patterns on the wall when she heard Dan's footsteps coming up the stairs, then he appeared in the doorway holding a tray.

He grinned at her, a beautiful smile that lit up his face, and she felt herself melt into the mattress. He wasn't annoyed with her. Not at all. 'Good morning, Mrs Marsden. I trust you slept well?'

She grinned back, grateful that her behaviour seemed to have been forgotten. 'Yes, dear husband, I did.'

'And are you ready for some breakfast?'

'I am indeed.'

He came and sat on the bed, carefully placing the tray between them while she shuffled up to a sitting position, aware that she was still in her underwear; he must have undressed her the previous night and put her to bed as she had no recollection of doing it herself. *Don't sweat the small stuff.* She decided that would be her mantra during their honeymoon and she would let him be masterful if that made him happy, let him organise everything. Wasn't that what she'd wished for so many times over the years – someone to look after her? How did she expect that to happen if she didn't ease off and give the man room to take control? And why would she care that he'd slept in this house with another woman? She was in the past and Chloe was the only woman he wanted in his future.

After a leisurely morning in bed, both of them relaxed and satiated, Dan suggested they go and explore the area and find somewhere for lunch.

'There's a few restaurants in the village, if I remember rightly. Lots of visitors come here because the sea is so shallow in the bay and the beach is perfect for kids. And then there's the dunes to explore and loads of trails in the nature reserve. What do you fancy doing?'

She gave him a lazy smile and looked into his eyes, her fingers caressing his cheek as they lay facing each other. She knew their relationship was going to need a bit of give and take to run smoothly. There was a lot still to learn and she was determined to enjoy the process of really getting to know him.

'That sounds lovely. A bit of exploring. A bit of eating.' She yawned. 'I feel pretty wiped out today after all that rushing around.'

'Well, there's nothing to do. For once you have nobody to look after.' He kissed her on the nose. 'All you have to do is relax and enjoy yourself. I am at your beck and call this week. It's all about you.' He stroked her hair and smiled. 'My gorgeous, lovely, wonderful wife.'

His words were like a balm to her thoughts, soothing all the little worries away. She stretched like a cat, from the tips of her fingers to her toes.

'Wow, I really stink.' She wrinkled her nose.

He laughed and nodded. 'Yeah, you really do.'

After showers then coffee on the patio enjoying the wonderful view, they finally decided to go in search of lunch. They were just about to leave the villa when Chloe stopped, seized by a sudden wave of guilt.

'I just need to give Gran a quick call,' she said, panicking that she hadn't thought to do it sooner.

Dan frowned and tried to pull her outside. 'Can't it wait? I'm so hungry I could eat a scabby donkey.' His eyes pleaded with her and she wavered, but only for a moment, her memories of past wrongs dragging her back inside.

She chewed at her lip. 'I'm going to be in so much trouble.' She could hear the panic in her voice, but that was nothing compared to the bedlam in her mind. 'Honestly, I should have rung last night, just to make sure the carer turned up and everything was okay. I'd never forgive myself if anything happened while we're away, and you know she hasn't been so good recently.'

She rummaged in her bag, trying to find her phone, and it took her a few minutes to realise it wasn't there. She frowned and went back into the living area, Dan following her, an exasperated look on his face.

'Please can we get something to eat and do this later?'

'No. No, we can't. I need to make sure she's okay.' He wouldn't understand, she knew, because there were a lot of things she hadn't told him and hoped he would never find out. But after what happened with her mum, she couldn't take any risks. She was sweating now as her search became more frantic. *What have I done with the damned thing*? She was always very careful with her phone, given her carer role, knowing that she needed to be contactable in case of emergencies. She hadn't used it since they'd left the UK, and could remember switching it off when she got on the plane.

She ran upstairs and checked all the drawers, under the bed, anywhere she might have been, while Dan did his best to help.

'I've lost it! I've lost my phone.' She was close to tears now, her panic making her feel light-headed. She was sure it had been zipped into a little compartment inside her handbag. A compartment that she always fastened because she'd lost a few phones and purses while travelling. Now her routine came as second nature.

He grabbed her arm as she hurried past on her way back downstairs to double-check. 'Hey, calm down. You can use my phone, can't you?'

She realised that Dan was right. She didn't need her phone to ring her gran, the number being etched in her memory. And anyway, they'd given the carer, who was being paid to look after her gran for the week, both of their phone numbers for exactly this eventuality. If there'd been a problem, they would have heard by now. The rational voice in her head carried on telling her that everything was fine, no need to have a meltdown about it. But something inside her refused to believe it.

She'd done that before, listened to that very same voice, and it had been a lie, a terrible piece of misdirection, because things had been the opposite of fine.

What if it happens again?

Dan pulled her to him and stroked her hair as she rested her head on his chest. 'Hey, sweetheart, no need to worry. I don't know what the panic is.'

No, and you never will, she thought as she pulled away, not able to look him in the eye. There was no way she could tell her new husband that she'd killed her mother. He never needed to know a thing like that.

CHAPTER TEN

Two weeks ago

Chloe sat at the little desk in the corner of the lounge looking at her list of things to do as she rubbed at the muscles in her neck. To be fair, she'd managed to get an awful lot done in a couple of weeks, but there was only another fortnight until their wedding day. It was a mad timescale and she still couldn't believe she'd let Dan talk her into it.

He'd come to see her during her lunchbreak the day after he'd proposed, looking like an excitable child. For her part, she was glowing with the sudden unbelievable romance of it all, the diamond engagement ring a novelty, surprising her when it caught her eye, making her smile.

'I'm taking you out to lunch,' he'd said, pulling her from her desk where she was about to tuck into an uninspiring ham sandwich, which she'd grabbed on the way to work.

'Go on then,' she'd said. 'Can't say no to my fiancé, can I?'

He'd pulled her along the corridor and round the corner to a little coffee shop, where he'd sat her down before coming back with paninis and coffee. Chloe's smile was so wide her cheeks were aching. She would have to admit that somewhere, in her heart, she'd imagined that he might change his mind, that he'd cool off once he realised what he'd done, tell her it had been a dreadful mistake.

'I've got news,' he'd said as he unloaded the tray and sat down opposite her.

'Go on then.' Chloe had bit into her panini, hungry after a morning of physical work.

'I've booked the wedding.'

She'd almost choked, and it took a moment of spluttering before she could sort herself out.

'Oh my God. Where? When?' A little voice had piped up in her head: *Aren't you supposed to involve me in this?* But she'd shushed it because he was looking at her with such a proud smirk on his face. 'Wow, you're speedy! We haven't even started talking about arrangements, have we?'

He held up a hand in apology, but there was laughter in his voice. 'I know. I probably should have asked you first, but Mum was so excited when I told her we were engaged, she went and asked the minister at the chapel where she's on the committee and the minister said we could have Wednesday, 26 September.'

Chloe's mouth had hung open for a moment, her mind shocked into silence. 'You are kidding me! That's only a month away.'

'I know. Couldn't be better, could it?'

She'd thought her heart might implode right then and there. She'd nodded, the speed of the whole thing and his obvious keenness to make her his wife having stolen her ability to speak. It was the exact opposite of her previous relationships, where she'd waited patiently and dropped subtle hints, which had been ignored until she'd had to accept the relationship was going nowhere. But Dan? He was determined to marry her; of that there was no doubt. Her face glowed, her heart pounding in her chest. *In a month, I will be this man's wife!*

'Fabulous,' she'd said, grinning like a loon, ignoring the fact that she would have liked a say in the venue and the timing. 'That's perfect.'

Now, sitting at the desk, she was a bit less thrilled because she'd seriously underestimated the amount of organisation that went into a wedding. Flowers and cakes and dresses and venues for the reception. Not to mention having to ask people at work to reorganise their time off so she could go on her honeymoon.

Dan was shouldering some of the jobs, though, and had found a lovely restaurant for the reception. He had also produced his side of the guest list, which had precisely three names on it: his mother and her best friend and her husband, who were like an aunt and uncle to him. Apparently, it was too short notice for any of his friends to come, although Chloe was now wondering if he actually had any friends, because he'd never mentioned any that she could think of; it was something she was going to have to ask him about.

On her side of the guest list, she was dithering. She'd asked friends from work, but only a couple were free. She sighed when she thought about the school friends that she was no longer in touch with. They knew what had happened with her mum, and her shame wouldn't allow her to socialise with them anymore. She was in touch with a few on social media, but only in a superficial way. So, at the moment she too only had three people to invite, including her gran. It wasn't quite shaping up to be the wedding she'd envisaged.

The real question that was bothering her was whether she should ask her brother and sister and their respective families. Dan would expect her family to be there, wouldn't he? But after the recent fracas, she wasn't sure she could face them.

She leant forwards, her head resting in her hands. She just didn't know what to do. Could she cope with all those painful memories surfacing when she was about to get married, or after for that matter? Her eyes widened. What if they made a scene in front of Dan, told him exactly what they thought of her and why? They might come just to spoil the whole thing. The idea made her pulse start to race, and a sheen of sweat appeared on her forehead, damp beneath her fingers. If the truth came out, there wouldn't even be a wedding.

She sat up and made a decision, nodding to herself as she crossed their names off her list. Her past wasn't going to be allowed at her wedding. Oh no, her marriage was opening a door to her future. A future where nobody was going to try and suffocate her with guilt. She would be free, at last, to be herself. And it was a door, she decided, that she was going to shut as soon as she walked through it. So, there it was: three people on either side, eight people in total, and wasn't that a nice number for a wedding party?

She picked up her phone and called Dan.

'Hey, gorgeous,' he said, which always made her want to laugh. *Gorgeous?* That was stretching things a bit, but she'd come to understand he genuinely meant it.

'I'm just finalising invitations and there's not going to be many of us. Just six guests.'

'Perfect! I was dreading the idea of loads of people, but the short notice seems to have whittled numbers down, hasn't it?'

'I was just wondering if you have any friends you want to invite. Someone as a best man, maybe?' She held her breath, curious.

'No.' His response was immediate and definite, leaving no room for argument, and she sat with her mouth open for a moment before she realised he'd moved the conversation on.

'Sorry, I missed that. Can we just backtrack a moment, so I'm clear about guests? I've got Gran, Lou and Poppy, and you've got your mum and your aunt and uncle.'

'Yep, that sounds about right. I was just saying that I've ordered my suit and I'm taking Mum to get her outfit at the weekend, so maybe we could all go together, and she could help you choose your wedding dress, given that your mum…'

Chloe's throat tightened, the connection between mums and wedding dresses unleashing a swirl of emotions that filled her chest. He was trying to be kind, she understood that, but the pain of her mum's death stabbed at her heart. What she would give to have her mum there, seeing her get married, helping her with the organisation. How much fun it would have been.

A sob stuck in her throat. *It's my fault that's not going to happen.* She couldn't even get her gran involved as she disapproved of the whole thing.

'You ridiculous girl!' she'd exclaimed when Chloe had told her the news of her engagement. 'You've only known him two minutes. What on earth is going on in that head of yours?'

'I love him, Gran,' she'd said, her face burning, her body rigid with anger. *How dare she talk to me like that? Like I'm a child?*

Her gran had laughed then, but not in a nice way.

The next day, when Chloe had told her the wedding date, she'd shaken her head, mouth working away as if she was having a whole conversation with herself, which she probably was – and her actions crushed the joy from Chloe's heart. Her gran had refused to get involved in any discussions about the wedding, and Chloe wasn't even sure if she'd be there on the day. *Why can't she just be happy for me?* Chloe had thought. But she knew why. Her gran didn't want to see her happy because she didn't think she deserved it. There, she'd said it, even if it was just in her head. But she was sure she was right.

Sod my family, she decided. *I don't need them. Not now I've got Dan.* They'd make their own family, his mum would become her mum – not a replacement but better than not having a mother at all – and she'd make sure that her kids never suffered the feelings of guilt that had plagued her life.

'Yes,' she said to Dan, imagining shopping with his mum, who was very excited about the whole thing. 'That sounds lovely. I could do with some help.'

'Are you sure?'

'Of course. It'll be fun.'

That's what she liked about Dan. Her happiness was important to him, and surely that was a good basis for their marriage, whatever her gran might say.

After they'd finished the call, she sat at the desk thinking that this was the first night since they'd met that they hadn't spent together. Not because he didn't want to see her but because she had wanted a bit of time to herself. To sort out wedding arrangements, she'd told him, but really, she'd wanted a bit of space to think.

Was she having second thoughts?

After she'd got engaged, everyone she'd told had been shocked. She could see it in their faces, even though they expressed their delight for her. They all had reservations, although nobody said so outright. It was there in their eyes, caught in snippets of overheard conversations. And then, when she announced she was going to be married just two months after meeting Dan, well, the comments had become a little more pointed: Are you sure you're not rushing it? How can you organise a wedding in a month? You're not pregnant, are you? On and on, questioning her, chipping away at her confidence, at her certainty that this was what she wanted.

She got up from the desk and went to run a bath, throwing in a bath bomb of essential oils to soothe her mind. She stepped into the water, breathing in the beautiful aroma as she sank into the bubbles.

Am I rushing things? She lay back and closed her eyes.

Well, there was no doubt that everything had happened very quickly, but did that make it rushed? Or did it just mean there was a natural rhythm to it? Everything had fallen into place so easily, she felt it was proof it was the right thing to do.

Do I love him?

Oh yes. There was no question in her mind. But was her gran right? Could she really know she loved him after only a few weeks, or did real love take longer to ferment? Was this an infatuation that would wear off? She sighed and sank lower in the water. Her love for Dan was all-consuming, it had devoured her, and she couldn't conceive of a life without him. The sun shone brighter, everything tasted sweeter, looked more beautiful when she was with him. Was it wrong to want more of that?

Does he love me?

Of that, she had no doubt. He loved her with a force and passion that she'd been unable to imagine before she'd met him. If he could, she thought, he would take up residence in her body, his need to be near her was so strong.

Overwhelming at times, the little voice said, and her breath faltered.

Perhaps a little claustrophobic, if she was being honest. She bit her lip, unable to keep her concerns at bay now that they had decided to make themselves known.

And why doesn't he have any friends?

She thought about that for a moment.

But I don't have any real friends either, she reminded herself.

That's because of what you did, came the answer. *So, what did Dan do?*

She stood and got out of the bath, unable to be alone with her thoughts a moment longer because there was no way her line of logic was helping. Her brain was addled; she wasn't making any sense. *Pre-wedding nerves.* They loved each other, no question about that, so why not get married quickly if the opportunity was there? She should be flattered that he was making all the moves, that he wanted to be with her forever, for things to move quickly. Wasn't that what she'd dreamed of? What every girl dreams of?

All good, she told herself as she put on some music and dried her hair, trying to drown out the negative voice that persisted in her head. 'Everything is good, good, good,' she sang until it was all she could hear.

CHAPTER ELEVEN

Now

Chloe's phone conversation with her gran was very short.

'Stop your fussing, girl. Of course I'm fine. That woman's here half the day. She's very nice, by the way. Doing a wonderful job.'

Her gran hadn't been in the mood for a chat and had put the phone down before Chloe had a chance to say goodbye. She sighed, a heaviness settling on her shoulders. *Would it hurt Gran to be civil?* She hadn't even said anything about the wedding, asked how things were going. Nothing. But then, she hadn't really spoken to Chloe at her wedding, except to say a cursory congratulations, and hadn't stayed for the reception, claiming she wasn't feeling up to it. Chloe had put her into a taxi and kissed her goodbye, almost glad that she wouldn't be there to sour the atmosphere. Their other guests, although few in number, were obviously delighted for them, laughing and chatting with Dan while she sorted out her gran.

Honestly, she's getting harder to deal with by the day. Chloe decided that once she was back home, she'd have a proper heart-to-heart with her, see if she actually wanted Chloe to carry on being her carer. Maybe Lucy and Mark had been right about that. Maybe it would be better for everyone if she just walked away and concentrated on her own life. Her marriage.

Lost in thought, she handed the phone back to Dan, who tucked it in his pocket. 'All good?'

Chloe nodded, her words knotted in her throat. She met his gaze, saw a glimmer of concern, and forced a smile. 'She's fine, just a cranky old bat.'

Dan pulled Chloe to him. 'Don't let her get to you,' he murmured into her hair, the warmth of his breath a soft caress. 'You've done more than your fair share of looking after her. I don't understand why your brother and sister can't take a turn every now and again. I know you don't get on with them, but I mean it's not like they live a million miles away, is it?'

Chloe sighed. This was something she had asked herself several times in recent years, and out came the justification she invariably settled on.

'Oh, they have busy lives, you know, with their jobs and kids and everything. I was always the single one and I'm the one who works in the caring profession. It's just natural, I suppose, that I'm the one who's taken responsibility for Gran.'

'She's mean to you, though, isn't she? A bit of a bully really?'

Chloe swallowed and picked at his T-shirt, removing invisible bits of fluff, not wanting to catch his eye because hers were filling with tears. He'd hit the nail on the head. That's exactly what her gran was: a bully. Chloe had put up with her behaviour because she'd wanted to be punished for what she'd done. But now... well, now things were different.

'You know,' he said, 'one thing we really need to make a decision on is where we're going to live now we're married. I know we've discussed it and gone round in circles, but by the end of the week, we really need to get it sorted. If you're not responsible for your gran's care, then we're free to live where we want, aren't we?'

Chloe tensed. 'I'm not ready to talk about this now. Nowhere near ready.'

'Well, I don't want to rush you, I just wanted to put it out there for discussion, you know? You're my priority now.' His cheek rested on the top of her head and his words rumbled through her.

'I want you to be happy and I'm not going to let your crabby old gran stop me from looking after you the way you deserve, okay? It's all about us now, you and me.'

She snuggled into his chest as his arm tightened around her. As long as he never found out the truth, then everything would be fine. If they moved away from her family, then the risk of him finding out was reduced, wasn't it? It was a tempting thought. But one of them needed to work, and at the moment that was her. Still, she could look for jobs elsewhere. Yes, maybe she needed to take a different perspective on their future, start to believe that she could leave the past behind.

'I'll definitely give it some thought,' she promised as they pulled apart and left the villa, ambling down the dirt track and into the village.

The view was breathtaking, the sea sparkling in the autumn sunshine, lines of boats bobbing in the bay, which formed a natural harbour. There were a couple of families on the beach, with young children playing in the sand, and she could see the lake behind a fuzz of trees in the nature reserve, the water speckled with birds, bobbing in little groups on the surface. Chloe breathed it all in. This was better, much better. *I'm on my honeymoon*, she reminded herself. *Just relax. Enjoy it.*

'Can we go out on a boat, do you think?' she said, pointing out into the bay. 'Over to that little island?'

He held her hand as they walked, and the feel of his warm skin against hers set her heart humming. She noticed the flowers and the insects buzzing around, little birds fluttering in the woods that bordered the track on one side, while the land fell away in rocky steps down towards the sea on the other.

'Oh yes, that's a great idea. Perfect conditions today, I'd say.' He squeezed her hand. 'Not so bad here after all, is it?'

She smiled. 'No, it's lovely and I'm sorry if I made a fuss yesterday, I just—'

'Don't mention it. It's forgotten. Yesterday was mad and we were tired, and I should have told you sooner, but who knows where the time went over the last couple of weeks? And I honestly didn't think you'd mind because this is like paradise, isn't it?'

'I don't mind, honestly I don't.' And that was the truth. In her new state of calm, she found that she really didn't mind the change of plans, the lack of coconut palms and the fact that the beach wasn't white and the sea wasn't quite that glorious turquoise colour. Just being here with Dan was enough.

He should have told me, though.

She swatted the thought away like a pesky insect and leant into him, enjoying the feel of his bare arm brushing against hers. Even the cool canopy of the trees on the wooded stretch of the track didn't seem so sinister today.

'So, is this like where you were living in Spain?'

He laughed. 'If only! No, I was in Barcelona. Definitely urban. But it's a lovely city. I'll take you there some time. I think you'd love it. Way better than Brighton, that's for sure. I can't wait to get out of the place.'

'I thought that before I moved down to look after Gran. But you know, it just sort of sucks you in. And it's just buzzing with life. Close to London if you want to nip up there for shopping or a show. After a while, you wonder how you could not live there.'

'Hmm.' He looked off into the distance and she could tell that he wasn't convinced. A prickle of unease worked its way down her back. Was where they lived going to be a sticking point? It wasn't something they had actually talked about in any great depth. In fact, they'd been so wrapped up in the all-consuming excitement of organising the wedding, that a lot of important subjects had not been discussed. *It's what this honeymoon is for,* she told herself. They had plenty of time to get themselves organised and on the same page about the direction of their future before they went home.

They walked in silence until they reached the village, each lost in their own thoughts, Chloe unsettled by the idea that Dan might not want to stay in Brighton after his mum fully recovered from her accident. Just something else to add to the list of things she didn't know about him.

She wondered now what they had talked about for the last two months, and the idea that she didn't know him at all wormed its way into her mind. Yes, she knew that his favourite colour was blue and he loved to read Lee Child and his favourite meal was Italian and his musical tastes were Ed Sheeran and George Ezra and he hated wearing a suit and loved the outdoors. But what did she know about the big things? His ambitions? What he wanted his life to be like? Apart from certain aspects of her family history, he knew almost everything about her because she had wittered on for hours, and she had loved the way he had listened. But what had he really said about himself? *Very little.* And that realisation brought all her other concerns bubbling to the surface again. *Why is that? Is he hiding something?* The very thought made her shiver.

The village was not a big place: all the restaurants sat along the beachfront, or on a stilted pontoon that stretched out beside the harbour. They checked them all out before Dan turned and pointed to the one at the far end. 'I think that will be the nicest place to sit for a while, don't you?'

'I don't mind.' She frowned. Her indifference bothered her. She should mind, shouldn't she? Did she have no opinion on what she wanted to eat? But it didn't seem to matter while the bigger questions preoccupied her thoughts, creeping beneath her skin, making her restless and twitchy.

The restaurant was light and airy, and they sat by the window, the breeze just slightly too chilly by the water's edge to sit outside.

Seafood seemed to be the only option and they feasted on prawns and calamari, deliciously fresh and beautifully cooked.

Once she'd had something to eat, Chloe started to relax a little. She fancied a glass of wine, and although she knew Dan wouldn't join her, it seemed the perfect end to the meal. Something light and crisp and ice-cold. *A spritzer maybe?* She was just contemplating her options when the waiter appeared and asked if they wanted anything else.

'Dessert?' Dan looked at her. 'Ice cream, maybe? I think I'll have something, what about you?'

'I'll just have a white wine and soda please. Dry white.'

The waiter bowed and walked off while Dan frowned at her. 'Wine?'

She shrugged. 'Why not? We're on our honeymoon, aren't we? It's not like I have to operate heavy machinery this afternoon, or make sensible conversation with clients. I just feel like kicking back a bit.' She wasn't sure why she was sounding so defensive. 'Anyway, what's wrong with wine? You never told me why you don't drink. Is it all drink you disapprove of? Or is it that you just don't like the taste?'

He gave her a brittle smile. 'Oh, it's what happens to people when they've had a drink that I don't like.'

'So, you don't want me to drink because it'll make me turn into someone you don't like. Is that what you're saying?'

He leant across the table and took her hand. 'Babe, if you want the odd glass of wine, don't mind me. It's just I'll never share a bottle of wine with you, or crack open a beer after work. It's not for me.'

The waiter returned with Dan's dessert and her glass of wine, condensation glittering on the outside of the glass. She raised it to him. 'Cheers,' she said and took a long drink. It was cold and sharp and sour and fizzy. And perfectly delicious. She looked at him and licked her lips. He lowered his eyes and started eating his ice cream while she took another long sip of her wine. Exactly what she needed. She felt it, icy down her throat, then the warmth of the alcohol in her stomach. Oh, that really was nice, and she was determined not to let his obvious disapproval ruin her enjoyment.

She called for the waiter, held up her glass when he came over and gave him a broad grin. 'Another one of these, please.'

Sod Dan, she thought. *I've earned a bit of a treat.*

It was only when she'd finished her second glass and she was feeling a little dizzy, having downed them pretty quickly, that she wondered whether her actions had been counterproductive. She took a big glug from her glass of water, hoping to dilute the effects of the alcohol.

He gazed at her. 'I was going to suggest we hire a kayak and paddle to the island, but I think we'd better save that for another day.' He folded his napkin and laid it carefully on the table. 'When we're fresh.'

Her eyes widened. 'You mean you think I'm pissed?' There was no mistaking the slur in her voice and she glowered at him. A kayak trip would have been fun. He could have mentioned that earlier, couldn't he? Before she'd ordered a second drink.

'No, I don't think that.'

But he does, really, she thought, *judging by that look on his face.* His jaw was clenched, eyes narrowed, lips pressed together. *Judgemental*, she decided, and it wasn't a look she liked.

'Anyway, I don't fancy kayaking today,' she lied. 'I'm still feeling a bit weird after all the rush yesterday. I just want to relax. Not do anything, really.'

'Shall we go back to the villa, then?' He sounded disappointed. No, frustrated would be more accurate, she decided, his tone of voice the same as a parent would use with a child who was playing up and ruining a day out.

Okay, if he wants to play that game, we'll play it.

'Yes.' She glared at him, got up from the table and stalked out of the restaurant, knowing that he had to stay and pay. She didn't want to walk back with him. What she needed was a bit of time to herself. *He's being odd,* she decided, and it was really bothering her. Not only had he been weird about her drinking, he'd also been on edge all through the meal, glancing around the restaurant, as if he was looking for someone, not really paying her much attention at all.

She stopped in her tracks as a thought hit her like a slap, stinging through her mind.

Wait a minute. Does he know a woman here? Is that it? Is that who he was looking for? Another thought piled into the internal discussion. *Perhaps she works in the restaurant?*

The idea mushroomed in her mind until it was all she could think about. But why would he bring Chloe here if he thought an ex-girlfriend would be lurking in the shadows? She breathed out as the voice of reason made itself known. *That's right. He wouldn't.* What on earth was she thinking? Why so suspicious? She hadn't felt like this back home; in fact, she'd felt the opposite. But then, ever since they'd said their vows, Dan had started behaving differently. He'd changed their honeymoon destination without telling her, he'd been bossy, taken charge of everything, and today… well, today he'd definitely been distracted. How could things have changed so much in the space of a day?

You're being ridiculous again. Nothing's changed except your mood. She nodded to herself. *It's the wine talking.*

She turned and started walking back the way she'd come, knowing she was in the wrong. She had behaved like a petulant teenager, and resolved to apologise so the day wouldn't be ruined, but when she neared the restaurant, she saw a scene that made her breath hitch in her throat. She crept into the shadows where she could not be seen.

Dan was talking to a woman. A very attractive woman, and a local by the look of her: dark-haired and olive-skinned, lithe and athletic. They were leaning against the wooden rail that bordered the decking outside the restaurant, standing shoulder to shoulder and having what looked like an intense conversation.

Way too intimate, Chloe decided.

Her heart started to race, and she chewed her lip in an effort to keep her emotions at bay. She told herself to go over and make her presence known, find out what was going on. Instead, she found herself turning and running away, back along the road towards the villa, completely overwhelmed by the situation. She was in a foreign land with a man who seemed more foreign to her by the day, and there was no way she was going to embarrass herself by bursting into tears in public. No, she'd go back to the villa and calm herself down. When the wine was out of her system and her thought processes were more composed, then she would confront him and find out who the woman was.

She slowed to a walk, the sun hot on the back of her neck, sweat dampening her T-shirt, and when she started up the track to the villa, she moved to the side where the trees cast a line of shade. She was feeling a bit queasy, wobbly on her legs, and really needed a lie down. She glanced ahead but knew that it was still a fair way up to the house and she'd have to walk through the long stretch of forest area on her own. The old fear crept up the back of her neck, pulling her scalp so tight it started a headache.

There was a large, flat boulder under the shade of an old olive tree up ahead, a perfect spot for a rest. Her body felt heavy and weary, and she lay down on the warm rock to wait for Dan to catch her up. He had the key, so she couldn't get in the house, and she really didn't want to walk through the forest on her own. No. She had to wait.

She woke with a shiver, the sun having disappeared, the sky a sheet of grey now, the sea ruffled by choppy waves. A cool breeze whispered through the trees. Her watch told her she'd been asleep for a couple of hours and she frowned. *So, where's Dan?* Why had he left her on her own for so long, knowing full well that she couldn't get into the house because he had the sodding key?

Is he with that woman?

Her teeth clamped tight as she visualised the two of them together. Then she stopped and rewound the image. Now she was feeling less woozy, what had she actually seen? They'd been standing very close, shoulders touching, faces just inches apart, so he definitely knew her, of that she was sure. They'd been having more than just a cosy chat, more than a casual conversation between people who'd just bumped into each other again. There was something strange going on, something that made her feel very alone and vulnerable.

She shivered as a fresh breeze brought goosebumps to her skin, and she looked around, thinking she might see him coming up the track, but there was no sign of him. Maybe he'd walked past and not seen her? Given how long she'd been asleep, that seemed the most likely scenario.

Oh God, she thought, looking in the direction of the house at the dark tunnel that disappeared into the trees. *I'm going to have to go through the forest on my own.* Her heart started to race. The wind rustled through the leaves, branches creaking, reminding her of her worst fears. She ran.

CHAPTER TWELVE

Yesterday

Chloe woke to find her wedding day was one of those still, drizzly affairs that September specialised in, but she wasn't going to let the weather dampen her spirits. Today was the day when everything would change for her, when she would become part of a married couple instead of being an ageing singleton. Finally, her dream was coming true. She hardly dared articulate it to herself, worried that she'd jinx the whole thing and Dan would change his mind, stand her up at the altar.

He wouldn't, she reassured herself. *He's not like that, and anyway, this is all his idea.*

The ceremony was scheduled for two o'clock, and at twenty past two, when she was standing next to the minister on the porch of the church, still waiting for Dan to turn up, she was having serious doubts.

'We'll give him until half past,' the minister said, with a forced smile. 'Must be some hold-up. But I have to be somewhere else at three, so we might have to rearrange it if he doesn't arrive soon.'

Chloe shivered. The dress she'd chosen was an off-the-shoulder ivory sheath which hugged her figure but provided very little in the way of warmth. She didn't have her phone on her, so she had no way of contacting him. The minister didn't have his number to hand either, so they just had to wait.

'It's a bit nippy, isn't it?' the minister said, obviously noticing the shivers that were trembling through Chloe's body. 'Tell you what, let's go inside for a few minutes, get you a coat to put on until they get here, shall we?' She put a comforting arm round Chloe's shoulders and was about to lead her inside when Chloe heard her name being called.

She turned, gasping with relief. 'Dan! It's Dan.' She watched him running up the path to the church while his mother paid the taxi driver.

'Oh, Chloe, you look beautiful,' he said with such love in his eyes that she couldn't be cross with him. He was here, that was all that mattered; she was sure she'd get a full explanation for his lateness in good time, but now the minister was ushering them inside.

'Timing's going to be a bit tight,' the minister said as she signalled to the organist to start playing. 'But at least it's just a short service, so we shouldn't have a problem.'

Dan, his mum and the minister hurried down the aisle while Chloe waited for everyone to get themselves in place and the wedding march began.

It's happening. It's really happening! A flutter of nerves flapped inside her chest, setting her heart racing.

With everyone in place, Chloe took a deep breath, picked up her posy of red roses and started her walk to the front of the chapel. She'd considered who she could ask to walk her down the aisle, but in all honesty, there was nobody she could think of, so she'd decided that it didn't matter. In this day and age, she didn't need someone to give her away. She could do that herself, but it felt a bit lonely, that long walk on her own, even though Dan was waiting at the end. It brought home how much she missed her parents. Her mum had died when Chloe was twenty-one and every day, in little ways, she felt the pain of her loss. Today, her wedding day, the consequences of what she'd done were almost overwhelming.

Clack, clack, clack went her heels on the stone floor, her footsteps echoing round the empty space, the chapel feeling huge with just a handful of people on the front two benches. There was something wrong about the whole thing, something that jarred and stopped her feeling the joy she should surely be feeling on her wedding day.

This isn't what it's supposed to be like.

If she'd had more time, if they'd been able to organise it on a Saturday, then they could have had more guests, made it feel like more of a celebration. But this… this felt sad rather than joyous. She almost turned and ran, but then she caught sight of Dan's face. The expression in his eyes pulled her towards him and she remembered his words from the day before, when she'd voiced her reservations about the wedding arrangements.

'This isn't about having crowds of people there that we hardly know, just so we can put pictures up on social media to prove what a fantastic couple we are. This is about you and me making vows to love and cherish each other for the rest of our lives.' He'd kissed her tenderly on the lips then pulled away, his hand stroking her cheek. 'Even if there were no guests, it would still be perfect for me. I just want to marry you, Chloe. The rest doesn't matter.'

She gave herself a mental shake as she finished her walk down the aisle. *That's all that matters*, she told herself. *Me and Dan, saying our vows, becoming man and wife. That's all that matters.*

She caught her gran's eye and smiled, but her gran didn't smile back. She was wearing her best black outfit, the only smart clothes she had which fitted, and she was crying. It looked like she was at a funeral.

Chloe swallowed and blinked before turning to Dan, gratefully taking his hand. She glanced at his mum, who was dressed in lilac with a matching fascinator and was beaming from ear to ear. That's more like it, she decided, looking at the rest of their guests who were also brightly dressed, also smiling. It was just her gran who was dampening the tone. *Forget her,* she told herself, before the minister cleared her throat and the service began.

It didn't take long. They'd decided against hymns – with such a small group, the minister had suggested it might be awkward. They'd gone for a couple of musical pieces instead, Chloe's two friends from work had done readings and Dan's mum had written a poem, but that was about it, and the service was all over and done with in just twenty-five minutes.

The wedding photographer hadn't made an appearance, and because they'd been running late, there was little time to take photos of them signing their marriage certificate. Dan's mum took a few, but her photography skills, from what Chloe had seen, were suspect to say the least.

'Never mind,' Dan said, completely unconcerned that there would be no official wedding photos. 'He was going to cost a fortune, and anyway, sometimes more casual shots have more meaning, don't they?'

Did he even book a photographer? Chloe wondered as they posed in the entrance of the chapel for some quick shots, not wanting to stand out in the rain, which had turned from a light drizzle to a proper downpour. Photos finished, they were about to dash round the corner to the restaurant that Dan had booked, when Chloe's gran grabbed her arm. Her face was pale, her eyes red-rimmed from crying.

'I'm not feeling up to the reception,' she said, her voice a bit wobbly. 'I'm just going to go home.'

'Oh, Gran, are you sure? You might feel better after you've had something to eat.'

'No, I want to go home.' Her meaning was very clear and there was no point arguing, so a taxi was organised and off she went.

Dan grabbed Chloe's hand as they ran through the rain, her friend's coat draped round her shoulders, and she couldn't stop herself from asking the question that had been playing on her mind. 'You were so late, Dan. I thought you weren't coming. You weren't having second thoughts, were you?'

He laughed. 'God no. I couldn't wait to get here, but we had… There was…' She glanced at him and saw a flash of anger cross his face. 'Well, it doesn't matter. We got here. That's all that counts.'

By that time, they had reached the venue and the rest of the wedding party were standing waiting for them, so nothing more was said until they'd finished eating and had done a quick round of speeches. It had been a fun gathering, with lots of jokes and laughter and Chloe decided it wasn't a bad thing to have a cosy little wedding after all; even if she had no family there, at least her friends had made an effort, and Dan's family was very enthusiastic and welcoming. That was all that mattered.

Still, the reason why he'd been late bothered her. Something had happened; she could tell by the way he'd brushed off her questions. And it reminded her of the incident with his car a few weeks earlier. The vandalism that could have been a warning, or a threat. She'd never got to the bottom of that, Dan always managing to evade her questions, waving it away as 'water under the bridge, doesn't matter'.

She seized her opportunity to have a quiet word with Dan's mum while he was chatting to his aunt and uncle. They were all getting ready to leave, in more of a rush than she'd anticipated because the flight times had changed, apparently.

Alma held both her hands and beamed at her. 'That dress was a good choice, wasn't it? You look stunning. And it's been such a lovely wedding, so happy. I can't tell you how delighted I am to welcome you to the family.'

Chloe smiled. 'Thank you! I did wonder whether you were going to make it at one point, though.'

The smile dropped off Alma's face. 'Yes, well, we had a bit of…' She stopped herself and flapped a hand. 'Oh, you don't need to know the ins and outs of it. All sorted now anyway.' Alma checked her watch. 'Probably time to get changed, isn't it? The taxi will be here in ten minutes.'

And that was the end of that conversation. Chloe was shooed into the restaurant toilets with her going-away clothes while Alma packed her wedding dress into a cover to take home with her. When Chloe emerged to thank the remaining guests for coming, she saw Alma and Dan having a whispered conversation, their frowns telling her that something wasn't right. Alma was nodding as Dan talked, a worried look in her eyes.

What is going on? What aren't they telling me?

She tried to ask Dan on the way to the airport, but he batted her question away.

'Doesn't matter, babe. Let's look forward to our honeymoon. It was just a little hiccup. Nothing for you to worry about.'

'But your mum—'

'Mum's so happy about us getting married. I can't tell you how excited she is.' He gazed at her. 'I love you so much, Chloe, so very much.'

He kissed her, long and deep, and soon she was thoroughly distracted, her concerns drifting to the back of her mind. Her head filled with the laughter and joy of her reception, the excitement of being part of a new family with a mother-in-law that she adored. Most of all, though, she knew that she loved her husband with all her heart.

CHAPTER THIRTEEN

Emotions are such fickle things, aren't they? One minute you can be the happiest you've ever been, then a moment later, all that joy has gone, evaporated. Doesn't take much to ruin a moment.

I can see it in her face, that she's uncertain, can see that she's not as happy as she should be on her wedding day. One minute she is radiating happiness and the next that pretty face of hers is scrunched up in a frown. Such an expressive set of features, she couldn't hide her feelings if she wanted to.

Poor Chloe.

I do feel a bit sorry for her.

She doesn't like it when she's not in control. That much is clear. Doesn't like not knowing.

Oh dear, I think she's in for a few nasty surprises.

CHAPTER FOURTEEN

Now

Chloe ran up the track through the forest as if the devil himself was snapping at her heels. A couple of times, she thought she heard footsteps behind her and turned, thinking it would be Dan, running to catch up. But the track behind her was empty, stretching back into an impenetrable gloom that could hide anything or anyone.

When she reached the house, her breathing was ragged, her legs aching after her sprint up the hill. She looked around, as if Dan would appear from somewhere, but she knew there was nobody home: the lights were off, and the place had that deserted feel about it. Shoulders sagging, she wandered round the back of the house, looking for an open window, trying all the doors, but everything was firmly locked, and she had no way of getting in.

She stood on the patio, arms wrapped around her shivering body, as she looked out to sea. She could see rain in the distance, sheets of it heading in her direction, and the wind was getting stronger. *Christ, I'm going to get soaked.* She glanced around, looking for shelter, and realised the only covered space was a little roofed area in the corner, over a barbecue pit – the rest of the shade on the patio was created by a large vine that crept over wooden beams, providing a useful canopy but no real protection from the imminent downpour.

A concrete seat had been created next to the back wall of the house and she plonked herself down, just as the first drops speckled the paving stones. Almost immediately, a torrent of water hissed against the ground, splattered on the windows and gurgled down the drainpipes, spraying her bare legs and arms with a fine mist. Her teeth started to chatter, and she brought her feet up onto the bench, arms hugging her legs and her chin resting on her knees in an effort to keep herself as dry and warm as possible.

How long is he going to make me wait?

It was completely out of order. He knew she couldn't get in the house. *What on earth is he doing? Is he punishing me for running off? For drinking?* It seemed fanciful, but the man she'd come on honeymoon with appeared to be a different person to the one she thought she knew. Yes, there were flashes of loving tenderness, but she'd caught his expression a few times when he thought she wasn't watching, and he'd looked… angry. Yes, that was it. Something was making him angry and it seemed to be her. Her body shuddered at the thought. She was rubbish at conflict of any kind, the sort of person who always went with a compromise rather than sticking up for herself. Growing up with her sister had taught her to be like that, and it was a mindset she'd never shaken.

She closed her eyes, listened to the sound of the rain, feeling exhausted and empty; completely alone. *This is what you wanted, isn't it?* The voice in her head mocked her. *Just you and Dan. Didn't want to bother with anyone else, did you? Well, look how that's turned out. Not even twenty-four hours married, and you already want to go home.*

Now she'd lost her phone she couldn't even ring anyone. In fact… She frowned, concentrating on that conundrum for a moment, trying to take her mind off the chill that was seeping down her neck, covering her arms and legs in goosebumps. *How did my phone go missing?* She hadn't used it after they'd boarded the plane, and it had stayed zipped in her bag in the overhead compartment.

Which could only mean one thing.

Dan took it.

But why?

The sound of a car engine stopped her train of thought and she unfurled herself, listening. She heard a voice, then the sound of a car door slamming. *Dan! Oh, thank God!* She stood up, her body stiff and aching, teeth chattering as she dashed round to the front of the house, the rain soaking through her clothes. She burst through the front door, slamming it behind her as if the weather was going to chase her indoors.

Dan's back was turned to her as he unloaded a couple of carrier bags in the kitchen area and he swung round, frowning. But his expression turned to concern when he saw her.

'Christ, Chloe, you're soaked. What have you been doing?'

For a moment, she couldn't speak.

'Me?' she said, pointing to her chest, a sarcastic tinge to her voice. 'Oh, I've just been hanging around for bloody hours waiting for you to turn up. That's what I've been doing. What about you?' She cocked her head to one side, waiting for his answer, pretty sure that she wasn't likely to believe a word he said.

He frowned and looked confused, then carried on unpacking the bags while he spoke. 'I came back to the house, but you weren't here. I thought you'd marched off in a strop somewhere and needed a bit of time to cool off. So, I thought I'd do something useful. I walked back to the village, the bus was there that goes into town, so I went and did a bit of shopping. Lots of tasty bits and pieces they don't have in the village. Stuff for picnics and easy meals. Then we don't have to worry about going out to get food.'

He wouldn't look at her. *He's lying.* Her hands bunched into fists, anger burning her cheeks.

'You didn't come back. I would have seen you.'

'But I did. Look, I left you a note on the front door.' He walked past her into the hall, opened the door and pulled something out of the letterbox. It was a damp, floppy scrap of paper and the ink was blurred round the edges, but the message was clear.

Sorry I've upset you. I didn't mean to. I've gone to get some shopping.
Love you so much, Dan xoxoxoxoxo

She stared at the note then glanced at Dan. She hadn't even checked the front door when she'd got to the house; knowing it would be locked, she'd gone straight round the back. *He must have walked past me.* That was possible, wasn't it? She'd been in the shade and he could have missed her if he'd been looking at the ground or out to sea. And she'd been asleep, so she wouldn't have heard him walk past. *But twice? He walked past twice?* She stared at the note again, not sure what to think. *He could have just put that there, to cover himself.*

She ran a hand through her hair, unsticking it from her forehead, shivering as water trickled down her neck.

He stopped what he was doing and sighed before walking towards her, arms held out, inviting a hug. 'Let's just rewind, shall we? Start again?' His eyes pleaded with her, his expression apologetic. 'Look, I'm sorry I went off with the key. I hadn't thought about that. We've both been a bit childish, haven't we? Not the best start.'

She fell into his embrace, wanting all the aggravation to end and for them to go back to how they'd been before they'd got married.

He seemed to read her thoughts. His cheek rested on the top of her head, his arms holding her tight. 'Let's pretend we've just got here. How about it?'

She nodded, her throat too clogged with emotion to speak. Her teeth chattered.

He pulled away from her, his hands on her shoulders as he bent to look at her face. 'Christ, you're freezing, aren't you? Let me run you a bath. Get you warmed up. And while you're relaxing, I'll make us something to eat. How about that?'

He didn't wait for an answer but bent and picked her up, slowly carrying her up the stairs and into the bedroom, where he set her down on the bed before disappearing into the bathroom. She sat shivering while she listened to him turn on the tap, wondering how he hadn't noticed her on the rock next to the track. Had he deliberately sneaked past? Or taken a different route through the trees? Had he even been into town or just grabbed some things from the village shop? Then she remembered the sound of the car and knew he must have got a cab. Or was it someone he knew, dropping him off?

She sighed. So many questions and no proper answers.

You're being stupid, she told herself. *Suspicious and stupid.*

He came out of the bathroom, his look of concentration turning to a smile when he caught her eye. *He loves me.* It was there in his face. *There's nothing going on, except me being a dick, creating problems where there aren't any.*

She smiled up at him. 'I'm sorry about lunch. I'm sorry about everything. I know I'm being...' She searched for the right word, but he shook his head.

'You're not being anything.' He sat beside her and pulled her close. She snuggled into the warmth of him, could feel the thump of his heart in his chest, could smell sweat and aftershave. 'We've had quite a time of it these last few weeks, haven't we? Getting everything organised, it was a lot to think about. So, we're both tired and a bit... strung out. Let's just leave it at that.'

She tipped her head and kissed him, loving him for not blaming her for anything, for understanding. Loving him for being the first person in her life who didn't try to make her feel guilty.

'You know what?' he said as he pulled away. 'I think I might go and start making that food before I decide that I need a bath too.'

She smiled at him. 'Oh, but I think you do, Mr Marsden. I think you definitely need a bath. You're smelling a little sweaty, if

I may be so bold.' Then she kissed him again and he pulled her to him and all the worries of the day were forgotten. It was time, she decided, to do what he'd asked: put all the niggles behind them and start their honeymoon again.

That worked for a while, but later, as she lay in bed, the unanswered questions came back to annoy her, demanding her attention, and she knew she wouldn't relax until she'd sorted out some proper answers.

Tomorrow, she promised herself. *Tomorrow, I'll make sure we have that conversation. Get everything out in the open. Find out what he's done with my phone, who that woman was and where he went this afternoon.*

CHAPTER FIFTEEN

That night, Chloe woke to the sound of shouting. Her heart was pounding, mind still blurry from sleep as her eyes searched the dark of the bedroom for the cause of the commotion.

'Get away from me!'

Dan's voice. He sounded panicked. *Oh God! An intruder.*

She could sense movement, heard feet scuffling on the tiled floor, before his voice startled her again. It was guttural and fierce now. 'Go on, just fuck off!'

Where is he?

A loud smack rang through the air and she sat up, gathered the covers around her more tightly, eyes straining to see. *Is that a shadow in the corner, over by the window?* She hardly dared to breathe as she wondered what to do. *Get out*, she told herself. *Just get yourself out of here.* Isn't that what Dan would want, for her to be safe? He was more than capable of looking after himself, given the size of him. She considered this for a moment. *But what if there's someone else downstairs. An accomplice?* Adrenaline surged round her body as she squinted in the dark, trying to see what was going on.

'Leave me alone! I haven't done anything!' Dan's words sounded more like a threat than a request. A flicker of silvery moonlight shone through the shutters, lighting up his profile for a moment before disappearing again. Her heart was racing so fast her breath was coming out in shallow gasps. Then she realised what she'd seen: Dan, staring at the wall. Nobody else.

With a sigh of relief, she understood. *He's sleepwalking. Having a nightmare. What should I do?* She frowned, trying to think, but she had no experience with this, nothing she could draw on to help, and there was no way she was going near him while he was in this mood. Shivers ran through her body and she realised that, for the first time, she was scared of him. His size had always been a comfort to her, but now he was behaving like the Incredible Hulk, she was helpless to stop him.

Escape. Get downstairs. Wait until it's over.

She was about to sneak out of bed and run for the door when renewed shouting startled her. He sounded much closer now. 'I didn't. I told you, I didn't do anything!'

Another flare of moonlight illuminated his face, which was turned towards her now, his features twisted into an expression of hatred that made her blood run cold. Suddenly, he dashed towards her, arms flailing, grunting and cursing under his breath as though he was struggling to push someone off him. Her escape route was blocked and she was rooted to the spot, unable to move while she watched the scene unfold. His shadowy bulk crashed into the bed, but he didn't seem to feel it, just kept coming towards her, his fists punching at the air, the bed, the pillows.

He's going to hit me.

She screamed and threw herself onto the floor, feeling the movement of air as his fist flew past her, landing where she'd been lying not a moment before.

'Oh my God, oh my God, oh my God,' she whimpered as she scuttled across the floor on her hands and knees and into the en-suite, where she banged the door shut and turned the lock. It took a moment for her to catch her breath before she could stagger to her feet and reach the light switch, relieved to banish the darkness. Things felt safer in the light.

She leant against the door, pulling big gulps of air into her lungs while her heart galloped and her mind tried to grasp what had just happened.

Christ, if I hadn't moved, I would have had his fist in my face.

A bloodcurdling cry came from the bedroom, visceral and unlike anything she'd heard before. A sound full of anguish and pain that seemed to go on and on, the air vibrating with the misery of it.

She moved away from the door and whatever was going on in the bedroom, flipped the toilet seat down and perched on it while she listened. Mercifully, the noise stopped. She heard a thump. Then nothing. She waited as the silence settled, arms hugging her chest, not sure what to do for the best. Eventually, after it had been quiet for a while, she unlocked the door and opened it a chink. A narrow beam of light illuminated her sleeping husband. He was sprawled across the bed like a starfish, leaving no room for Chloe. Which was fine, she decided, as she crept out of the bedroom and into the room next door, making sure she turned the lock.

Sleep eluded her as she tossed and turned, listening for footsteps, or shouts, unable to forget what she'd just experienced. That was one humdinger of a nightmare he'd been having, and it made her wonder what had got him so stirred up. Or who. Because he'd clearly been speaking to someone. Finally, she fell asleep with that thought in her mind.

She woke to the sound of tapping on the door.

'Chloe? Chloe?'

The handle rattled, and she blinked awake, wondering where she was for a moment, before she remembered. *He was sleepwalking.* She lay on her back, waiting for her brain to come awake, all the questions from the night before flooding into her mind. *What's he so worried about?*

'Chloe, what are you doing in there? Open the door.'

Oh God, he won't know he had a nightmare, will he? What did he think when I wasn't there when he woke up? Is he going to be mad at me for locking myself in here?

She cringed and swung her legs out of bed, unsure which side of her husband she was going to see when she opened the door.

She gave him a welcoming smile, not wanting another day to start badly. No, today she needed answers, and the only way to get them was if he was relaxed. She caught the hurt in his eyes and put a hand round his neck, drawing him close, a lingering kiss the only way to break the awkwardness between them.

He pulled away and gazed at her. 'What's going on? I just don't understand.'

She sighed and took his hand, led him into the bedroom, pulling him down to sit next to her on the bed. 'You had a nightmare last night. Did you know that?'

He frowned. 'Did I?'

'You were sleepwalking. Shouting. Telling someone to get off you.'

He looked away.

'It was pretty scary,' she continued. 'I went to hide in the bathroom. Then, when you fell asleep, I came in here.' She watched him, willing him to say something. 'I was really scared, Dan.'

Finally, he met her gaze, a frown creasing his forehead. 'Oh God, I'm so sorry. I thought I'd grown out of that stuff. I used to do it when I was a kid. I was... Look, I know this sounds daft, but I was bullied at school for a while.'

Chloe's eyes widened. She couldn't imagine that this hulk of a man ever got bullied.

He saw the incredulity in her gaze and shrugged. 'I was small when I was little. Only started growing when I was fifteen.'

She was silent for a moment. There was something in the tone of his voice that made her doubt the truth of his words, but she couldn't say exactly what it was. *You're being paranoid*, she told herself. *Why can't he have been bullied as a child?* Lots of kids were and it did tend to have a lasting psychological effect. She reached for his hand. 'Do you want to tell me about it?'

He sighed and was silent for a moment. 'Not much to tell, really. No reason for the bullying except I was the weedy kid in glasses.'

'Glasses?'

'Yeah, I was short-sighted. But I had laser treatment a few years ago, so it wasn't a problem when I was playing rugby. The club paid for it.'

'Right.' Of course, he'd told her he used to play rugby. But if the club had paid for it, then that suggested it was a bit more serious than a game with the lads on a Sunday morning. *So many things I don't know about him.* 'So, what level were you playing at?'

He put her hand to his lips and kissed her fingers, one by one. 'Do we have to talk about rugby, Mrs Marsden? You see, I'm on my honeymoon and I've got much more interesting things to be doing.'

She shivered as he leant over and kissed her neck, his hands travelling down her back. And that was it. Conversation over. Once again, he'd deflected her questions, leaving her feeling that the longer she spent with this man, the less she knew about him.

CHAPTER SIXTEEN

Over the next few days, Chloe's doubts about Dan had faded to a niggle at the back of her mind. She was emotional, she told herself, a bit overtired after the blur of the last two weeks, and once she relaxed, everything had a logical explanation. Even her phone going missing. After all, they'd slept for a little bit of the journey on the plane, easy for someone to steal it from her bag if they'd wanted to. She was, by her own admission, an over-thinker. And that was clearly the problem here. It was all in her mind, making connections where there weren't any, and she had to let it go, trust the intuition that had led her to agree to marry Dan in the first place. If she could only put all her stupid worries behind her, then maybe she could start enjoying herself. Besides, Dan was being the perfect husband. He was attentive and considerate and did all the cooking and had organised some days out. She didn't have to do a thing.

As time moved on and she couldn't find the right moment to ask him all those questions that had seemed so important, she found that she didn't need the answers anymore. That would just sour the atmosphere, and she'd be mortified if the problem lay with her overactive imagination rather than anything real.

Once she'd put her concerns out of her mind, her hopes for the honeymoon started to become a reality. They went kayaking in the bay and landed on a deserted beach, where they had a picnic. They snorkelled in the crystal-clear waters, hiked through the nature reserve and explored the area. He was easy company again, now that she wasn't behaving like a spoilt teenager, and his love for her was so apparent, he might as well have had it tattooed on his forehead.

On the next-to-last day of their honeymoon, they took the water taxi to Colom Island, which sat just off the mouth of the bay. It was midweek and only Dan and Chloe were on the small inflatable motorboat that could probably hold a dozen people at most. After the downpour on their first day, they had been blessed with beautiful weather, and today was no different: the sea shimmered in the sunlight and the island ahead of them seemed to float above the water on the heat haze.

'Isn't it gorgeous?' Dan said, his arms around her shoulders as he held her to him.

'Hmm, it really is. I almost never want to leave.' She turned to him and laughed. 'And it's just as good as the Maldives.'

Dan had been right. The place was beautiful and quiet, the villa was better than a hotel would have been – more private and cosy – and over the past few days the bond between them had grown stronger than ever. Yes, he was always alert to potential danger, pernickety about security and keeping everything locked, but she could live with that. Being protective was hardly a fault when all was said and done. And being without her phone was actually quite liberating. She'd borrowed Dan's to ring her gran a couple of times and as the carer had Dan's number, she knew she'd be in touch if there was a problem. She glanced at him, the grin on his face telling her that he was delighted by her response.

He kissed the top of her head. 'I love the Spanish way of life, don't you?'

She nodded. 'It is pretty relaxed, I'll say that for it. And the idea of a siesta in the middle of the day, then being out and about later in the evening when it cools down, is a nice way to live.'

'The language is lovely as well, isn't it? And I do believe you're starting to pick it up, after just a few days. Imagine if we could actually live here for a while, you'd be fluent!'

She laughed. 'In your dreams. I can manage "hello" and "thank you", but that's about it. I'm not great at languages. Not like you.'

'So much cheaper living here than in Brighton. We've hardly spent anything on food.'

'Hmm. It's not just food in Brighton, is it? I mean, transport alone eats up so much money, then rents are going through the roof. You get used to living in something like a rabbit hutch, thinking it's fine, then you come here and have a whole house to yourself and…' She shrugged, not quite ready to think about going home yet, to her job, looking after her gran and all those other chores that went with day-to-day life.

'It's a healthier way to live, no doubt about that.' He smoothed her hair away from her face, an earnest look in his eyes. 'Stress is such a killer, isn't it? Not to mention air pollution.'

She nodded, eyes scanning the horizon, aware that she hadn't felt this relaxed for a very long time. Not since her holiday before her mum died, all those years ago. Nine years of stress and guilt about what she'd done – what effect had that had on her body? And all those car fumes she was breathing every day during her commute to work. Dan had a point, she supposed. But she did love the hustle and bustle of living in a city.

She squinted at him, the sun in her eyes. 'You don't think it might get a bit boring here after a while?'

'What? You can't mean that.'

'Well… The village is lovely, and all this wonderful countryside to explore is great, but Menorca is only a very small island – even the capital city isn't much more than a town.'

He huffed. 'Cities aren't everything, though, are they? We both love being active and doing stuff outdoors. Why would we choose to live in a city when the countryside would offer more of what we like doing? And it would be so much healthier, less stressful. Cheaper.' His eyes searched her face. 'Imagine how much better off we'd be living somewhere like this.'

She realised, with a jolt, that he was being serious. This was something he wanted her to consider, and she was paralysed by the thought. *Leaving the UK? Christ!* It had never occurred to her that would be on the agenda. Dan's mum was better, so that freed him up, but she had her gran to consider. Surely they'd live in her apartment? Especially since Dan wasn't working at the moment. It was where they'd spent all their time together since they'd met, and she felt it wasn't an unreasonable assumption. But it was clear that he had other ideas. A weight settled in her stomach and she started to feel a bit queasy as the boat bounced over the waves.

Not now, she decided, hoping that her breakfast wasn't going to make a reappearance. *I just want to enjoy a bit more fun before we get down to discussing anything like that.* Because she knew there were compromises to be made, negotiations to be had, and it would all get a bit heated if they couldn't find common ground.

'I think you'd just get used to it,' Dan said, breaking into her thoughts. 'Once you'd slowed down and adjusted your expectations. I think you'd find pleasure in different things.'

'Hmm.' Her eyes slid away from his and took in the island ahead of them. It wasn't that she didn't like the idea, it was just that she had responsibilities. Ones that she couldn't shed in an instant. Caring for her gran was absolutely non-negotiable. Then there was her job, which she really enjoyed and had no intention of giving up. They hadn't talked about that either.

The tone of the engine changed as the boat slowed, the landing jetty not far away now. In the future, when her gran was no longer with them, would she consider moving abroad? She decided to open her mind to the possibility, play along for a while and see what she felt about the idea.

'Earth to Chloe,' Dan said, giving her a nudge. 'We're here.'

Chloe flashed him a smile. Only one full day left before they went home. Maybe this was as good a time as any to hammer out some of the essential details of their married life. She'd just have to get her timing right, because there was no storming off to be done here and it was a few hours until the water taxi would be back to collect them. She took a deep breath and reached for Dan's hand as she got out of the boat.

They found a path leading over the island, stopping at the highest point to have their picnic and enjoy the views back towards the mainland. On either side of the bay, low rocky cliffs edged the sea, which lapped at the shore in little crested waves, like pieces of lace on the water. Viewing the land from here, it all looked surprisingly green, with the shrubby dunes on one side and the wooded slopes on the other, ending at the top of low, rocky cliffs.

'Isn't that magnificent?' Dan said as he laid out the picnic blanket and started unpacking the rucksack they'd brought. 'Seriously. Just imagine living here. You'd have this great big playground all year round and the town just six miles away. Honestly, it only took a quarter of an hour to get to the supermarket, and that was on the bus. I only got a taxi back because it started raining.'

He passed her a chunk of bread and the cheese they'd bought from the village shop, then dug around in the rucksack for olives, spicy sausage and the bottles of water.

The bread smelt delicious and she was so ready for food she felt like her stomach had turned itself inside out. She pulled off a piece and stuffed it in her mouth, followed by a chunk of cheese.

'Mmm, that cheese is amazing. Why does it always taste better when you're having a picnic?' Now that she'd started eating, Chloe couldn't seem to get it down fast enough.

'I could get a job in a bar or a restaurant.'

She looked at him, eyes narrowed. 'What? You're not kidding about this, are you? You want to live here?' She could hear the disparaging tone in her voice and cringed, aware that she'd have to tread more carefully.

He shrugged. 'Play along with me…' He leant across and kissed her cheek. 'Let's pretend life's simple and we could decide to stay.'

She laughed and chewed a couple of olives while she thought. 'Okay. But what would I do in this wonderful world of yours?'

He handed her a couple of slices of sausage and another piece of bread. 'You could… find a job at the hospital. Or do private consultations for holidaymakers, at one of the resorts maybe, or travelling round the island. Or look after the elderly people. Lots of ex-pats in Menorca, you know.'

She laughed.

He looked at her, his eyes studying her expression, she thought, assessing how she felt about the idea. 'I'm sure you'd have no trouble getting a job even though you don't speak Spanish yet. But I'm fluent, so it would be easier for me to pick up something quickly.'

He was trying to sound nonchalant, but there was a graveness to his voice that brought a surge of panic to her thoughts. *Am I going to have a say in this, or has the decision already been made?* She stopped chewing and stared at him.

'I could earn the money at the start.' He handed her a bottle of water, unaware of the effect the conversation was having on her. 'We could have a house, a whole house, not just a scabby little apartment.'

She bristled. 'My apartment isn't scabby.'

He nodded. 'Your apartment is definitely scabby. And it smells. Of damp.'

Her eyes widened. She'd always thought of her apartment as cosy and had thought he felt the same. 'It does not,' she said, defensively, the attack feeling personal now. *Oh God, what else doesn't he like?* She suddenly felt vulnerable. *Is he going to try and change me, change my whole life?* Surely that wasn't what marriage was about. She moved herself away from him slightly and took a deep breath, getting ready to stand her ground because she sensed there was more to come.

He carried on talking, oblivious to her discomfort. 'You're probably just used to it. But honestly, it really does smell pretty horrible.'

'Right. Good to know.' She turned away from him and gazed at the view so he wouldn't see her hurt, hoping they'd come to the end of that particular conversation.

'Just think, you could eat this lovely fresh food all the time. And we all know that the Mediterranean diet is the healthiest on the planet. That could be us. Super healthy.'

She snapped her head back to look at him, angry now that he could be so insensitive and not even realise. 'Oh yes. And I suppose we could have a lovely villa like the one we're renting. No smelly little basement apartments for us.'

'Exactly.' He beamed at her. 'Imagine waking up to that view every morning.'

She looked back towards the land, working out the geography from this angle, her eyes travelling up from the village until she found their villa, sitting on top of the little bluff above the sea. The windows glinted, the whitewash gleamed.

'Look.' She pointed. 'That's where we're staying, isn't it? Up there?'

'Oh yeah. That's our house. Sounds nice that, doesn't it? Our house.'

Nip this in the bud, now, she told herself. *Otherwise he'll get even more carried away and think it's real.* She sighed. *Go on, do it.*

'In another life maybe. But we can't just up and leave. We've both got responsibilities. I mean, it's a fun game, but it just wouldn't be possible. Not at the moment. Besides, don't you think a little island like this might feel a bit claustrophobic after a while? I kinda like living in a city.'

'You probably haven't thought about it as a possibility, though, have you? Not properly. You know, worked out what you really want out of life, looked at the pros and cons of things. I reckon this place has a lot going for it.'

Oh God, he means it! He wants to live here. Her mind started scrabbling for counterarguments, things that would make him change his mind.

'What about your mum?'

'She's doing great. She doesn't need me anymore.'

'But would you want to live this far away?'

'You're making it sound like it's on the other side of the world. It's not that far away, is it? Flights are dirt cheap, especially off-season, and wouldn't it be a nice place for her to come on holiday?'

Christ, he's thought of everything.

Chloe shook her head. 'You know I can't leave, don't you? I've got Gran to look after. There's no way I can leave her on her own.'

Dan started to say something, then closed his mouth, his jaw clenched as he looked out to sea.

Stalemate.

They were silent for a while, both lost in their thoughts, Chloe's mind whirling in dizzying circles. Taking responsibility for caring for her gran was the only way she could make amends for her mother's death. It was her penance. But Dan didn't know anything about that. And she couldn't tell him because he wouldn't want to be married to a killer, would he?

She sighed and leant back against a rock, suddenly tired and apprehensive about the inevitable conflict that lay ahead. Her eyes drifted over to the headland and back up to the villa as she let her thoughts wander, hoping they'd find a solution to what seemed an impossible situation. She tensed and frowned.

'Dan, is that somebody standing on our patio, or am I seeing things?' She sat up, Dan following her movement, both of them gazing in the direction of the house.

'Bloody hell, you're right.'

The figure was just an outline against the whitewashed walls, but they seemed to be moving around the building.

'He's looking in the window. Is it a he? Or is that long hair?' Nowadays, she realised, hair length really wasn't a determining factor when it came to gender.

The person disappeared for a moment.

'It could be the gardener?' she suggested. 'Or someone who does maintenance, maybe? Or the letting agent?'

Dan got to his feet to get a better look. He reached down for the rucksack, unzipped a pocket and pulled out a pair of binoculars that they'd found in the villa and had been using to watch the wildlife. 'Christ!' he muttered under his breath.

'What? What is it?' She scrambled to her feet, but he didn't reply because he was busy with his phone and his expression told her to be quiet. He spoke in Spanish, quick forceful words which she didn't understand, and before she knew what was happening, he was packing up their belongings.

'What's going on, Dan? Is there a problem?'

He didn't answer, his body tense, a stern expression on his face that made him look like a different man. He set off walking back to the jetty, the water taxi visible in the distance, heading their way. He'd obviously called and asked for it to come back and pick them up early. She hurried to catch up, put a hand on his arm and tried to pull him to a halt, anger burning in her chest.

'For God's sake! You could at least answer. I'm not a child, you know. What's going on?'

He stopped. 'I don't like the idea of someone prowling round the house, okay? Remote areas like this, it could be a burglar.'

'Yeah, well, that's just shattered the fantasy, hasn't it? Why would we be safer here than Brighton?'

She heard him sigh as he strode ahead, and she hurried after him.

'You didn't answer me.'

He stopped and turned, glowering at her. She shrank back, aware of the tremor in her legs. All the things she was about to say slid back down her throat and she could almost feel herself shrinking under his gaze.

'I'm your husband,' he said with forced patience, towering over her. 'It's my job to protect you and keep you safe. So, you just need to trust me to do that, okay?' He looked away from her at the advancing water taxi. 'I'm going back to make sure the house is secure. Then I'll contact the letting agents and see if they sent anyone up there. Get it all checked out. Once we're sure everything is above board, we can relax.'

He'd never talked to her like that before and there was a look in his eyes that forced her to comply, silently tagging along behind him as they made their way to the landing stage. Never, for one moment, had she imagined she would be scared of Dan, but after his nightmare and the way he'd lashed out with his fists, she understood what he was capable of. Clearly there was a side to his character that he'd kept hidden. One that seemed to be edging its way out into the open. Her stomach swirled. *Is this the real Dan?*

'I want you to go and sit in one of the restaurants and I'll come and get you when it's all checked out, okay?'

She shrugged, unwilling to argue with him while he was in this mood. 'Whatever,' she said, her annoyance clear. In her eyes he was overreacting, their day out unnecessarily cut short. She'd watched the person looking round their house, and their actions were leisurely rather than furtive. Surely, if they'd wanted to break in, they would have just thrown a rock through a window. And even if they had broken in, what was there to take? Everything of any value was with them in the rucksack.

Why is he being so paranoid?

As soon as they reached the landing stage, Dan jumped out and she clambered after him. Her mind pondered the question as she watched him stride down the road towards the villa while she found a seat outside her favourite café.

She thought over their time together and realised there had been a few incidents now that had gone unexplained. Things that had bothered her at the time and he had brushed away. Like the vandalism of his car and him not wanting to report it. *That was strange, wasn't it?* And his lateness for their wedding. She'd never had a proper explanation for that either, but something weird had happened that day. Something that had got him and his mum jumpy. Then there was his terrifying nightmare, and his explanation hadn't sounded completely genuine.

He's definitely hiding something. And whatever it is frightens him. Her hand shook as she took a sip of her orange juice.

All the concerns that she'd wafted away as being unimportant flowed back into her mind, and her eyes narrowed. *He's running away from something.* That was the only answer she could come up with. *All the talk about moving here... is that what it's about? He's frightened to go back?*

Her mind whirred through all the possibilities, a whole list reappearing for closer scrutiny, until a new thought popped into her head. *Is this to do with that woman?* Another incident that he'd waved away as unimportant: a conversation with a local, he'd said, asking about activities and where to hire kayaks. She wasn't buying that explanation anymore. *Maybe it's not what I thought. Maybe it's something that happened here that's pulling him to want to stay. Something that would have consequences if he left.*

Her head was throbbing now, her hand grasping her drink a little tighter as her thoughts muddled together. This theorising was getting her nowhere. *It can't go on. No more messing about, you've got to confront him, get him to tell you the truth.*

That's when she saw the woman who'd been talking to Dan on their first day, as if she'd popped out of Chloe's mind and materialised before her. But this time, she was pushing a baby in a buggy. Chloe's eyes widened, nausea stirring in her belly as a new possibility presented itself. *Oh my God. Tell me that's not his baby.* She stood, snatched up her bag and followed the woman up the street, her jaw set. It was time to know the truth.

CHAPTER SEVENTEEN

It was a little while before Chloe got back to the café, her eyes sore and hidden behind her sunglasses. She ordered a glass of wine, needing something to take the edge off her shock, and downed it in one before ordering another.

Ten minutes later, Dan appeared, a familiar smile on his face. 'All sorted,' he said as he flopped onto a chair on the other side of the table. He reached over and took her hand. 'Sorry I've been so long, but it took a while to get hold of the letting agent.'

She glared at him, mouth pinched, glad that her eyes were hidden.

'What?' he said, as she studied him in silence.

'I don't know what's got into you, Dan, I really don't.'

'What do you mean?'

'Well, I've realised there's so much I don't know about you, and now I'm your wife, I really need to understand.' *That's it. Give him an opportunity. One last chance to tell the truth.*

Her jaw clenched.

His smile faltered.

'There wasn't a problem at the house, was there?' Her question made him let go of her hand, and he sat back in his chair.

'No. It was the guy who does all the maintenance.' He fiddled with his sunglasses, wiping the lenses on his T-shirt rather than looking at her. 'He'd got his dates mixed up and thought he was scheduled to do work today, when it had been moved to next week.'

Chloe nodded. 'So, you were just being paranoid?'

He didn't reply.

'Tell me… who did you think it was?'

Dan frowned, and his voice sharpened. 'For God's sake, Chloe. It was an easy mistake to make, seeing someone who looks like he's casing up the joint. That would worry anyone.'

'But you've been so jumpy this week. You can't deny that, can you?'

'What do you mean?'

'Well, wherever we go, you're looking around, as if you're expecting to see someone. Or maybe you are? Do you know someone who lives here, is that it?'

Come on. This is your chance. Tell me.

Dan shook his head and her heart felt heavy. 'No. I don't know why you'd think that.' He put on his sunglasses so she could no longer see his eyes. 'What's with all the questions anyway? I'm trying to be a good husband, that's all.' His mouth twitched, a little pout, and she wanted to slap it off his face.

'Well, you've sort of flipped into this Jason Statham persona.' She tried to keep her voice light, playful, so he might decide that now was the time to tell her. *Very last chance*, she decided, studying his face. 'It's making you all jumpy and that makes me feel jumpy.'

He sighed, his hands playing with a beer mat on the table. 'I love you so much, Chloe. If anything bad ever happened to you, it would destroy me.' He looked at her. 'I'm sorry if I'm getting it wrong, but I just want to keep you safe.'

Chloe huffed. 'But you're way over the top, Dan. That's the problem. Just look at this place! It's a sleepy little village on a sleepy little island in the middle of the Med. I think we're as safe here as we could be anywhere in the world.' She leant forwards. 'Why don't you tell me what's really going on? Stop treating me like an idiot and tell me the truth.'

He gazed at her for a moment, his expression unreadable.

Chloe exploded. 'You're a liar! A sneaky, horrible liar. I know your secret. I know why we're here. Let's forget all this cloak and dagger stuff. Let's forget you being the noble protector of your helpless little wife, shall we?' She stood and leant over the table, her body trembling with indignation.

'Chloe! What are you doing? Keep your voice down.' Dan looked around, but the rest of the tables were empty and anyway, Chloe didn't care who heard what she had to say.

She jabbed a finger at him. 'I gave you a chance to tell the truth, but no, you wanted to keep up the pretence. Well, it's over. Our marriage is over.'

Dan gasped as if she'd hit him, his mouth hanging open. 'What? What are you talking about?'

The wine made her voice a little slurred, but her anger came through loud and clear. 'I met Sofia while you were gone. And a lovely little baby.' Her face crumpled as she struggled to hold back her tears. 'Who, I believe, is your son.'

She turned to leave, but Dan grabbed her arm and pulled her to him. She struggled against him, tears trickling down her cheeks. 'Let me go. I don't want you near me.'

'Shh. Shh. It's okay.' His arms tightened around her, preventing her from escaping. 'Just calm down, will you, and let me explain.'

'Let you make up more lies?' she shouted, still squirming. 'You must be joking.'

'No, you don't understand.' His arms clasped her so tight, it was hard to breathe.

Suddenly she understood there was no point in fighting him and she stilled. *Let him tell his lies then you can get away.* 'Go on then,' she said with a sneer. 'Make me understand, why don't you?'

He loosened his grasp and walked away, heading towards the house where Sofia lived. She stared after him for a moment then followed. *I've got to know his version of events*, she decided. *If I'm going to call time on this marriage, I've got to be sure.* But there was no arguing with the fact that Sofia had a baby and Dan was the father. No arguing at all. Sofia had told her, straight to her face.

She watched him knock on Sofia's door, somehow distant from the emotional drama of it all. *How is he going to try and wangle his way out of this one?*

Sofia answered and started gabbling in rapid Spanish, hands flying around, while Dan nodded and replied, both of them casting glances at Chloe, who stood a little distance away. *They're cooking up a story*, she decided, reluctant to get any closer.

Then Sofia beckoned to her. 'Come, come,' she said. 'You ran away before I could explain properly.'

Chloe hesitated.

'Please,' Dan said as he walked towards her. 'Listen to what she has to say.'

A voice in Chloe's head screamed at her to go, not to listen to any more lies. The evidence was plain to see, and she wanted no part of their cover-up story. She shook her head, started backing away, but he grabbed her arm and pulled her behind him, bundling her into Sofia's house before she could resist. The door closed, leaving the three of them standing in a dim hallway.

'Just listen, will you,' he hissed into her ear.

'I tried to tell her.' Sofia stood with her hands on her hips. 'My English. You know it's not too good.'

'Sofia is a friend. A gay friend.' He waited for that to register. Chloe stopped struggling and looked at Sofia, who nodded. *Gay?* 'She lives in Mahón with her wife, Gina.'

Sofia went into another room and came back with a photo of her and another woman in wedding dresses, to prove that his words were the truth. 'This is her father's house. He runs the water taxi and owns the house we're staying in.'

'No letting agency, then. So that was a lie as well.' Chloe's head was spinning and she felt nauseous.

Dan gritted his teeth. 'For God's sake. I'm trying to explain.'

'Oh, please do. Don't let me stop you.' She shook herself free from his grasp and turned to look at him. He still had his sunglasses on. *Still hiding*, she thought, preparing herself for more lies.

'Sofia and Gina wanted to start a family and asked me if I would help them.'

Chloe huffed as she looked Sofia up and down. 'Yeah, that must have been a real chore.'

'I was merely a sperm donor. That's it. Completely impersonal, no sex involved.'

'That's right,' Sofia said. 'We never had sex. And anyway, Gina had the baby, not me.'

Chloe closed her eyes, completely bemused by the story she was being told. *Is this the truth?* She felt dizzy, dots appearing in front of her eyes. She steadied herself against the wall but couldn't stop herself from sliding to the floor as everything went black.

She awoke in the back of a taxi as it bumped its way up the track to the villa. Dan sat beside her, holding her hand.

'Nearly there,' he said. 'You fainted.'

She drew her hand away from his, closed her eyes again as she remembered Sofia and Gina and the baby. *What have I got myself into? More to the point, do I believe him?* It was too much to deal with and she gazed at the trees as they drove up through the forest, hardly noticing when they finally emerged at the house.

Dan waved a couple of notes at the driver before getting out and hurrying round to her side, ready to lift her out.

She batted his hands away. 'Leave me alone,' she snapped, edging her way out of the car, holding onto the door as she steadied herself. She still felt a bit sick and her legs were definitely wobbly, knees threatening to buckle.

'Let me help you,' Dan said, his face full of concern. 'Please, Chloe.'

She relented as she gazed at the villa and the path she would need to negotiate. He scooped her up and she resisted the urge to kick and scratch and lash out in any way she could, settling instead for grinding her teeth.

As soon as they were in the house, she wriggled from his grasp and hauled herself upstairs and into the spare bedroom, where she locked the door, leaning on it while she debated whether she was going to be sick or not.

She heard his footsteps, then he banged on the door, the vibrations jarring through her body. 'Chloe, we have to talk. Let me explain.'

'Let you tell me more lies? Yeah, I don't think so.'

She crawled into bed, and after a while he went away. In the silence, there was one question that refused to leave her mind. *Why would he bring me on our honeymoon to a place where he has secrets?* It didn't make sense. If the child meant nothing to him, if he was the biological father in name only and intended to play no part in the child's life, why come back? *And why would he be trying to persuade me to stay here?*

She desperately needed answers to so many questions, but she felt so tired, so weary of it all, that she couldn't face him. Her eyelids refused to stay open and she fell asleep.

CHAPTER EIGHTEEN

It was morning when Chloe awoke. She lay in bed for a while, listening to the sounds of Dan in the kitchen while she ran through the events of the previous day. The existence of the baby didn't explain everything, she realised. Although it might explain why they were here, and in this house, there were other things that didn't make sense.

She got out of bed and wandered into the master bedroom to get showered and dressed, deciding that as they'd be going home tomorrow, she only had to get through today, then she'd be on her way back to normality. Today, she thought, she'd go into town and stay there, unable to face the possibility of running into Sofia again. She wanted to be around people rather than stuck out here with only Dan for company, trying to trick her with his lies. Maybe a day out, in an environment where she felt safe, would help her get everything in perspective.

Her stomach was playing up – the queasiness she'd felt yesterday was still there, and she wondered if it was the stress that was getting to her. She sat on the bed and was towelling her hair when Dan came in. The sight of him looking so worried and sad was like a punch to the heart, making her eyes sting. *How has it all gone so wrong?*

He sat next to her on the bed, not too close, respectful. 'I'm so sorry you had to find out like that. You've got to believe me, I wanted to wait for the right moment.'

Anger flared in her chest. 'I don't think there's ever a right time for something like that. But you should have told me. And why bring me here, for God's sake? Of all the places in the world we could have gone, why did we end up here?'

He sighed, his voice unsteady when he eventually spoke. 'Because it's the safest place I know.'

She was shaking with frustration. 'Safe? Why are you so worried about being safe? This was our honeymoon. What we needed was romantic, not bloody safe. And it might seem safe to you, but for me… with your baby here. That's right, Dan, the baby you didn't tell me about. And staying in the house owned by their relative. Christ! It's unbelievable that you'd think for one minute that was okay.'

She stood and paced around the room, the strangeness of the situation more apparent now she'd said it out loud.

'I'm sorry, Chloe. Really, I am, but I did have your best interests at heart.' His eyes shone as they followed her movements. 'I love you so much, you're my whole world, babe. And if anything happened to you, well I'd—'

'Stop it!' she yelled. 'Just stop it.' Her hands knotted in her hair as she paced. She looked at him, took in his dishevelled appearance, the fact that he was on the verge of tears, and suddenly it made sense. 'Have you got some mental health problem you didn't tell me about? Is that it? Some sort of paranoia? Because that's what it feels like.'

His shoulders slumped, a look of confusion in his eyes. 'No. No, what are you talking about?' He looked away. 'It's nothing like that.'

'Well, what is it then?' She tugged at her hair. 'What the bloody hell is going on? Because this… your behaviour ever since we got married… well, it's not normal.'

He sat in silence and she screamed her frustration at the ceiling. 'I can't cope with you. I really can't. I'm going into town. I need to get a phone.'

His head whipped up and he blinked. 'You don't need a phone. You can use mine.'

She shook her head, her voice slow and determined. 'I need my own phone and I'm going to get one, okay?'

He thought for a moment, then stood. 'Okay.'

She glared at him. 'Who invited you? I'm going alone.'

He shook his head, jaw set. 'You're not, Chloe. I'm coming with you.'

'I don't want you to. Why can't you understand? I need a bit of space.' She turned and ran downstairs before he could argue, pulled on her trainers and grabbed a fleece off the peg.

His footsteps thudded behind her. *Handbag! Where is it?* She couldn't get to town without money, and she rushed round the living area, wondering where she'd left it. Normally, it was hung over the back of a dining chair. But not today.

She could feel the bulk of him behind her and she turned, backing away. 'Don't try and stop me,' she warned, her eyes frantically scanning the room, but her bag was nowhere to be seen. She couldn't remember much about arriving home yesterday, so she really wasn't sure where she'd left it. *Dan carried me in.* But had she brought her handbag? *Christ, did I leave it in the village? Or the taxi?*

Dan blocked the doorway, arms folded across his chest. 'Either I come or you're not going.'

'What do you mean?'

'You're not going to get far without any money, are you?'

Her eyes widened as she realised what that meant. 'You've got my bag?'

He nodded. 'I'm just keeping you safe, Chloe.'

'Oh, for God's sake. I feel like a bloody prisoner now.'

He stared at her, his gaze unnerving.

'Well, you'll have to give it back to me tomorrow, when we go home, so you might as well give it to me now.'

He shook his head. 'I'm sorry, but that's not happening.'

'What?'

'We're not going back.'

Chloe held onto the top of a chair while she stared at him, not sure if she'd heard him right. 'What are you talking about? Of course we're going back.'

He shook his head. 'No, we're not. We can't at the moment. We have to stay here.'

'Christ, Dan, you're not making any sense! I know it's a nice daydream and I'm sure if you were still single that would be an option for you. But I've got to go back to look after Gran. You know that.' Her heart raced, her head filling with panic, pressing at her skull. *He can't mean it. He can't.* 'And I've got my job. I can't just walk out of that, can I?'

'It's not safe for us to go back. There's… an issue I need to sort out first and I have no idea how long it will take. So, in the meantime, we have to stay.'

She held the chair tighter, trying to find words that were out of her grasp, while he carried on speaking. 'I've sorted out a job in town here, working in a bar for now until I can get something better. And I've spoken to Sofia's dad and we've agreed a winter let on the villa. So, we have a home and we have a source of income.'

'No! No, we can't stay. Haven't you been listening to me? I've got Gran to look after. And a bar job won't give us enough money to live on.'

'Well, we could look for physio work for you. And I can do private tutoring or see if there's TEFL work around.' He sounded so rational, so calm, but to Chloe it felt like madness.

She sank onto the chair, the enormity of what he was saying starting to sink in. 'I don't speak Spanish. Nobody's going to give me a job.'

'You might not need to. Why don't we just have a look and see what there is?'

'But I don't want to stay, Dan. I don't.' Her voice wavered as she fought to control her emotions, the whole situation spinning away from her. 'I need to get back.'

He pressed his lips together and gazed at her for a moment before speaking. 'I'm afraid you don't have a choice.'

CHAPTER NINETEEN

Chloe stared at her husband as though seeing him for the first time. She'd never seen that expression on his face, the way his lips thinned to nothing, his eyebrows drawn so close together they joined into one dark line, the grooves down each side of his mouth, the set of his jaw.

She kept his gaze for a long moment and finally looked away, blinking back tears. *Gran was right, wasn't she? Marry in haste, repent at leisure.* How many times had she said that to Chloe over the last month? But Chloe had thought she'd known better. She wiped her eyes, determined to try and change his mind.

'You can't do this to me, Dan. You can't keep me here.'

He swallowed, but his expression didn't waver. 'Look, I can't go into details at the moment, but it's for your own safety.' He sat opposite her and reached for her hand. 'You've got to trust me.'

She snatched her hand away and shook her head, frustration sharpening her voice. 'I don't understand. It's still not making sense. Why wouldn't I be safe? You're going to have to explain that to me if there's any chance of me staying.' She glared at him, her anger an unstoppable force now, pushing its way into her chest, quickening her breathing. But he didn't speak, just stared at the table, picking at the wood. She got up and pushed her chair back, jabbed a finger at him. 'You're being ridiculous. Overprotective and ridiculous!'

Her eyes scanned the room and found the door, but Dan was at her side before she could make her escape, holding her arm, squeezing it a little too tight. She winced, tried to slip out of his grasp, but his grip tightened.

'Come on, babe, let's just talk this through and you'll understand it's not as bad as you think it is.' He tugged her over to the sofa and pulled her next to him. 'Let's sit here for a minute while you calm down.'

They sat, his hand still holding her arm until she finally relaxed, acknowledging to herself that now was not the time. If she really wanted to get away, she would have to choose her moment because she would never be a match for him, would never be strong enough or fast enough to get away while he was alert to what she was doing.

She closed her eyes. *What's changed? Why is he being like this? Or… has he always been like this?*

Her mind took her back over their brief relationship, replaying it like a movie. From their first date, he'd always picked her up from her apartment and taken her home. In fact, the only time she'd been on her own was when she came home from work and went to look in on her gran. Other than that, they'd been together. She'd enjoyed his attentiveness. Had revelled in it. But was it a sign of possessiveness, of paranoia: an irrational fear that something bad would happen to her if she was on her own?

Then he'd insisted on organising the honeymoon, changing the destination without telling her, taking them to a remote villa, away from people. *So, what's so scary about people?* Had something happened to him in the past? She thought about his nightmare. *Is this some sort of PTSD symptom playing itself out?*

The more she thought about it, the more it made sense, in which case, the solution might be to get him to talk. If she could get to the bottom of his behaviour, then maybe he would see that there was no threat. That it was all in his imagination. And then she could go home, even if he didn't come with her.

It was inconceivable that she should leave her gran to cope on her own. She needed looking after, and Chloe was the only member of the family available to do that. In any case, she owed it to her gran to stay with her to the end, then she would feel like she'd repaid her debt. *You can't repay a mother for killing their child.* She knew her gran's pain would never diminish, but it was the best Chloe could do and the only way she could live with her conscience.

But you're married now. You've got someone else to think about. From Dan's behaviour, it was clear that he had problems. Surely, he needed her support as well. Hadn't she promised to love him in sickness and in health? *After all those lies he's told you?* It occurred to her then that he might be having some sort of breakdown. Her heart skipped a beat.

She looked at him, sitting next to her, gazing out of the window, his mind clearly somewhere else, and she was torn as to what to do. She decided that her things were probably in the house somewhere, it was just a matter of looking when Dan was occupied doing something else. *Yes, that's my first challenge.* Her pulse started to speed up as she thought about it for a moment.

'I'm not feeling great, Dan.' She stood up. 'I'm going upstairs for a lie down.'

His body tensed at the sound of her voice, his hand clamping her arm before he pulled her back down.

'Ow!' She glared at him. 'Let go of me! That hurts.'

His eyes widened, and his hand dropped from her arm, leaving red rings where his fingers had been. 'I'm so sorry. I didn't… It's just… You have to stay with me. Don't go dashing off anywhere.' He held her hand, a little too firm to be comfortable, his palm sweaty.

She glowered at him, her body tense, her mind darting around, uncertain what she should do for the best. *Run for it?* Then she remembered that the doors were locked. Her heart beat faster.

'I need the loo.' It was her get-out-of-jail card, a request he couldn't ignore.

He looked sheepish then. 'Okay.' But he kept her hand firmly in his and she cursed inwardly as they walked to the cloakroom under the stairs, where he let go of her hand but waited outside the door.

All Chloe wanted was a bit of space, a few moments to herself, to get her head round what was happening and work out how she was going to deal with it. She couldn't think with him glued to her, watching her every move.

She perched on the toilet, her heart thudding in her chest, her whole body shaking with the force of each beat. Dan was really freaking her out now, the whole thing escalating to a different level. If he wasn't such a big man, then it might not worry her so much – she was fit and strong with her physio work, not to mention her love of exercise, and she would think of herself as a match for half the men she knew. But Dan was in a class of his own. He wasn't just a big man, he was huge and could use force to make her do what he wanted. A point he had proven earlier. No, she had to be smart about this. The first thing she had to do was get him to talk about what was happening; maybe then she could use her powers of persuasion to make him see how unreasonable he was being.

Moving to Menorca… What was he thinking, just springing it on her like that? But he was deadly serious. He wasn't going to let her go home. And all that talk about her safety sounded like deluded ramblings. She sighed and leant her elbows on her knees, head in her hands. *What on earth am I going to do?*

'Chloe, are you okay in there?' From the loudness of his voice, Dan was obviously listening at the door.

'On my way,' she called and flushed the loo, then ran the tap. Maybe if she pretended to be okay with everything, she could find a moment when he was more relaxed to discover what was really going on. If she suggested a walk, then she might have the chance to get away – even without money, she could get help, couldn't she?

She had to push past him to get out of the cloakroom door. 'Sorry, my stomach isn't feeling great. Maybe a bit of indigestion. Can we go for a walk, see if that'll settle it down?'

He studied her face for what seemed like a week before nodding, and she let out a quiet breath of relief. She'd feel better if they were outside because at the moment, whether she wanted to entertain the thought or not, she was a prisoner.

'Okay. If that's what you want.' He delved in his pocket, pulled out the key and unlocked the front door, then reached for her hand as they walked down the path, gentle now that the tension seemed to have ebbed out of him.

'You know that I love you more than anything, don't you?'

His words caught her by surprise, touched a vulnerable place in her heart, and a lump formed in her throat. She squeezed his hand, waiting for her flush of emotions to subside before saying, 'And I love you too, Dan. I really do.' This was her opportunity, she realised, and she forced herself to go on. 'But I can't leave Gran. I just can't, I know you won't understand, but after Mum died…' She tailed off, taking a deep breath.

Maybe I should tell him?

The thought made her breath hitch in her throat, but it seemed like her only option. If he understood… properly understood her situation, then perhaps he'd have a rethink and they could go home. And if he was worried about her safety for some reason, then she'd let him be her bodyguard until they'd sorted out the problem. *There must be a compromise, and if I make the first move, then…*

'Dan, there's something I need to tell you.' She stopped and looked up at him, swallowed down her fears before she spoke. 'When Mum died, it was… it was my fault. I… um…' There was no easy way to say it. She took a deep breath and the words tumbled out. 'I was responsible for her death. I killed her.'

He frowned, clearly confused. 'What do you mean?'

She started walking again, her eyes fixed on the ground, her face burning with shame.

'After uni, I moved back home to stay with Mum, had a few weeks off before I started looking for jobs. A bunch of mates off my course organised a last-minute trip to Thailand and invited me along. We'd shared a house for three years and had become very close and this was our big adventure, a blow-out before we all went our separate ways.'

She could feel him staring at her but knew she wouldn't be able to carry on if she caught his eye. She'd never told anyone what had really happened, not a soul knew the real truth, not even her family, and it would be too easy to back out. His hand found hers and their fingers intertwined, giving her the encouragement to carry on.

'Anyway... Mum wasn't well before I was due to go.' She sighed. 'No, the truth is she'd been really poorly with flu, stuck in bed for over a week. And with her being epileptic, she had to be careful because any illness made it worse. I did think about staying, but she shooed me off, said she could look after herself and I deserved a holiday after getting my degree.' Chloe shook her head, knowing that she should have made a different decision, shouldn't have listened to her mum. She gave a hollow laugh, eyes stinging as she remembered their last conversation, how insistent her mother had been. 'She was so proud of me. Wanted me to have a life she hadn't managed to have herself. She'd never had the money to travel when she was young, never had the freedom.'

Chloe's body started to shake with the effort of keeping her emotions in check and she sank onto a boulder at the side of the path, Dan sitting next to her, his hand squeezing hers.

'It's okay,' he said. 'You don't have to tell me if it's too painful. I understand.'

She shook her head, voice cracking. 'No. No, you don't understand. But you need to because then you'll know why...'

She stopped herself, couldn't risk angering him before he knew the whole story. 'So… Mum asked me to get her prescription for her epilepsy meds before I went because she was running low. I stuffed the thing in my pocket and forgot about it. I left the next day. It was a really early flight, so I didn't see her before I went and I just… I left the jeans on my bedroom floor, with the prescription still in the back pocket.' She bit her lip, hardly able to get the words out. 'She told me not to bother ringing while I was away because it was too expensive. Three weeks later, I came home and…' A sob burst out of her chest, the moment still raw and unreal. 'Mum… She was dead. She'd had a fit and choked.'

Dan folded her into his arms, hugging her to him as she cried, the memory all too fresh, the hurt still raw. 'Oh, babe, that's awful, but you didn't kill her.'

'I knew she wasn't well, I mean seriously not well, and couldn't get the prescription herself. I promised her I'd get it before I went away because she had to have her meds every day. She trusted me completely. And I just didn't… I was so focused on my holiday, going off and enjoying myself, I forgot all about it. Her death was completely preventable. If she'd had her meds, she wouldn't have had a fit and she wouldn't have died. I should have put her first instead of thinking about myself and my stupid trip. What did that matter, compared to my mum's life?'

'You didn't kill her, Chloe.'

'I did.' She gulped back her tears and wiped her face with the back of her hand. 'Anyway, the rest of my family is pretty sure that I did. They don't know about the prescription, but they all blame me for her death because I was the one who was at home, I knew what was going on. My brother and sister were in London, Gran was in Brighton, while we were in Leeds, hundreds of miles away. And they didn't know Mum was ill and they didn't know I was going away and leaving her on her own.' She lay her head against his chest, grateful for his embrace. 'I missed the funeral, so I didn't get to say goodbye. My brother and sister didn't talk to me for years. And they still hate me, if our last get-together is anything to go by.'

'So that's why they weren't at the wedding?'

'I didn't invite them in case they came and made trouble. Gran wasn't as bad – you know, she's so old-school, she's of a generation who don't tend to make their feelings known. But there's been a strained atmosphere since Mum died and our relationship isn't what it used to be. She blames me too.'

He stroked her hair and she held him tighter, thinking that this was what she wanted, this closeness, not all the strangeness that had been pushing them apart all week. Perhaps now he'd understand.

'It wasn't your fault, babe. You shouldn't be punishing yourself, whatever your family says.'

'You don't know, Dan. You weren't there.'

'So that's why you don't want to leave your gran?'

'I couldn't go through that again, being blamed for someone's death because I didn't care enough. I owe it to Gran to look after her. I took her daughter away from her.' She looked up at him, blinking back her tears. 'That's why I can't stay here. Not now. Maybe in the future we could think about living abroad, but I'm not sure how much time Gran's got left and I need to be there for her. Mum died alone. I can't let that happen to Gran.'

He released her from his embrace, his eyes locked on hers. 'I understand the situation. I really do. And if I felt you'd be safe going back to Brighton, then there wouldn't be a problem. But it's not safe. That's the thing you need to understand. Your life would be in danger, and I know that sounds weird and melodramatic, but it's the truth. You have to trust me on this and stay here with me.'

She gazed at him, wondering how she could change his mind.

'How about asking your brother and sister to take a turn at looking after your gran? They're not too far from Brighton.'

She pushed away from him, her head feeling like it might explode. 'Weren't you listening?' she snapped. 'They won't talk to me. If I rang them up, they'd slam their phones down. They both have families, they're busy with their jobs. They don't have time to do what I do for her. And they don't know how to clear her chest.'

'Well, we could pay for the carer to stay a bit longer, how about that? From what your gran has said, things have been fine this week, haven't they?'

Chloe shook her head, weary with the effort of her confession and his inability to understand. Her head was aching, the sun hot on the back of her neck. 'It's costing a fortune and we don't even know if we're going to be able to earn enough money to live on over here. At least at home I have a job, somewhere to live. Here we have nothing.'

He kicked at a stone on the path, clearly frustrated by her unwillingness to do as she was told. 'You're wrong.' He pointed back up the track. 'We have a house, I have a job and the cost of living is way lower here than at home.' His eyes bored into her. 'We're staying, Chloe, and that's that.'

The look in his eyes chilled her, the tone of his voice telling her that he meant what he said.

CHAPTER TWENTY

Chloe let the afternoon drift along according to Dan's wishes, trying to act as though she had accepted his decision about not going home. They wandered over the hillside behind the house, exploring tracks she hadn't been on before, but which seemed familiar to Dan, while her mind gnawed at the problem like a dog with a bone. It was no good telling her she wasn't safe without a proper explanation.

Didn't he say we couldn't go back yet? So, this could be a temporary thing.

He has something to sort out, something that he is obviously very concerned about. A mess that needs clearing up, maybe.

Is it me he's concerned about or himself?

Maybe he's committed a crime?

She wasn't sure where the last thought had come from, pushing itself to the front of her mind, but she had to consider it. Was he running away from something he'd done? *Christ, the possibilities are endless. Maybe if I reassure him, he'll be more willing to open up.*

'Okay, Dan, I give in,' she said, when they got back to the house and were sitting on the terrace. 'I'll agree to stay for now. If that's what you think is best, that's what we'll do.'

He let out the longest sigh and reached for her hand, knotting his fingers with hers. 'Oh, babe, I'm so glad you understand. I really am.' He squeezed her hand then put it to his lips before holding it against his cheek, and despite all her reservations, the feel of his skin against hers still made her heart flutter. 'If you can just trust me to sort things out, then everything will be fine.'

And if I don't trust him? What was the consequence he was so worried about? She puzzled about it while Dan went and made them a drink, but didn't like where her mind was taking her. *You've been watching way too many films.* Life wasn't like that. It wasn't that dark. Not for people like her.

'I don't want you to worry,' Dan said when he returned, putting glasses of freshly squeezed orange juice beside the loungers. 'Everything will be fine, you'll see. Another few months and it will all be different.'

She looked at him. 'Different how?'

He turned to her, his eyes hidden behind his sunglasses, but his mouth twitched just a little at the corner and she knew she'd hit the spot.

'I think we'll relax into island life and you'll come to love it. I miss living in Spain. It's such a wonderful country and the people are so centred on family. It'll be a lovely place to settle.'

She felt her breath catch in her throat. That was a crass comment regarding family given the fact he'd fathered a son, who lived close by. She mustn't forget that element of the situation, however much he played it down. And this wasn't sounding like a short-term solution at all.

She frowned and turned to him, wishing he'd take his sunglasses off so she could see his eyes, work out what he was feeling. 'But I thought you said once you'd sorted something out, we could go back to England?'

'Well, I think we should leave our options open.' He swung an arm around, indicating the panorama that stretched for 180 degrees in front of them – Colom Island to the left, and the headland stretching out to the right with nothing but sea between. 'What could be more wonderful than living in a place like this?'

It was the most beautiful view, there was no denying it, and for a holiday location it was perfect. But living here?

'If it's only for a few months, until whatever it is that's bothering you has been resolved, then I'm willing to go with it. But I can't promise to be here forever.' She shook her head. 'That's unreasonable.'

His voice hardened, no longer soft and loving. 'I'm your husband, Chloe. We're a partnership now and we do what's best for us as a couple. At this point in time, living here is going to be the best option.' He picked up his drink and took a sip. 'It's not open for discussion. We're staying. Both of us.'

'But why? Maybe if you could explain it to me, then I could understand, but at the moment…' She sighed, unable to find words that wouldn't anger him, because it was clear his patience was wearing thin.

He put his drink down and swung his legs to the ground, leaning forwards. 'I'm sorry, it's just… I can't explain. Not yet. You have to trust me.'

She jumped up, exasperation making her voice shrill. 'How can I trust you when you don't trust me enough to tell me what the hell is going on?' Her eyes felt like they were going to pop out of her head, her voice getting higher and higher as her frustration wound up within her.

He ran a hand through his hair and grimaced. 'I'm sorry. There are things you don't need to know.' He stood and pulled her to him, and the smell of him, the warmth of his body next to hers, created all sorts of confusion in her mind. Instinctively, she responded to him, but why should she accept his behaviour?

His voice softened, and she allowed herself to submit to his embrace. 'I promise I'll make it up to you. I wasn't thinking about your gran. I'll admit I was only thinking about you. But isn't it time Lucy and Mark shared some of the burden? Why is it up to us to pay for care? And it's not as if your gran hasn't got any money. I mean that house of hers must be worth well over a million. It's the only one on the row that hasn't been turned into three apartments, and they sell for half a mill each.' He huffed. 'She's loaded. We're not. I know it sounds harsh, but it's time you put yourself first for once. Put us first. And leave your family to sort themselves out. This is the start of our new life together and I think Menorca will be a great place to live for a while.'

'A while?' She clutched at the phrase. 'How long is a while?'

He let go of her, threw up his hands, annoyed again. 'I don't know. As long as we want.'

'But what if I don't want to in the first place?' she snapped.

'So, let me ask you this. If your gran wasn't your responsibility, what would you feel about living here?'

His question made her pause and it took a moment to find an answer. How long had it been since she'd put her needs before those of others? Not since her mum had died, and that was over nine years ago. His words stuck for a moment until she rattled her mind free of such selfishness.

'I can't think like that. Gran is my responsibility. Yes, maybe my brother and sister could be more involved, but we've got a routine, and everything works fine.'

'So, your gran's health is going to dictate how we live our lives? What about me? Your husband. Where do my needs come into your thinking?'

'No… I didn't mean…' She stepped away from him, a hand to her forehead as she tried to think. They were getting nowhere. He kept turning the conversation around and she was exhausted. 'You're impossible to talk to!' she shouted before storming inside, slamming the patio door behind her.

Men. Bloody stupid men. He'd turned her thoughts upside down and inside out, but she had to admit there was something in his argument. *He should have discussed it with me first.* Then she might have got used to the idea, but springing it on her in this mysterious way, giving her no choice in the matter… That was plain wrong, and she wasn't going to let him do it to her. *I'm going whether he likes it or not.* The thought shocked her for a moment before she gritted her teeth and committed to her decision. *It's my life. It's me who has to live with my conscience.*

She grabbed the rucksack that they used for their excursions and stomped upstairs to the bedroom. She'd thought they were booked onto a flight in the morning, but now she realised that was a fantasy. He'd booked one-way tickets. There was nothing stopping her getting a flight, though, and there were bound to be spare seats at this time of year. Obviously, she couldn't take her suitcase because he'd notice, but she could squeeze a couple of outfits and essentials in the rucksack and he'd never know.

The plan formed in her mind as she quickly stuffed belongings in the bag. She would go back to Brighton, talk everything over with her gran and see what she thought, check whether she'd mind if they put alternative care plans in place for a little while. *Maybe I'll contact Lucy and Mark, suggest they could be more active in terms of looking after Gran for a few months.*

That thought made her insides clench. Could she really bring herself to contact them, let alone ask for a favour? Something about the vitriol in their last conversation still lingered and she had no intention of letting either of them wound her like that again. That was the problem with harsh words: once they were said, they could never be taken back, and their imprint was stamped on her mind forever.

She had the number for the taxi firm that Dan had been using, having picked up a card from the kitchen worktop when Dan wasn't looking; she just needed to find her handbag, then she'd be good to go. While Dan was cooking their meal, she'd borrow his phone to ring her gran, something she had done a few times, so he wouldn't suspect anything. Then she'd book her flight and the taxi to pick her up from the village in the morning, and she'd creep out while he was asleep, be gone without him knowing until it was too late. Once she was at the airport, then what could he do to stop her? *Nothing*. She nodded and zipped up the bag, stuffing it under her side of the bed, hoping he wouldn't look under there as part of his nightly security checks.

Where would he hide my handbag?

She was about to start looking when footsteps thundered up the stairs, and she dashed into the bathroom and started running a bath before coming back into the bedroom just as Dan appeared in the doorway.

'Are you okay?' Dan looked worried.

'Fine. I'm fine. Just thought I'd have a bath to see if that will help me relax a bit.'

He ran a hand through his hair, face pinched with tension. 'I'm sorry. I've made a complete mess of everything.'

They stared at each other for a moment.

'What I don't understand is why this place is safer than anywhere else.' She shrugged. 'If I understood that, maybe I could find this situation easier to accept.'

Dan sat on the bed and she leant against the wall, almost too weary to stand up.

'Nobody knows we're here, for one thing. Only your gran knows we're in Menorca and not the Maldives, and I'm assuming she's not told anyone, given that she doesn't actually go out. And this place is a private house, not a holiday let, so it's not on any database anywhere. We didn't book a package deal, so there's no holiday rep expecting us to be anywhere.'

His words brought a chill to her skin. He was right. They were invisible and something about that scared her. He could keep her prisoner here and nobody would report her missing. Because she wouldn't be. And would her gran really care enough to alert the authorities if she didn't hear from her? No, she wouldn't, because Chloe was with her husband. Technically, she was right where she should be. Technically, she was safe. So why was her body trembling at the prospect of a future where she was locked in every night and escorted everywhere she went? Why was the bigness of her husband a worry rather than something that made her feel secure?

She gazed at him. What would happen if he had another nightmare, lashed out and she couldn't get away from him? Her shoulders tightened.

She noticed the fine lines drawn down each side of his mouth, the contours of his face, the clump of hair that flopped over his forehead, refusing to stay back. Her heart lurched. *What will he do when he realises I'm gone?* She closed her eyes, a hurricane of conflicting emotions whirling inside her head, making it ache.

At a subconscious level, there was no doubt that she wanted to be with him, but the sensible part of her brain was yelling at her, telling her this was no way for her husband to behave, his expectations over and above what could be classed as normal. He was either deranged or had done something bad, and neither of those scenarios pointed to a rosy future.

Her eyes blinked open. 'If I'm so safe here, why do you lock the windows and doors every night and hide the keys?'

He looked at the top of her head, avoiding her eyes. 'Simple security measures, that's all. It's not good practice to leave keys on the insides of doors and windows because a burglar can get to them.'

'But you said we were safe here, so why would you even need to think about that?'

He frowned, his stare boring into her. She stiffened and held her breath.

'Why all the questions?' His voice was sharp, angry. 'I'm not sure what you're accusing me of here. I'm only trying to look after you and you keep throwing my efforts back at me as if I'm doing something wrong.'

She gritted her teeth. *Leave it for now.* He had an answer for everything and she had to accept that talking wasn't going to get her anywhere. The conversation had only made her more determined to leave. Once he was asleep, she could turn the house upside down if necessary to find the keys because he was a sound sleeper. *Unless he has a nightmare.* She'd just have to make sure he was relaxed before he went to sleep. *Make him think that everything is okay, back to normal.*

'I'm sorry.' She looked at the floor. 'I just feel all jumpy and on edge. Worried about Gran. It's such a big thing, leaving her.'

His voice softened. 'Now that you've explained it all – now I know what happened to your mum – I understand how protective you feel. But like I said, your circumstances have changed. You're married now. The responsibility needs to be shared. And anyway, she has the carer going in every day, so there's nothing to worry about.'

Chloe nodded. 'I know. You're right. I'm going to have a nice long bath and then ring her while you make dinner. Try and explain it to her and see what arrangements we can make for now to tide her over. Okay?'

He gazed into her eyes for a long moment while her heart pounded.

What can he see? Can he tell I'm lying? Can he?

CHAPTER TWENTY-ONE

Chloe waited until Dan was fast asleep, his breathing deep and settled, then, with her pulse thudding in her ears, she crept out of bed and over to the chair where he'd draped his trousers. Quietly as she could, she dipped a hand in his pockets but found only coins and a few receipts. She tried his shoes, but there was nothing in them either.

The bedclothes rustled as Dan moved and she held her breath, still crouched by the chair in the corner of the room.

'Chloe?' His sleepy question floated in the air.

Can he see me? Her heart raced faster as she tried to work out what to do.

More rustling. She tensed.

'Chloe!'

'I'm here,' she said, standing, hoping he hadn't noticed her movement. 'I was just wanting to get a bit of air in the room. I can't sleep I'm so hot. And being next to you doesn't help. It's like sleeping next to a radiator.' She sighed, trying to make her frustration clear, hoping he'd take pity. 'I wanted to open the window. I know you said the bugs would get in, but if I just open it a crack there might be a bit of a draught, something to cool the air in here.'

He was silent for a moment, then she heard the movement of bedclothes, and through the gloom she could see a dark outline sitting on the edge of the bed. She thought she heard a slight scraping noise. *His bedside drawer?* That would make sense. The lamp flicked on and she squinted in the sudden light, watched him walk over to where she was standing. She held her breath, heart pumping so hard she felt dizzy. He unlocked the window and left the key in the lock before turning to her. She leant against the wall, all the strength draining from her legs. *It's possible now.* But she knew she had to be patient.

'There you are. That better?'

'Thank you,' she said and wrapped her arms around him, tipping her head back for a kiss.

They'd made love that evening, before going to sleep, and he smelt of sex, reminding her how good their union had been. Despite everything that had happened, all her reservations had been wiped away by the strength of her love for him, the fierce passion that he instilled in her. It wasn't something she had any control over, wasn't something that could be rationalised in any way. She loved him and that was that.

Should I really go? she wondered now, feeling safe and warm in his embrace. *Or should I bide my time for a few days, see if things settle down.* She leant her head against his chest, the decision tearing at her heart.

What about Gran?

She had spoken to her earlier in the evening, as planned.

'You don't have to ring me so often, you know.' Those had been her first words. Chloe had tensed. Not a 'thank you for bothering to check that I'm safe and well'. Or a 'how are you, love – are you having a nice honeymoon?' No, a telling off. A dismissal, as if she didn't matter. *Maybe in Gran's world, I don't.* She'd have to admit it was a thought that popped up on a regular basis.

She reminded herself that her gran was not comfortable chatting on the phone and had never been one for long conversations. It would be easy to make wrong assumptions. She'd swallowed her hurt and waited a moment before responding so she could be sure that her voice would be steady. 'I like to know that everything's okay, Gran.'

'Well, the woman's coming in and doing my food and she does my chest-clearing exercises really well. Better than you, I think. Not so rough. I quite like her, actually. Nice and cheerful.'

Little barbs, as usual. Nothing nice to say and Chloe wondered whether Dan had got it right. Her gran clearly wasn't bothered if she was there or not, and Chloe was getting worked up about something that didn't matter.

But it matters to me. What if she dies while I'm away? That was the constant fear nagging away at the back of her mind. What if the same thing happened again, and a relative died while supposedly in her care? She'd never forgive herself.

I've got to go back for my peace of mind, she'd decided. *I can organise a longer-term arrangement with the agency, get it properly sorted out.* Then she might be happier about coming back and helping Dan to sort through whatever problem he was struggling with. It was the only possible option. Not going back was no solution at all, not if she wanted to have a clear conscience.

Now, she lingered in her husband's embrace, unsure whether she was about to destroy the most important relationship of her life. She clung to him until he gently pulled away, his eyes dark in the dim lamplight, a playful smile on his lips.

'Have you cooled down now? Because I can tell you, I'm starting to heat up here. Shall we go back to bed?'

She took his hand, her mind on nothing more than her love for her husband and her burning desire for him. *Perhaps I won't go.*

They fell asleep wrapped in each other's arms until Chloe woke suddenly, a nightmare of being chased making her heart race and her eyes snap open. It took a moment for her to understand where she was and to realise it was just a dream, however real it had felt. The night was no longer black and the golden light of dawn crept across the sky, filtering through the shutters. She was wide awake. She wriggled free of Dan's arms and sneaked into the bathroom, where she sat on the loo, jumpy and anxious while she worked out what the nightmare had been about. What was her brain trying to tell her?

I've got to go back. Then the worry of whether Gran's all right can't chase me around. That's what the dream was about. I've got to go.

The previous evening, she'd managed to find her handbag while she was upstairs on the pretext of talking to her gran. Dan had been busy cooking, and since her phone conversation had only lasted a couple of minutes, she'd taken the opportunity to have a scout around. It had been hidden under the wardrobe in the spare room, pushed right to the back, where Dan's long arm could reach but hers couldn't. It took a bit of jiggling about, but she'd finally manoeuvred it out with the toilet brush.

Everything was in there, so he'd obviously been using her bag as a place to store all their valuables – easier to carry with them when they went out, she supposed. He must have taken her passport from her make-up bag, and his passport was there too. She'd stared at it for a moment then tucked it back in her bag. *Without it, he won't be following me anywhere*, she'd decided, with a sigh of relief. Quickly, she'd found her bank card, booked her flight and put everything in the rucksack, ready for her escape.

I'm ready. I can go, she told herself now.

She brushed her hair, splashed water on her face to wake herself up, and crept back into the bedroom, hardly daring to breathe. The key was still in the window lock and she slipped it out, wriggled the rucksack out from under the bed and crept downstairs, where she dressed.

As a last-minute thought, she wrote him a note on the back of an envelope she found in her bag.

Gone back to sort out Gran's care.
Chloe x

She put it on the table, weighted with a mug.

Time was moving on, and she knew she'd have to hurry if she was to be in the village by seven o'clock to meet the taxi. With no sign of the door keys anywhere, a window was her only escape. The one in the dining-room was reasonably large, and she managed to squeeze herself out, having dropped her bags down first. At least it was getting light now; she pushed her worries about the dark forest to the back of her mind and jogged down the track, focused only on getting to the airport.

The taxi was waiting, idling outside the shop, and she got in, desperate to get going in case she changed her mind and ran back to her husband. She twisted to look out of the rear window, heart pounding, breath rasping in her throat as she scanned the road, imagining Dan appearing behind them.

Her mind was like a nest of snakes, thoughts weaving in and out, contradicting each other. One minute she was recalling a loving moment, the next the fear she'd felt when he was in the middle of his nightmare, or when his face took on that hardness round the jaw and his eyes narrowed, his voice clipped and firm.

As they drove through the countryside towards the airport, she thought about the questions he wouldn't answer, his conviction that she was in danger for a reason he wouldn't articulate. *It doesn't make sense.* And neither did coming here on their honeymoon, to a place where he had a son. There was no sense to any of it, no working it out. Was he having some sort of breakdown and needed her support to get through it? Or had he done something wrong and was running away? Whatever was happening, he had no right to control her, no right to keep her prisoner. And she had every right to sort out her responsibilities in her own way. *Because it's me who has to live with the consequences.*

But what was the consequence of going against his wishes? *Am I making the biggest mistake of my life?*

CHAPTER TWENTY-TWO

By the time Chloe boarded the plane, she was feeling decidedly queasy, her stomach churning, her bloodstream full of adrenaline as she constantly checked over her shoulder to make sure Dan hadn't appeared. Exhausted, she collapsed into her seat, gratefully tucking into a pastry she'd bought in the airport. She hoped it would satiate the hunger that gnawed at her belly and allow her to sleep for the rest of the journey, but it seemed to make things worse and she found herself dashing to the toilets to be sick. *Nerves,* she decided, but at the back of her mind, another possibility appeared, one that she really couldn't entertain. *It's just the crappy airport food*, she reassured herself, settling back in her seat. But the idea had hooked into her thoughts like a leech, sucking everything else away until it was all that was left.

I'm pregnant.

Her hands went to her mouth, eyes wide. *I can't be.* But as she started working out dates, it became obvious there was an odds-on chance she was. A few years ago, she'd gone on the contraceptive pill, but it had disagreed with her so badly she'd had to stop. In all honesty, when she thought about it now, they'd been a bit slapdash about contraception. She covered her face with her hands. *Oh, Christ! I can't even think about it.*

'You all right, love?' The passenger to her right, a middle-aged woman with an abundance of suntanned flesh spilling out of her summer clothing, frowned at her. 'You're looking a bit peaky. Isn't she, George?' The man sitting next to her leant forwards and peered at Chloe, who gave them the best smile she could muster.

She shook her head. 'I'm fine, thanks. Just feel a bit queasy.'

'Well, you just let us know if you need to get out in a hurry, won't you?'

Chloe nodded. 'Yes. Yes, I will.' She took the sick bag out of the back of the chair in front and held it up. 'I'll keep this handy, just in case.'

'Want a mint?' The man held out a packet and she took one, smiling her thanks as she popped it into her mouth.

She closed her eyes and flopped back into her seat, her body not sure how to respond to this new situation. She was hot and flustered, claustrophobic in the confined space of the cabin. An urge to scream was building inside, all the frustrations and uncertainties and fears of the last week coming together, the pressure pounding behind her eyes.

A baby. I'm going to have a bloody baby.

At this point in time, that was the last thing she needed.

The rest of the journey was uneventful, the plane full of holidaymakers, chattering and laughing and sleeping off the excesses of the night before. She tried not to think about what she'd just done by leaving Dan, and the fact that she now had another person to think about; a new development that completely changed the dynamics of her situation.

By the time she got out of the airport it was almost one in the afternoon, and she decided she would go and check on her gran first. Then she'd do a bit of grocery shopping, get a pregnancy test and go back to her apartment to give herself some quiet time to think about things.

Everything felt a little different, she decided, as she walked up the familiar street to her gran's house. She noticed the noise, the smells, the drabness of the buildings, how busy the streets were, teeming with traffic and people. She was out of step with her old world, as if she'd jumped off the roundabout and couldn't get back on again. Thoroughly bemused, she finally arrived at her gran's house and let herself in.

'Oh, you're back,' her gran said as Chloe walked into the lounge, scanning the room to check everything was as it should be. The windows sparkled, she noticed, making the room seem brighter. There was no dust on any of the surfaces, and the carpet was devoid of biscuit crumbs, which normally littered the floor around her gran's feet.

'I am.' She smiled at her gran, who was looking better than she had been when they'd left, and bent to give her a hug. 'It looks nice in here.'

Her gran nodded, knitting needles clacking to their usual rhythm. 'Oh yes, Janelle had a tidy round yesterday. But to be honest, she's done a bit of housework every day she's been here, and the place hasn't looked so clean and tidy in years.'

Chloe nodded, relieved that employing the carer had worked out well. 'She's done a good job.' She sat on the settee next to her gran, noticed that there was a bit more colour in her cheeks, more of a sparkle in her eye. 'You like her then?'

'Oh yes, she's so funny. Irish, you know. Really good company. And she makes a lovely cup of tea, just how I like it. And she did a roast dinner on Sunday and we've had all sorts of different things to eat.'

Chloe couldn't remember when she'd last heard her gran sounding so cheerful, each compliment about Janelle feeling like a criticism levelled at herself. *You're being oversensitive*, she told herself, forcing the smile to stay on her face while she thought of something else to say.

Her gran stopped knitting and frowned. 'Your husband not with you?'

Chloe chewed her bottom lip, willing the tears to stay away, but just the mention of Dan and the memory of the tension between them, brought a lump to her throat. She shook her head and studied her nails for a minute before she was able to mutter, 'No.'

'Oh, he's gone to see his mum, has he?'

Chloe took a deep breath. 'No, he's still in Menorca.'

The knitting needles stilled while her gran looked at her, head cocked to one side like a little bird, a puzzled frown crinkling her forehead.

Chloe flopped back on the sofa, took a deep breath and told her everything that had happened.

'So, he's still out there and you came back because of me?' Her gran sounded incredulous.

Chloe turned to look at her. 'Of course I did. I couldn't leave you here on your own, could I?'

Her gran put her knitting on the arm of the sofa and turned to Chloe. Her lips pursed before she spoke. 'Look, I know we've not always seen eye to eye, but I don't really need looking after.' There was exasperation in her voice. 'You've got your own life to lead, especially now you're married.' She gazed at Chloe for a long moment. 'I know you think I'm helpless, but I'm not. I've still got all my faculties. Can still look after myself. I never asked you to be my carer, did I? You just took that on yourself.'

Chloe opened her mouth to speak, but her gran held up a hand to shush her before carrying on. 'I can't say it hasn't been helpful. But I knew things would change and I have been thinking about the future, you know? I mean, it would have been a bit of a surprise if you'd moved over there, but you didn't have to come back for me.' She sighed and was quiet for a moment before continuing. 'I've really enjoyed having Janelle for company. In fact, I was thinking about seeing if she'd stay on permanently. You know, we get on so well, it's lovely having her here. Then that would relieve you of your duties, wouldn't it? And you can go back to Menorca.'

'But I don't want to—'

Her gran gave Chloe one of her fierce looks, and she knew not to speak. 'No, just listen to me. We should have had this conversation a long time ago, and it's only since you've been away, and I've had some good long chats with Janelle, that I've realised a few things. Things that have probably been making both of us unhappy.' She put a hand on Chloe's arm. 'I don't want to be a duty and I feel like I am. You squeeze me into the rest of your life and it's all got to be part of a routine for you. I don't want to be part of a routine. I know I'm old, but I've still got a life to live and I want to make the most of it.'

Chloe could feel the heat rushing to her cheeks because there was an element of truth in her gran's words. 'Oh, Gran, it's not like that. I want to look after you. Really, I do.'

Her gran shook her head, slowly. 'Look, let's be honest with each other, shall we? Events happen in life that change the way we see things. Our priorities change. The way we think about life changes. Dan coming along has changed the way you see things, and Janelle coming along has changed the way I see things.'

Chloe frowned, unsure what was coming next.

Her gran stared out of the window. 'I know I haven't always been very fair to you, love, I realise that now. When your mum died…' She paused and looked away before pulling a hanky out of her sleeve and dabbing at her eyes. 'Well, it was a shock. And grief does funny things to us, I'm afraid.' She sighed and looked at Chloe, her eyes glistening. 'I'm sorry to say you became the scapegoat. We all want someone to blame in a tragedy, don't we?' She nodded. 'I can see now that I felt as guilty as you did about her dying so suddenly and none of us realising how poorly she was, but…'

Chloe tensed, sure she was going to be told once again how she should have informed another family member that her mum wasn't well before she'd gone off on holiday, then they would have known to check on her. But she hadn't – she'd just swanned off without a backwards glance. Familiar emotions swirled in Chloe's chest, blocking her throat, making her bite her lip to stop her tears.

'The thing is, nobody was to blame. Your mum was old enough to look after herself. She could have rung the doctor and asked for her meds to be delivered. But even then, there's nothing to say she would have survived. Flu is a nasty illness, and for epileptics, it's especially dangerous. We don't know, do we?' She sighed. 'Janelle has helped me to put it all in perspective. Someone from the outside looking in… Well, it all looks different, doesn't it?'

Chloe reached for her gran's hand as a tear rolled down her cheek.

'The problem for me…' Her gran stopped and pressed her lips together for a moment before speaking again. 'I've promised myself I'm going to be honest with you. And the thing is, you look so like your mum, you even sound like her, have all her little mannerisms… it's like she's here. But then I remember she isn't, and it's like losing her all over again. Having you here… I can't get over her death because I keep getting muddled up and thinking she's still alive.'

'Oh, Gran, I didn't know you felt like that. Have I been making it worse, when I was trying to make things better? I thought if I looked after you, then you might find it in your heart to forgive me.'

Chloe's gran squeezed her hand. 'I've nothing to forgive you for, love. But…' She swallowed and looked out of the window for a moment, obviously choosing her words carefully. 'Now I don't want you taking this the wrong way, but I do think I need some time on my own to get things in perspective. You being here every day… and you being so like her… it's not allowing my grief to heal.'

Chloe stared at her gran, trying to see if she meant it. *She's sending me away? Doesn't want me here?* The breath went out of her as if she'd been winded, all her efforts over the last few years diminished to a point where they counted for nothing.

'Anyway, I want you to know that Janelle took me to the solicitor's on Friday and I've finally sorted out my will. It was all left to your mum, but now she's gone, well, it's shared between the three of you. So that's all done now.'

Chloe frowned. 'But Lucy said you'd left everything to her and Mark. She told me. Said I was looking after you just to get your money.'

Her gran tutted and shook her head. 'I don't know what's got into that girl sometimes.' She sighed. 'I probably shouldn't tell you this, but she and Mark did try and persuade me to cut you out. I didn't commit to anything at the time, so she was wrong to say that. Anyway, I've told them both what I've done and, if I'm honest, they're both being a bit unreasonable about it. But it's my decision. When I go, the three of you share what's left. That'll make up for what happened to your mum's house. I know they bullied you out of your share and you let them, but they can't this time.'

'Oh, Gran,' she said quickly. 'Let's not talk about dying.'

'I just wanted you to know and I needed to get that off my chest. I'm sorry if I've been a bit mean to you. I could feel myself doing it, but couldn't seem to stop. It just felt easier if there was somebody to blame rather than having to accept that I could have kept in touch with your mum more, I could have played a part in keeping her alive.'

Chloe sniffed back her tears, wiping her cheeks with the back of her hands.

'I understand. Honestly, I do. I know you all blamed me, but I blamed myself just as much.'

'Well, let's change that. Let's just accept it was a tragedy. Just that. Nobody did anything to cause it. Shit happens, as Janelle says.'

Chloe's eyes widened. She'd never heard her gran use language like that.

'So, you think Janelle will stay on?'

'Well, I've asked her to. She's going to leave the agency first, then we're going to have a private arrangement. More flexible that way. If I'm paying Janelle, then I'm in control of what happens, and if I want to go shopping, I can pay her to come with me. Or we can have days out, you know, that sort of thing.'

Her gran smiled, and Chloe understood that, as much as anything, she needed a companion. Janelle seemed ideal for the role.

'Anyway, let's talk about you. What's going on with this man of yours, then?'

Chloe sighed and looked at the ceiling, her emotions threatening to overflow again. 'Like I said, he didn't want me to come home at all, said it wasn't safe and we had to stay in Menorca until he got some problem sorted out. But he wouldn't tell me what it was.'

'Well, that's very odd, isn't it?'

She sighed. 'I'd say it was totally out of character, but I've begun to realise that… I don't know him at all.'

Her gran gave a little laugh. 'That's right, love. After a lifetime together, you may know someone a little better, but you never completely know a person. You can only see what they want to show you.' She was quiet for a moment, thoughtful. 'He does sound a bit controlling if you ask me. Not letting you come home. At least he could have tried to persuade you rather than tell you. You'll have to nip that in the bud, my girl. You don't want him thinking that just because you married him, he's in charge of your life.'

Chloe looked out of the window, watched people hurrying to and fro. 'No, I don't think it's that. He said it was his job to keep me safe and he couldn't do that if we came back here.'

'How peculiar.'

'Half the time I felt I didn't know him at all, and then he'd soften and become the Dan I love again.'

Her gran put a gentle hand on her knee. 'I was married for forty-five years and let me tell you, it's a constant struggle. There's always a compromise to be made, but you have to be careful that it's not you doing all the giving and him doing all the taking. It takes time to get used to being a couple. You can't know after a week.'

Chloe took a deep breath and looked at her gran, deciding that she needed to share her latest concern. 'And there's another thing that's sort of freaking me out, Gran. I think I might be pregnant.'

Her gran's mouth hung open for a moment before she covered it with her hands. 'Oh, my goodness. A baby! Honestly, you know how to complicate things, don't you?'

Chloe sighed. Complicated didn't begin to describe her predicament. 'I don't know what to do.'

Her gran gave her a quick smile. 'I think we should have something to eat. Tea and cake? You're so pale you look like you might faint. And if you are pregnant, you've got to think about that baby as well.'

A cup of tea was her gran's answer to everything, but Chloe's mind was stuck on Dan's behaviour. *Should I have just done what he asked?* Because now she'd created a whole new set of problems to deal with.

CHAPTER TWENTY-THREE

Trust is something unseen, something that we take for granted. But it can be broken so easily. Snapped like a twig, then it can't be put back together again. There is a price to pay for breaking trust, and Chloe is going to find that out.

She almost left the island without me knowing. Thank goodness I woke up when I did. She's sneaky, that's for sure.

I'm going to have to keep a close eye on her from now on because she is the key to everything. It hit me yesterday – a moment of clarity, if you like. She is the key.

And I see her.

I see her sitting in her grandma's front room.

CHAPTER TWENTY-FOUR

Chloe felt a lot better once she'd had something to eat, and while her gran had her afternoon nap, she sat down at the kitchen table and tried to work out what she was going to do. Now that her gran had made it clear she didn't need her – and, in fact, didn't want Chloe to look after her – she was free to go back to Menorca.

If I want to.

She sat for a moment, trying to decide if she did want to go back. Or should she wait for Dan to follow her home? If he did, then that proved he loved her. If he didn't, then maybe that told her something else. Then she remembered that she had his passport and he wouldn't be going anywhere without it. *Unless… what if he reports it as lost or stolen?* Surely there'd be measures in place to get him back home? Yes, he might be delayed, but he had other ID, other ways to prove that he was Daniel Marsden.

Already she missed him, felt alone and strangely vulnerable. But even if she did decide to go back, she couldn't just up and leave with so many loose ends to tie up. If she was going to relocate over there, then she wanted to do it properly. There were responsibilities that had to be addressed.

There was her job for starters. And her apartment. And then there would be loads of paperwork that needed sorting out.

The baby.

She had to find out for definite if she was pregnant, because she couldn't understand how she felt about the situation until she knew it was real. If it was, then it would be a major factor when it came to making plans for the future. Did she want to bring up a child in that house in Menorca, isolated, up a bumpy track? *Imagine trying to push a buggy up and down that!* And she wondered how practical it would be if Dan was out at work. Then there was the question of income because she wouldn't be working with a baby, not for a little while anyway. *Can we even afford to live there?*

Staying in Brighton would be a better option. She'd get maternity leave from her job and would be able to go back part-time if she wanted. Dan would be able to get work if he looked. Plus, there would be Dan's mum to give her a hand. In Menorca she'd have nobody to help, and there'd be Dan's other baby. She gave a shudder. That would be a horrible situation. *No, I'm not going to do it. He'll have to come back here and sort out his problems.*

That brought Dan to the top of her pile of worries. He'd be going frantic, especially with his paranoia about her safety. At least if he was back here, she could encourage him to get some therapy, work through his fears with somebody who knew how to help him.

I can post him his passport. He'll come back if I'm here, won't he?

She sighed and rested her head in her hands, tiredness making the list of jobs seem unsurmountable. But there was one thing that overshadowed everything else: the pregnancy test. That had to come first, then she could use the news to soften the conversation with Dan. *He'll be happy about a baby, won't he?* She thought about it for a moment, remembered that he'd trained as an infant teacher, recalled the tone in his voice when he'd told her anecdotes about the kids, who he'd obviously adored. Yes, she was sure he wanted a family.

But what if he won't come back? Will I wait to go to Menorca until he's sorted out his problems? It was almost too much to take in: the idea of becoming a mother, moving to a Spanish island, living in a rural community all at the same time. It was all so different, so alien to her, it was hard to believe she would settle. A whole new stream of worries sped through her mind; feeling isolated, not coping as a new mum being left alone with a baby, feeling homesick. So many things made her certain that Menorca wasn't a viable option.

But I love Dan. And he loves me. Of that she was sure. If she stayed here, he would come back, and would have to accept that this was where their married life would begin.

With that thought in her mind, she let herself out of the house and walked down the road to the high street and into the chemist. She quickly chose a pregnancy test kit and presented it to the cashier, feeling strangely embarrassed about the whole process. She tapped her card on the reader, but it refused to scan. She pushed it into the reader instead, but it still wouldn't work. Her faced burned as she tried the PIN again, with no luck.

The cashier gave her a sympathetic look. 'I'm really sorry, but unless you have another card, I'm afraid I can't complete your purchase.'

Chloe sighed. 'No, I only have this one. I've no idea why it isn't working, but I'll nip to the cash machine.'

With her eyes on the ground, she dashed out of the shop and hurried down the street to the cashpoint. She fed her card into the machine, but instead of letting her take cash, the machine swallowed it. She stared, irritated, then started pressing buttons, but nothing worked; her card was gone.

She leant against the wall, her head resting on her arm, trying not to cry. *It must be some technical problem*, she decided, knowing that there was plenty of money in the account. She'd collected debts at a rapid rate when she'd been a student and it had taken her years to get her finances under control. Now she didn't have a credit card and only spent money that she had.

She stormed back to her gran's house, muttering under her breath. The bank had no branches on the high street anymore and she'd have to phone them to find out what was going on. In the meantime, she had no money. She'd been planning on buying a replacement phone, just a cheap pay-as-you-go one to tide her over until Dan returned hers. But if she hadn't any money, she couldn't do that. *Why is life so bloody difficult?* she thought as she let herself into her gran's house, banging the door behind her.

Her gran was sitting at the kitchen table doing a Sudoku puzzle.

'I think you're getting yourself all steamed up about nothing,' she said after Chloe told her what had happened. She went to the kitchen drawer, got out a purse and held up some notes, waving them in the air. 'Here you go, have this to tide you over. Go and get that test kit, then at least you'll know for sure and that'll be one less thing to worry about.'

More like one more thing to worry about, Chloe thought, but she took the money and hurried back to the shop, stopping to buy a basic phone and a SIM card, ready to ring Dan and try and make peace with him.

Of course, the test was positive. *But I knew that, didn't I?* she thought as she sat on the edge of the bath in her gran's house, looking at the lines on the plastic stick. Lines that told her the future was going to be very different.

I'm not ready. That was her next thought, given all the uncertainties that had been thrown up in their relationship over the last week. But then, who was ever ready for a baby? Surely this would reset their relationship. Bring them back on a more even keel.

He'll come back to the UK for his baby. She was sure of that, but it wasn't the sort of subject she could send a text message about. This needed to be a proper conversation. She was so tired all of a sudden, so very weary, that she couldn't contemplate talking to him just yet. What she needed was a lie down. Then she'd ring him.

She stumbled into one of the spare bedrooms, the one that had always been hers whenever she came to stay, and curled up on the bed, falling asleep almost as soon as her eyes were shut.

*

The sound of a door shutting woke her much later. It was pitch-black and her phone told her it was three thirty in the morning – the sound must have been one of her gran's nocturnal visits to the bathroom. She squinted at her phone, eyes sticky with sleep and struggling to focus, hardly able to believe that she'd slept for almost twelve hours. Her conversation with Dan would have to wait until morning, and with that decision made, she made a quick trip to the bathroom herself before getting back into bed and falling asleep.

CHAPTER TWENTY-FIVE

She woke early, had a quick shower and hurried downstairs to retrieve her rucksack. She had a lot to sort out today, and talking to Dan was top of her list. Her mind was clearer after her long sleep and she was adamant she was staying in Brighton.

She popped her head round the kitchen door, the smell of fried eggs turning her stomach, and she had to dash into the downstairs loo. It was a little while before she was confident that her stomach had finished emptying itself, and when she went back into the kitchen, her gran gave her a knowing look.

'The test was positive then?'

Chloe gave a wry smile. 'You guessed.' She leant against the worktop, not sure if she was going to have to dash to the loo again.

'Ginger biscuits always worked for me. Now, let's see... I'm pretty sure I've got a packet somewhere.' Her gran got up from her chair, opened a cupboard, took out an oblong tin and held out a packet of Gingernuts. 'There you are – glass of water and a couple of biscuits and you'll be fine.'

Chloe swallowed the bile that crept up her throat at the thought of food but did as she was told, and after she'd nibbled her way through a biscuit, her queasiness did seem to subside. She picked up another. 'I'm sorry I just crashed out yesterday, can't believe I slept so long.'

Her gran was gazing at her, an unnerving stare, making Chloe remember that she'd been sacked from all caring duties. Practically banned from the house.

She doesn't want me here. A spear of hurt jabbed at her heart and she felt suddenly awkward, unwanted, the urge to leave making her restless.

'I hope you didn't mind me staying too much?' Chloe start to gabble. 'I'll get out of your hair, get back to my flat and see if I can get this mess sorted.'

Her gran looked away and poured herself another cup of tea from the pot, carefully stirring in milk then a couple of spoons of sugar. 'Your young man rang yesterday. When you were asleep.'

Chloe stopped chewing. 'What? Why didn't you wake me?'

'Well, I came up, but you obviously needed the rest after all that dashing about. Anyway, I thought it'd be better if you rang him back when you were good and ready, not half asleep.'

She thought about it for a moment, adrenaline coursing round her veins. *Oh God. What's he going to say? Am I ready?* Not quite, she decided, finishing her biscuit. And anyway, she wouldn't be ringing him where her gran could hear. No, this was between her and Dan. She pulled her phone from her pocket. 'Okay... well, I'll just take his number, then I'll ring him back later.'

'Phone's on the hall table. It'll be on there, won't it? I've no idea how these mobile things work.' She sipped her tea. 'You can get it on your way out.'

I've been dismissed. Chloe bristled, her hurt turning to anger. 'Yes, right. I'm going.' She'd go back to her apartment, then she'd have a bit of peace and quiet to sort everything out.

'No need to come rushing back. Janelle's coming over this morning. We're going to play chess and she said she'd make pizza for lunch.'

'Chess?' Chloe wasn't sure she'd heard properly.

'Oh, yes, she's a big fan of the game and she's been teaching me. Turns out I'm not a complete duffer. Anyway, it's fun learning something new.'

'I didn't know you liked pizza either.' In all the time Chloe had been looking after her gran, she'd been a fussy eater and often shunned the meals Chloe had prepared.

'Neither did I until she brought some that she'd made at home. So much nicer than shop-bought stuff. It's become quite a favourite, I have to say.'

Chloe wondered how Janelle had managed to get her gran to become so experimental. They'd obviously really hit it off. It was something she should feel pleased about, something that lessened the burden of responsibility. But somehow she felt shunned.

What the hell did I rush home for?

'Right, okay. Well, I'll see you later.'

She transferred Dan's number from her gran's phone and left the house, resisting the urge to slam the door behind her.

Outside, she hurried down the road, deciding that she should ring the bank before she spoke to Dan because without access to her account she wasn't going anywhere. Her heart lurched when she thought about her husband and the worry she must have put him through by dashing off.

Why did I think I had to leave him like that? What was making me feel so nervous?

As she walked, she tried to convince herself that she'd done the right thing, that she'd had good reason to behave as she did. She rehearsed the points she wanted to make during their conversation, so he would understand her decision to go. First he'd been so controlling, changing their destination without telling her; that was unforgivable. Wanting to organise everything. He wouldn't hire a car and he stuck to her like glue. Then there was his paranoia about security, not letting her have a window open, hiding the keys. She'd felt suffocated. The fact that he already had a baby and the parents lived nearby, yet he chose that very place for them to go on their honeymoon; that was plain weird. And finally, wanting her to up and leave everything, saying she couldn't go back and keeping her as a virtual prisoner.

None of that can be justified, can it?

Once she'd laid it all out in her mind, she decided her behaviour had been quite rational. It was definitely Dan who was being odd.

He was right about Gran, though. Maybe he's right about other things. Perhaps the windows and door keys were just sensible precautions. And controlling their trips out was because he knew the area and wanted to make sure they had a nice time. And there was an innocent explanation about the baby, it being a favour for gay friends.

But what about the keeping me safe bit? Why won't he explain that to me?

By the time she got to her apartment, her head felt like it was full of knots, all her thoughts tied together into an unfathomable mess.

A cup of tea. That's what she needed. And a sit down. She couldn't believe how weary she felt, her limbs like lead, as she walked down the steps to her basement apartment. She inserted her key into the lock. Or at least she tried. But it wouldn't fit. She looked at it to make sure she had the right key and tried again, frowning. *Weird.* Still it wouldn't fit. *Christ! Another problem to sort out.*

She sank onto the bottom step, staring at the door for a moment as if that alone would make it open, before resting her elbows on her knees, hands tugging at her hair. How she wished there was someone to help her, but in Brighton, she was on her own. *Just stop feeling sorry for yourself and get this sorted out.* With a sigh, she sat up straight and got her phone out of her bag.

It only took a few minutes to google the property company and get their number, and she leant against the wall while the phone rang, grateful that at least the weather was being kind and it hadn't started raining. Thankfully, they answered quickly.

'Hello! I'm sorry to bother you, but I've got a bit of a problem. For some reason, the key to my apartment won't work.'

'Oh dear,' the operator said, her voice warm and sympathetic. 'Let me pull up the details.'

Chloe answered all the questions required to make sure of her identity, then the line went quiet for a moment before the operator came back on.

'Um, I'll just pop you on hold for a moment while I check something. Bear with me, please.'

Chloe sighed, cold now after sitting on the stone steps, and she walked back up, jigging about to warm herself up. A movement in her peripheral vision made her turn. A man wearing a baseball hat, thick neck, broad shoulders walked on by and disappeared behind a neighbouring hedge. She frowned and glanced around, hoping for people to come along the pavement, but it was quiet. A tinny tune played in her ear while she waited, staring at the hedge, not sure if she could make out the shadow of a person behind it, or whether her eyes were playing tricks. The hairs rose on the back of her neck. *Is someone watching me?*

'Hello. Sorry to keep you waiting.' The voice distracted her, and she hoisted her rucksack up on her shoulder to stop it slipping off as she walked back down the steps.

'No problem. I just wondered if you could send someone out to open the apartment for me. I know I'll have to pay. But I really need to get in and I don't understand why—'

'Let me stop you there. I think there's been a misunderstanding because I've just spoken to my manager to make sure I've got this right, and it appears we received written notice from you, saying you were leaving the accommodation with immediate effect. The locks have been changed, I'm afraid. We do it as a matter of course when a tenant moves out.'

Chloe shook her head, completely confused. 'No, no you've got that wrong. I haven't given notice. My stuff is in there!'

'I'm sorry, but we have a letter here and the signature matches the one on your tenancy agreement.'

Chloe put a hand to her forehead, hardly able to grasp what she was hearing. 'But I didn't send you a letter.'

'Excuse me for a moment while I get my manager for you. Perhaps he can help you to resolve the situation.'

Before Chloe could say anything else, the tinny music was back in her ear. *What the hell is going on?* She knew she hadn't written a letter. *So, who did?* Her body chilled as she realised it could only be one person. Dan. *So, does that mean he had the move to Menorca planned before we left?* Because if he did, then everything was far more premeditated than she'd imagined, his behaviour even more unacceptable.

'Hello. Can I help you?'

A man's voice, smooth and calm, came on the line. She could picture him, with slicked-back hair and a sharp suit, a smarmy smile on his face.

She swallowed and tried to get her thoughts in order. 'Yes. There seems to have been some confusion. I understand you've had a letter from me giving notice, but the thing is, I didn't send one. It must be a forgery.'

There was a moment's silence before the man spoke. 'What? But why would someone do that?'

Chloe opened her mouth to speak, then closed it again. That was a very good question and one she couldn't answer. Maybe it wasn't Dan. Maybe someone else wanted to cause trouble for her? *No, that's a daft idea.* But then this whole situation was crazy.

She sighed. 'I don't know, but that's what has happened. I've just come back from my honeymoon and found that I can't get into my apartment because you have apparently changed the locks. And all my belongings are in there and—'

'No, I'm afraid that's incorrect. Your belongings are not in there. The place was empty when we took it back.'

Chloe's legs weakened, and she leant against the wall. 'What? No, it can't have been. Everything was there when I went away a week ago.'

'According to my file on that property, it had been emptied and cleaned, and your deposit will be repaid in full.'

Chloe's eyes widened, her voice rising as panic whizzed through her mind. 'But where's all my stuff? It was all in there. It was!'

'Um… I'm really sorry but I honestly can't help you. All I know is that we took the property back, inspected it and changed the locks, ready for reletting.'

'But… but…' Chloe could feel the tears stinging her eyes. 'There must be someone who can help me. This… It's all wrong.'

A sigh crackled down the phone. 'If you say this letter is a forgery and someone has taken all your belongings, then that's a matter for the police, I'm afraid. There's nothing more I can do.'

'The police?'

'Yes. I don't think I can really be of much help.'

Chloe sighed, a sound of defeat that rippled through her body. 'Okay, well thank you,' she muttered before she rang off, her hand clasped to her forehead, a headache pounding behind her eyes. The day was going from bad to worse. Instead of solving problems, they seemed to be stacking up around her like a wall, boxing her in.

She heard a rustle, a cracking of twigs, and she turned, suddenly frightened, sure that someone was watching her. The noise seemed to come from the hedge and she wondered if the figure she'd seen earlier was still there. Her eyes narrowed, her frustration igniting into anger. She shot up the steps from her apartment and dashed down the path to the gate, running down the pavement so she could see the other side of the hedge. There was enough going on without creeps spying her, and she'd be happy to give them a piece of her mind. But nobody was there. She glanced up and down the road, saw people coming and going in both directions, no clue if one of them had been watching her.

A wave of dizziness caught her by surprise and she had to sit on the wall for a moment until it passed. Her life was spinning out of control and she couldn't seem to stop it. In fact, the harder she tried to sort things out, the worse they became. *Oh, Dan. What's happening?* She felt like weeping and closed her eyes for a moment to try and regain control. *I will not show myself up. I will not.*

After a few moments, she managed to calm herself down and understood that she had very few options open to her. She had to go back to her gran's whether she wanted to or not. The bank card situation needed sorting out first, otherwise she had no access to money. Then, if she was calm enough, she'd ring Dan. She definitely wasn't up to it yet, not if he'd written the letter to surrender her lease on the apartment. *If he had… what then?* Her mind fizzed with answers that she didn't want to hear.

CHAPTER TWENTY-SIX

Chloe shivered in the cool breeze as she walked back to her gran's. Tiredness dragged at her, each footstep an effort, and when another thought crawled into her head, she had to stop and sit on a wall for a minute.

Work!

She'd forgotten about work. She was supposed to be in for her shift in the morning, but she couldn't see that happening. There was far too much to sort out and her mind would be too preoccupied to focus properly. Anyway, she'd have to go and talk to the police in the morning about her apartment and her belongings because there was no way she could do it now. Her head was pounding like a blacksmith was in there bashing away at his anvil. Tension bunched her shoulders, the pressure building inside her like she might burst.

Think of the baby, she told herself as she sucked in a few deep breaths. *Stress is not good for babies.*

Oh, and there was another thing… She needed to see her GP, to make sure she was having all the proper maternity checks. Her to-do list was becoming endless.

She sighed and got back to her feet, plodding down the road like an old woman. It seemed to take much longer than usual to walk the ten-minute journey to her gran's house and she practically fell through the door, almost too tired now to stay standing. She bumped into the hall table, sending a pile of magazines sprawling all over the floor, and couldn't stop the frustration from bursting out of her in a long, loud scream.

Footsteps hurried from the kitchen and a tall, middle-aged woman with dyed purple hair dashed towards her.

'Oh my goodness, what happened? Are you okay?' She stopped and surveyed the sea of magazines, which had slid in every direction, creating a barrier of slippery paper between them.

Chloe leant against the wall. 'I'm sorry. You must be Janelle?'

A smile lit up the woman's face, the warmth of her personality clear from the laugh lines that creased around her eyes and mouth. 'That I am, and you must be Chloe.'

'That's me.' Chloe nodded and looked at the mess, psyching herself up for the inevitable job of picking it all up.

Janelle flapped a hand and pointed to the chair next to the hall table. 'No, it's all right. I'll do it. You just sit and sort yourself out for a moment. Won't take a minute for me to clear this lot up.' She crouched on the floor, gathering the magazines as she spoke, while Chloe stood where she was, too surprised by the encounter to think about moving. 'Sure, it's my fault anyway. I shouldn't have left them there, but I was going to put them in the recycling bin, then I got distracted and forgot all about them.'

Five minutes later it was all done, and Janelle stood, the magazines clasped in her arms. 'I'll take these out now. Your gran's in the kitchen if you want to go through. We were just having a cuppa and a quick game of chess. Easier in the kitchen, with the table.' She laughed. 'We tried in the lounge, but we kept knocking the damned board over.'

Chloe stood aside to let her pass. She watched her disappear out of the front door where the recycling boxes were stored, leaving Chloe feeling like an outsider in a home she had known since she was a child.

She trudged into the kitchen where her gran was sipping a cup of tea while she studied a chess board. She glanced up and smiled, then frowned. 'Chloe, you're back! I thought you were going to stay at your apartment?'

'Oh, Gran, you wouldn't believe what's happened now. I can't get in. The landlord changed the locks because they said I'd sent a letter relinquishing my lease.'

Her gran looked a bit taken aback. 'You didn't say you were moving.' Her frown deepened, the corners of her mouth pinched downwards into that disapproving look Chloe had come to know so well. 'But then I seem to be last to know about everything.'

Chloe sank onto a chair, resisting the urge to lay her head on the table and cry. The last thing she needed was her gran getting all uppity with her. What she wanted more than anything was Dan. She wanted him to come and take her away, sort out all this mess and tell her everything would be fine. Because right now, nothing in her world was fine and she had a growing mountain of problems to address.

She sighed. 'I didn't tell you because I didn't send a letter. It wasn't me.'

Her gran huffed and shook her head, impatient. 'I'm sorry, Chloe, I don't think I'm following you.'

Chloe ran a hand through her hair, too tired to explain. She saw the time on the clock which was hung on the wall behind her gran: 11 a.m. *Oh God, I've got to ring work, get that sorted out. And the bank.*

Chloe rummaged in her bag for her phone, catching her gran's quizzical look.

'I'm sorry, I've just got a couple of calls to make, then I'll explain it all.' She heaved herself to her feet. 'I'll um… go in the lounge, if you don't mind. I can hardly think straight, and I've got such a mess to sort out.'

She bumped into Janelle in the hallway.

'Sorry, love, are you going already?' Janelle smiled at her, but Chloe couldn't bring herself to smile back, anxious now to get the calls made.

She held up her phone. 'Just got a couple of calls to make, then I'll come and join you.'

'Right you are,' Janelle said, walking past her and settling back down at the kitchen table without a backwards glance.

Chloe slipped into the lounge, closing the door behind her, and blew out a breath, weariness pulling her body onto the sofa. *Come on, just make the calls. No big deal. Let's get this sorted.* Of course, this was going to be harder with a new phone as she hadn't got the direct number for work. She took a deep breath and got on with the job of finding the number for the hospital. Then she had to wait for the switchboard, which took a few attempts, the engaged tone beeping in her ear for quite a few minutes before someone actually answered. Finally, she reached a voice she recognised.

'Anna! Thank goodness. It's Chloe.'

'Oh, you're back! Go on, tell me, did you have a fab time? I thought you would have posted some pictures, but obviously you were…' She coughed. 'Too busy.'

Chloe could almost see Anna's cheeky smile, see the lifted eyebrow. She forced a smile into her voice. 'Well… um, I'll have to fill you in next time I see you. I just wondered if Marie is there? I need a quick word.'

Marie was in charge of the physio unit, and she needed to tell her that she wouldn't be able to do her shift the following day. Already she was feeling bad about it.

'Yes, sure, I'll go and get her for you. But you should be warned, you're not her favourite person at the moment.'

Chloe frowned. 'What? Why?' She wondered what she'd done wrong, but when Anna didn't reply she realised she'd put her on hold. Her palms felt sweaty. Marie was not someone you wanted to get on the wrong side of; with a sharp tongue and a talent for sarcasm, she'd seen her reduce fellow team members to tears. Chloe's pulse whooshed in her ears as she waited, unable to think of what she might have done, nervous about Marie's reaction to the news she was about to give her regarding her shift the following day.

'Chloe.' Marie's voice was cold and snippy. 'I'm surprised you've got the nerve to ring after that little stunt.'

'Stunt?' Chloe frowned, confused. 'What stunt? I'm sorry, I don't know what you're talking about.'

Marie huffed down the phone. She was clearly fuming, and Chloe's body tensed, ready for a verbal onslaught. 'You could have spoken to me. That would have been the proper thing to do.'

'I'm sorry.' Chloe's voice wavered. 'I'm not sure what I've done.'

'If you wanted to resign, firstly you should have had the manners to come and tell me in person instead of sending an email. And second, you're supposed to give a month's notice.' Marie's voice was getting louder and Chloe had to hold the phone away from her ear. 'We're understaffed as it is, as you well know. But to just walk away like this… well, it's indefensible. So, if you think I'm going to give you a reference, then you've got another think coming!'

Chloe gasped. 'But I haven't resigned! I just had a week's holiday, for my honeymoon, you know that.'

'Well, how come I got an email last Monday saying you weren't coming back? I've had to get HR involved, of course. We've got an agency guy filling in. But honestly, Chloe, I thought you were better than that.'

Panic fluttered in Chloe's chest. 'I'm sorry but there seems to have been a misunderstanding. I haven't resigned!'

'So, you've changed your mind, have you?'

'No. No, listen to me.. I never sent that email. I didn't.'

Marie huffed.

'I was ringing to say I wouldn't be in tomorrow because I've come back and there's loads of weird stuff going on that I need to sort out.'

'Stuff that's more important than your job? You know I can't stand unreliability.'

A headache hammered through Chloe's skull, making thought almost impossible as her life crumbled around her.

'I'm sorry, Marie. Believe me—'

'You know I can't abide excuses.' The phone buzzed in Chloe's ear as Marie hung up.

Chloe leant forwards, her fingers rubbing at her temples. *What the hell is going on?* She definitely hadn't sent an email to Marie, so who had? *Dan.* That was the only answer. Was it him doing all this, to make sure she couldn't come back to her life in Brighton, giving her no option but to move to Menorca? He'd taken her phone, hadn't he? So, he'd have all her contacts and access to her email. Her hands curled into fists by her side.

How could he? Just wait till I speak to him!

The conversation she needed to have with Dan had now turned upside down in her mind, and instead of asking him to forgive her for running away, she'd be wanting answers to some bloody difficult questions. *What's all that rubbish about wanting to keep me safe?* Gran had been right. It was melodramatic nonsense, designed to scare her. But the only person scaring her was him, if she was honest with herself. What sort of man would do this to his wife? Take her life away from her?

She looked at her phone as a headache boomed inside her skull, making her wince. *Not yet,* she told herself and slumped back on the settee, eyes squinting against the pain.

So many things still to do. But each task she tackled seemed to bring new horror, as she watched her life being taken apart, piece by piece. She hardly dared ring the bank, but that had to be her next job. She closed her eyes and tried to relax a little before she tackled anything else, thinking her blood pressure must be sky-high by now. Her hand gravitated towards her stomach, aware of the new life growing inside her. She needed to rest. Make sure she was eating properly. And she definitely needed to calm down.

There was a weekly class that she did with pregnant women, a whole exercise routine that she knew off by heart to help keep them flexible and make sure they were ready for the rigours of childbirth. She knew what was to come, knew how her body would change, which ligaments would loosen, which exercises would help. In her mind, she ran through the relaxation exercises they did at the end of each session, and after a few minutes, she was asleep.

She woke with a stiff neck, and checked her phone just as the time ticked over to 2.43 p.m. *The bank!* Immediately she was wide awake. She had to get that sorted out because she couldn't function without money and wasn't going to demean herself by begging from her gran. She took a deep breath, found the number for the bank's central call centre and settled in for a bit of a wait while another round of tinny music rattled in her ear.

'Good afternoon,' said a bored, robotic-sounding voice. 'My name is Lisa, how may I help you?'

'Oh, I've got a problem with my debit card. The cash machine took it.'

'Okay. I'll just take you through security, then I'll have a look for you.'

Chloe answered all the questions and waited while she was put back on hold. When a voice came on the line again, it was somebody else.

'Hello, Miss Black, and thanks for holding.' It was a different woman's voice, well-spoken and older. 'My colleague has passed your call on to me. I've looked into your query and it seems that your card was taken because your account is closed.'

Chloe gasped, appalled at what she was hearing. 'No! No, it isn't closed. I haven't closed it, what are you talking about?'

'It's recorded here that we've had signed documentation closing your account. The paperwork arrived last Thursday. So that's why your card won't work. The balance has been transferred to your new account.'

Chloe's jaw squeezed tight and she could hear her teeth grinding. She couldn't speak, could hardly breathe and disconnected, knowing that there was no way she could carry on the conversation. Then she looked at the phone, wishing she had asked the obvious question: *What new account?*

CHAPTER TWENTY-SEVEN

Poor Chloe.

Who would want to be in her shoes right now? Not me, that's for sure. But from my point of view, everything seems to be working out just fine.

I can see her now, as she sits on the sofa, her face covered by her hands, shoulders shaking. Yes, poor thing is sobbing her heart out.

I should apologise to her, because none of this is her fault really. But I can't feel bad about it. I won't let myself.

Sometimes it's a matter of no pain, no gain, isn't it?

CHAPTER TWENTY-EIGHT

'Chloe? Are you okay?'

Janelle's voice startled Chloe and she looked up, blinking back the tears as she tried to control her sobs. She swiped at her cheeks with the back of her hand, fumbled in her pocket for something to wipe up the snotty mess.

'Here,' Janelle said, pulling a pack of tissues from her pocket before sitting beside her. 'What on earth's the matter? Is it that husband of yours? Your gran told me he'd been playing up a bit. And you know, when you're pregnant, all those hormones do funny things to your emotions.'

Chloe tried to speak, but her breath juddered in her throat as sobs forced themselves out. She shook her head, not sure she wanted to tell Janelle anything, and a spark of anger flared at the thought her gran had told this woman everything. A woman she'd only known for a week. Practically a stranger. *How dare she?*

'Chloe, what's going on?'

The sound of her gran's voice made Chloe focus on the packet of tissues in her hand, not sure what to do anymore, who to trust. But then she remembered a favourite saying of her mother's – a problem shared is a problem halved – and she decided she could really do with her problems shrinking because they were swamping her right now. Her money had gone to a mysterious account, she was homeless, all her possessions had disappeared, she no longer had a job and her husband was acting strangely. She could do with someone putting a positive spin on that lot.

Her sobs finally subsided, and she started to explain everything that had happened since she'd arrived back in Brighton.

'Oh, my days,' Janelle said, shaking her head. 'That's one heck of a mess you've got on your hands, isn't it?' She shuffled up the sofa and put an arm round Chloe's shoulders, giving her a hug. She smelt of something floral, her body soft and comforting, but she was a stranger and Chloe tensed. A hug wasn't going to be the answer.

'Right, well, first thing is to ring that husband of yours and find out what's going on,' her gran said.

Chloe nodded.

'You give him a call and we'll give you a bit of privacy.' Her gran wagged a finger. 'But you stand up to him, young lady. None of this submissive nonsense just because he's your husband. You're allowed to have your own life and it's not for him to decide how you live it!'

'Or where you live it,' Janelle chimed in.

Once she was on her own, Chloe sat for a few minutes, dazed by how quickly her life had been taken apart. She'd been solid before she'd met Dan. Unexciting maybe, but solid, held in place by routine and responsibilities. Yes, it had felt like she was holding her breath, waiting for her future to spring to life, but she'd felt calm, a contentment of sorts. Had she really been so desperate for a relationship that she'd blocked out all the warning signs of trouble? She'd revelled in Dan's attentiveness, never imagining it might be the precursor to control. How could she have foreseen this? That he'd whisk her life away without discussion, taking it on himself to make decisions that weren't his to make, to shape her life in a way that she didn't want.

Finally ready, she rang his number. Instantly, a woman's voice told her, 'Sorry this number is no longer available.'

She frowned and tried again, with the same result. Then she remembered that Dan had bought a new SIM card, a local one because he said it would save money. Had he changed it after he'd rung her gran? Or maybe there was a problem with his phone? *What the hell?* If his number wasn't working for some reason, she had no way of talking to him.

Her mind ran round in frantic circles before she realised she could still message him. Not ideal, but at least she could have a conversation of sorts.

'What now?' she muttered to herself when her Facebook page wouldn't load. She tried Dan's page, but that wouldn't come up either. She went to her email, but it said her password wasn't recognised. Same with her Messenger account, and her Instagram and Twitter accounts seemed to have disappeared as well. Gone. In social media terms, she no longer existed and her list of contacts had vanished.

Her fingers rubbed at her temple. *Why would he do this?*

She lay down on the settee, too tired to sit up anymore, her thoughts racing. *Perhaps it isn't him?* She had to open her mind to other possibilities, didn't she? She chewed her lip as she pondered the question, looking for an alternative explanation. *Who else might want to get me out of Brighton? Cause me so much hassle?*

After a moment, her thoughts settled.

Lucy and Mark.

Her eyes widened. Now that was a definite possibility.

She never thought of them as individuals anymore because they seemed to act in unison where she was concerned. Her sister the leader and her brother right behind her, backing her up. *Lucy and Mark.* That's how it had been for years, ever since their father had died. As the firstborn, there had been a time when Lucy was the only child, when all the attention had been focused on her. Their father had been in the habit of taking Lucy for trips out, to give their mother a chance to have a rest and the habit continued when the other two children had come along. As soon as Lucy was old enough to ride a bike, their father had taken her out on cycling trips almost every weekend. It was their thing, something that happened whatever the weather, experiences that only they shared. When their father died, it had struck Lucy the hardest and she had latched onto Mark, who adored his oldest sister and would do whatever she said.

Overnight, the family dynamics changed, and Chloe remembered life at home as being fraught, all the way through her teenage years, until Lucy left home to go to university. There was a familiar theme to the dramas, she remembered.

'You don't care about me!' Lucy would yell at their mother when she'd tell her that she couldn't have whatever it was she'd asked for. 'You only care about Chloe.'

Their mother would sigh, exhausted by the strain of being a single parent and the demands of her fractious daughter. 'You know that's not true. I care about you all equally.'

'But you spend all your time with her. You don't take me to the allotment, do you?'

'You don't like gardening, Lucy,' their mother would answer, evenly.

'I might do if you asked me.'

'I have asked you and you've never wanted to come.'

'You don't ask me either,' Mark would pipe up.

'Because you get bored and want to come home five minutes after we've got there.'

'You treat me as an unpaid babysitter, while you two go off for hours.' Lucy would round on Chloe then, to make sure she knew she was in the wrong as well.

'An hour at the most,' their mum would point out, and it was true. 'It's never more than an hour.'

'I hate you!' Lucy would yell. 'I hate both of you.' And she would run off crying, with Mark on her heels.

Chloe would always go and give her mum a hug after these explosions of temper, knowing how much her mum struggled to do everything on her own. Chloe did whatever she could to help, wanting nothing more than to ease her mother's pain, to make her life a bit easier. *Why couldn't Lucy see that?* But it wasn't in her nature. Lucy's life was all about Lucy and nothing was ever going to change that.

Chloe knew that her mother didn't have favourites, didn't love her more than the other two, but there was no getting away from the fact that they were similar people, liked doing the same things and always had so much to talk about. Lucy hated that and always tried to wedge herself between them, causing trouble. Chloe rationalised her behaviour as being part of her grief; that's how her mother had explained it to her. Nothing personal, she was just lashing out.

After their mother's death, Lucy's hatred had notched up to another level. Chloe had missed the funeral, arriving home the following week, only finding out what had happened when she'd rung home the day before she left Thailand. Lucy and Mark were staying at their mother's house, which was still Chloe's home, as they started to sort out her affairs.

'Oh, it's you,' Lucy had said when Chloe had walked into the kitchen after depositing her bags in the hallway. 'How dare you even show your face?'

Chloe had stepped back as Lucy advanced towards her.

'I live here, Lucy. It's my home.'

Lucy had sneered. 'It's not your home anymore, so you can pick up your trash and get out.'

Chloe had stood her ground then, told herself not to be intimidated. 'It's always been my home. You're the ones that moved out. You and Mark.'

'But you're responsible for her death. You do know that, don't you? That's what everyone thinks. You bloody killed her. You knew she was ill, and you still went off, without telling any of us she was really poorly.' Lucy's face had been inches away from Chloe's. She could smell the garlic on her breath, could see the open pores on her nose. 'Would it have been so hard to let us know, eh? Would it? She'd still be alive. Has that occurred to you? If you'd bothered to make a couple of phone calls, we'd still have a mother.'

Chloe had shaken her head, tears welling up, filling her throat. She had no answer, no words to explain, nothing that would make any difference.

'I'm sorry,' she'd murmured.

Lucy had slapped her face. Chloe's head had whipped to the side and she'd staggered backwards, so shocked that she couldn't speak.

Lucy had had a manic look in her eye and Chloe knew she was winding herself up into one of her furious tantrums. 'Sorry! You're sorry? Oh, well, that's all right then, isn't it? That all fine and dandy.'

Another slap, even harder this time, had made Chloe dash into the hallway, pick up her bags and leave. She'd stayed with a friend until Lucy had gone back home a couple of days later, and she'd let herself back into the house, feeling like an intruder in her own home.

The intimidation had continued until Chloe agreed that she didn't deserve her share of the inheritance, and as an executor of her mother's will, she'd signed it over to Lucy and Mark. Compensation for their loss, Lucy had said. It was only right. If Chloe had cared more, their mother wouldn't be dead.

Now, in her gran's lounge, the memories made her shiver. *Is Lucy making trouble again? Looking to take her share of Gran's inheritance?* It would be a considerable amount. *It's a possibility*, she decided, especially after her gran's comments about her will.

'Any luck?' Janelle popped her head round the door. 'We're having a cuppa and cookies if you fancy some?'

Chloe gazed at her and sighed. 'All my online accounts have gone. And Dan's. I can't contact him.' Her voice was hardly more than a whisper, but the desperation was clear.

Janelle came into the room and perched on the edge of the armchair, frowning. 'Well, that's a bit odd, isn't it?'

Chloe nodded, too exhausted to even speak.

'Tell you what. Come and have something to eat, then we can have a chat about it, see if we can work out what the heck is going on. How about that?'

Chloe realised she hadn't had any lunch, remembered that she had a baby to think about now, and after a moment she slowly rose to her feet. Even if she didn't feel like eating, she had to force something down for the sake of this new life growing inside her. A life that Dan knew nothing about.

She followed Janelle into the kitchen where the smell of freshly baked cookies filled the air. Her stomach rumbled while Janelle poured the tea, and she began to explain what had happened.

'Oh, it's turned into a terrible mess, hasn't it?' her gran said, as if it was Chloe's fault. There was no answer to that one, but then her gran didn't expect it and carried on talking. 'Look, I've got to say this, and I don't want you to take this the wrong way… but I can't have you moving in here, so I don't want you to think that's an option. It just brings everything back – all that sadness – and it confuses me sometimes when I think you are your mum. It's not good for my blood pressure. Or my mental health.'

Janelle stayed quiet, but Chloe could see this was something they'd spoken about, could tell by the little glance exchanged by the two women.

Chloe ate in silence while she considered her options before realising that she didn't have any. With no money, no accommodation and no way of contacting people, she was completely stuck.

'I need to talk to him, Gran. Get this sorted out.'

'Well, there's only one way to do that, isn't there? You'll have to go back to Menorca.'

Chloe looked down at her plate, picking up crumbs on her finger, wounded by her gran's words. Nobody cared about her.

Not her gran, or Lucy or Mark. She'd alienated her workmates by making the department short-staffed and couldn't get in touch with anyone else. She was alone. Completely alone.

'Look, I'll pay for you to go,' her gran said, a steely gleam in her eyes. 'You can stay here tonight and go back tomorrow morning. Get it all sorted.' She sighed and her voice softened. 'Marriage is difficult in the beginning and you've only been wed a week. This is probably all some sort of silly misunderstanding. But you won't know unless you actually go and talk to him.'

So there it was. Her gran was throwing her out. Going back to Dan and getting some answers was her only option.

CHAPTER TWENTY-NINE

I almost missed her again!

My goodness, she darts around like one of those little fishes, turning this way and that. Thank goodness I saw her getting into the airport taxi.

Back to Menorca we go, then.

I can feel the pressure building, like a boil about to burst.

Time to speed things up now, I think.

Time to reach the finale.

Time for Chloe to hear a few home truths.

CHAPTER THIRTY

As soon as the plane took off, Chloe finally slept, her thoughts having kept her tossing and turning for most of the night. Her gran had paid for the ticket, a return coming back in a couple of days, and given her a small amount of cash to tide her over. She seemed enthusiastic to see her go, if Chloe was being honest, not at all concerned that Chloe might be heading into danger of some sort, and she'd left with a feeling that she wasn't welcome anymore. Now she was devoid of any family ties, she really needed to sort out the situation with Dan, and decide how she wanted the future to be for her and their baby.

A tap on her shoulder woke her, the smiling face of an air hostess beaming down at her. 'I need you to put your table up, please. We're just coming in to land.'

Chloe did as she was asked, rubbed her eyes, and glanced out of the window. There was nothing to see except a billowing cushion of clouds below them, blue sky above and the plane seeming to hang in the space between. Next to her, an elderly couple were doing a crossword puzzle and taking no notice of her whatsoever. She closed her eyes, wishing she could go back to sleep and wake up to find it had all been a crazy dream. That she and Dan were just starting their honeymoon, off to the Maldives, to that beautiful hotel she'd been looking forward to, very much in love.

I do still love him, though, don't I?

Her heart clenched at the thought, the fact that she was even asking herself that question. There was no doubt that she'd been missing him. No doubt that he filled her thoughts, that she felt empty without him. But there was something else now. Questions, uncertainties and, yes, an element of fear. If he was trying to force her to live in Menorca by wiping out her existence in the UK, then that was seriously twisted behaviour. And he'd definitely misjudged her. She'd been bullied enough by her sister without Dan starting. *No*, she told herself, hands clenching in her lap. *I won't put up with it.* Once she knew the truth, she could work out what she was going to do about it, but in the meantime, she needed to keep an open mind.

It might not be Dan.

Now that was an even scarier thought, one she hadn't allowed herself to consider too much. Dan she could deal with, she thought, because he loved her. Of that she was certain. If he was doing this, it was a mistake, assumptions made that shouldn't have been, him trying to be the masterful husband, getting everything organised so she didn't have to worry about anything.

Who else would want to rip my life away from me?

She watched as the clouds filled the horizon, the plane starting its descent. It could only be someone who was jealous. Or someone who didn't want her to be happy. The faces of her brother and sister sprang into her mind again. *Could it be them?* Were they trying to make sure that she was out of the way, not contactable, so she couldn't collect her share of her gran's estate. *Gran's house is worth a lot of money.* They would hate to share that windfall. Hate it.

She frowned. It was a possibility she should consider. Given the failing health of her gran, were they circling, like vultures, eyeing up the millions that her gran's estate would provide when she died?

The plane thumped onto the runway, sending a shudder through the cabin, and she braced herself against the seat in front until the speed decreased and the plane started to taxi to its resting place next to the terminal. *Not long till I see Dan.* She took a deep breath, her pulse starting to speed up. The thought both thrilled and scared her. *How on earth is he going to react to me running off like that?*

For the first time, she tried to put herself in Dan's shoes. He'd told her they couldn't go home because it wasn't safe, for some mysterious reason. Was that real, or imaginary? Something he'd created to make her do what he wanted? But suppose she *was* in danger. He'd be frantic by now, wouldn't he? No word from her for over twenty-four hours. *But he could have rung me*, she reminded herself. She chewed at her lip as she waited to get off the plane. *Why didn't he ring Gran again?*

Her frown deepened, her mind ticking through everything that had happened all over again as the queue to get off the plane finally started to shuffle forwards and she walked through the terminal to the taxi rank.

As she started the journey back to the villa, the possibilities swirled like a grey mist, blocking any clarity of thought. She was just going to have to be brave, apologise to Dan for freaking out, tell him exactly what had happened and ask him if he knew what the hell was going on. There was absolutely no point trying to second-guess what lay ahead of her.

It was raining, a damp, drizzly day that blurred the landscape and filled the roads with enormous puddles. Quite different to the sunny paradise she'd left a couple of days before, but completely in keeping with her mood. Her stomach griped and churned as they drew close to the village, a headache stretching across her forehead. She needed food – or rather, it seemed like the baby did – and she decided to stop for a quick breakfast in one of the harbourside cafés before walking up to the house. The fresh air would help her think and a good breakfast would give her energy and the resolve to stand her ground if it came to an argument.

*

A little while later, she made herself leave the comfort of the café and start the final part of her journey. The rain pattered on the hood of her raincoat, seeping through her trainers until her feet squelched. She shivered and thought she should have brought more layers, until she reminded herself that she couldn't do that because she had no clothes in Brighton. All that she owned was either here or stored in a mysterious location somewhere.

Her jaw hardened, her shoulders bunching under her jacket as anger flared in her chest. She stomped through the forest without a thought for her surroundings, no fear of what might be lurking in the trees, her mind too busy sorting out what she was going to say.

Given the gloominess of the day, she was surprised that there were no lights on when she reached the house. She was even more surprised when she found the door was locked. She checked her watch, finding that it was almost 11 a.m., so Dan would be up and about by now. In fact, he was probably out, getting shopping. *Or looking for me.* She cringed. *What if he rang Gran and went to the airport to meet me and I missed him? Why hadn't he rung again while I was in Brighton? Or maybe he did, and Gran didn't tell me?* Now that was a thought she needed to consider. *Gran was very keen to pack me off to Menorca again.* Perhaps that was because she'd spoken to Dan.

She sighed and went round the back of the house where she could sit out of the rain. Ten minutes later, she heard the sound of a car engine, coming closer. Her heart jumped in her chest. *He's back.*

She decided to wait for the car to leave before she made her presence known, not wanting any sort of scene in front of a stranger. The door slammed shut and she heard the engine start to fade. She crept round to the front of the house, tried the door and walked in, stopping when she saw Dan in front of her, taking off his jacket.

'Dan.'

He whirled round, eyes wide when he saw her. She found herself unable to move. He stepped towards her, and from the look sparking in his eyes, she wasn't sure whether to stay or run.

'What the hell?' His eyes moved up and down her body as if he was doing an inventory. 'Christ!'

There was anger in his voice and she edged away until her back hit the wall and she could go no further. Her chest felt tight, her heart pounding.

'I'm so sorry, Dan,' she gabbled. 'I'm sorry I went home. But I couldn't think about leaving Gran.' She looked down at the floor and thought about that for a moment. 'Actually, you were right.' She swallowed, understanding what an idiot she'd been, thinking she was needed when the opposite had been true. 'She doesn't want me to look after her. The carer, Janelle, seems very capable and they seem to have struck up a real friendship.' Heat spread up her neck. 'Oh God, I'm so sorry.'

He moved to her and folded her into his arms, pulling her to his chest. She breathed in the smell of him, felt the warmth of his body against hers, but she couldn't relax.

'I was so worried.' He pushed away, his hands on her shoulders, eyes level with hers as he pinned her to the wall. 'You've no idea what you put me through. No idea. Knowing you were out there on your own, without me to protect you.' His voice was full of anguish and Chloe felt like a child again, when she'd gone out to play with a friend and not told her mum, coming home well after dark. It had only happened once because she got such a telling-off.

She looked away, and forced herself to stand her ground, spell out why she'd gone. The situation was of his making and there was no need for her to take all the responsibility. 'Look, I've said I'm sorry, but you were being so paranoid and then saying I couldn't go home and not listening when I told you how worried I was about Gran. To my mind, it was major control-freak behaviour.'

He straightened up and ran a hand through his hair, his mouth a thin line. 'But you didn't need to go running off. After everything I've said to you about being in danger, didn't you think about how worried I'd be?' He scowled at her. 'Did that even cross your mind?'

She cringed. 'To tell you the truth, Dan, you were scaring me.'

'Scaring you?' He looked incredulous, his voice getting louder, his fingers digging into her shoulders. 'Me, your husband who loves you more than life itself – I was scaring you?'

She winced. *And you're starting to scare me now*, she thought as she watched the colour of his face grow darker, the vein popping out on his forehead. It felt claustrophobic in the hallway, his body seeming to fill the entire space, leaving no room for air. 'You're hurting me.'

He looked puzzled then realised how tightly he was holding her, and his grip loosened enough for her to wriggle free. She ducked past him and walked into the living area, wanting to put some distance between them until she'd properly had her say and found out exactly what was going on. She could hear him following her and she went and sat at the dining table, somewhere she felt more in control, where he couldn't be too close.

'Dan, will you sit down? I really need to talk to you.'

'Talk to me? Now you want to talk to me!' He was pacing up and down, hands gesticulating as he spoke. 'Shouldn't we have done the talking before you decided to run off? Honestly, Chloe.' He took a deep breath and sank down onto the chair opposite, like a deflating balloon. She could see the redness in his eyes, the tears glistening on the surface, and her heart clenched.

'What happened to loving each other for better or worse, and all of that?' His voice cracked with emotion, the anger gone for now. 'What about those promises we made only a week ago? I promised to cherish you and that's what I've been trying to do. Trying to keep you away from anything that might cause us trouble.'

'Oh, Dan.' She reached for his hand across the table, wanting to soothe his pain. 'You went a bit over the top, don't you think? I felt like a prisoner being locked in every night, not being able to have any fresh air in the house, you taking control of everything we did.'

'There was a reason, and if you trusted me, then you would have known…'

'Known what?'

He gazed at her, his thumb caressing the back of her hand. 'I only want to look after you.' He shook his head slowly. 'I can't imagine how you would find me scary. I can't tell you how much that hurts. You thinking I might harm you in some way.'

She squeezed his hand and looked away, shuffled in her chair. 'Well, no… I didn't…' She ground to a halt, unsure now exactly what she did think. He looked like a broken man, trying his best not to cry, and she felt like her heart was breaking. She slipped her hand from his grasp, went round the table and held him in her arms, a tear working its way down her cheek. Had she broken them? Had she ruined everything before they'd even got started?

'There's so much I have to tell you.' She kissed his cheek, then his mouth, and he responded so gently that she wondered what on earth she *had* been thinking.

'I'm just so relieved that you came back,' he murmured. 'I can't tell you what was running through my mind.' He swung her onto his lap, her head resting on his shoulder, his arm pulling her close. She found his hand and linked her fingers with his, their two wedding bands side by side. *For better or for worse. Let's hope we've got the worse out of the way*, she thought as she relaxed into his arms, finding it hard to believe that he was the one behind all her troubles, the one who had taken away her life.

CHAPTER THIRTY-ONE

They stayed wrapped up in each other for a while. Chloe didn't want to think about anything except the moment, the fact that they loved each other, that he wasn't angry with her anymore and she hadn't ruined everything. He was the first to speak.

'Sorry, babe, but my leg's gone to sleep, I'm going to have to move.'

She shuffled over to sit on the chair beside him. 'Dan…' She swallowed, readying her little speech, about everything that had gone wrong while she was away, but that wasn't what came out. What she said instead was, 'I'm pregnant.'

His mouth fell open, but his expression of disbelief soon changed to a massive smile. 'For real? You're actually pregnant?' His eyes shone, and he grabbed her hand in both of his. 'Definitely?'

She nodded, glad that he was pleased about it happening so soon. She hadn't even acknowledged to herself that he might not be ready for a baby. That fear had been pushed right to the bottom of the pile, given everything else that had been going on. They had been so bad at planning their future, and this was the worst possible time to be talking about a baby, but clearly her subconscious had decided it was her priority. She let out a slow breath. *At least he knows now.*

'Well, that explains things, doesn't it? Why you've been so grumpy and paranoid.'

She frowned, his words scratching at her. 'Sorry? Me paranoid? I'm not the one who's been making the place into a prison every night, am I? I'm not the one who says we can't go home, who's worried about a mystery danger. I'm not the one who changed the honeymoon plans without any discussion whatsoever. I'm not—'

'Chloe.' He held up a hand in an attempt to stop her flow. 'Let's not go there.'

'Where?' she snapped. 'Where don't you want to go?'

'Come on, babe. Don't spoil the moment. I'm just trying to say that we've been a bit tetchy with each other this last week and it wasn't like that before we got married, and maybe the pregnancy has something to do with it.' He smiled at her, his hand reaching for her, but she slapped it away and got to her feet.

'Are you for real? Is it going to be hormones to blame for everything now?'

He grabbed her arm, the tightness of his grip reminding her of his superior strength as he pulled her towards him, his eyes not moving from hers.

'I love you so much, babe. You mean the world to me. The absolute world.'

'I love you too, Dan. But…' She sighed. *Don't start again*, she told herself. *Save it for another day. There are more important things to talk about.* 'A lot's happened since I last saw you. And it's been freaking me out and I need to know who's behind it.'

He frowned, looking concerned now. 'What do you mean? What sort of things?'

She sat down, took a deep breath and went through all the events of the previous couple of days: the gradual discovery that her life in the UK had been wound up by somebody. She turned to him. 'Dan, I know you want us to move over here… Was it you? Did you do all that?'

He jerked back in his seat, hurt written all over his face. 'How could you think that? How could you?'

She gazed at him, saw his chest heaving as he ran a hand over his hair while he fought to find the right words.

She reached out and grabbed his hand, panic tearing through her. Was she ripping their love apart with her accusations? Creating scars that would never heal? Pain flared in her chest and she knew then how deeply she loved this man, how even the thought of losing him was destroying her.

'I'm sorry. I'm so sorry,' she stammered. 'But I can't see who else would even want to do those things to me. It makes no sense. Unless…' She bit her lip, her mind presenting her with the only other alternative.

'Unless what?'

'Unless it's Lucy and Mark.'

'But why would they do it?' His voice was harsh, incredulous. 'That doesn't make sense either.'

'Well, it sort of does. I haven't told you what happened after Mum died, have I?'

He sighed. 'I'm beginning to think there's a lot of things you haven't told me.'

She scowled and grabbed her hand away from his. Anger swirled in her belly, and the willingness to share a painful part of her past evaporated as quickly as it had materialised. 'You know just as much about me as I know about you,' she snapped. 'Don't go making out that I've been secretive, because that's not it.'

'So, what is it, if they're not secrets? You told me about your mum dying the other day. How you blamed yourself for not getting her prescription, not making sure she was all right. That was a secret, wasn't it?'

'Christ!' She flung her hands in the air. 'Why are you being so argumentative?'

He closed his mouth and took a deep breath as if he was sucking his words back in, deciding not to say whatever had been on the tip of his tongue. He looked down at his hands, not willing to meet her eye, and she knew she'd hit on something.

'Come on, Dan. What is it you're not telling me? You're the one who thinks I'm in danger. And you know what? After all the stuff that's been going on, I'm beginning to wonder if you're right.'

She had to stand her ground here. Had to find out exactly what was behind all her troubles. Then she remembered something else. Something that had really been puzzling her.

'I tried to ring you, you know?' Her eyes narrowed as she remembered her panic when she couldn't talk to him. 'But it said your number was unavailable. Why was that, do you think?'

His lips twitched but he still wouldn't look at her.

She frowned. 'I could have let you know I was safe if I'd been able to ring you. And I wanted to tell you about the baby, but I couldn't. And ask you about all these other weird problems that just started piling up.' She nodded. 'You weren't there when I needed you, Dan.' A headache thudded at the base of her skull, the tension pulling her muscles tighter and tighter. 'Then I thought I'd message you instead, but neither of us appears to have any social media accounts anymore.' She rubbed her neck, waiting for his answer. 'You had Gran's number, and I know you rang her once. You could have rung back to speak to me, couldn't you?' She glared at him. 'I'm interested to know why you didn't.'

He ran his tongue round his bottom lip, his hands fiddling with the zip on his fleece. She waited for his response, watched him pull the zip up and down, up and down.

'Okay, I'll admit I did delete our email accounts and social media when I knew you'd gone back.'

His admission was like a slap and she reeled back against the chair, speech impossible for a moment.

'But why? It's not for you to do that!' Anger flushed her cheeks, sharpened her voice. 'Delete your own if you want, but my accounts are nothing to do with you.'

He wavered for a moment before speaking and she wondered if she was going to get the truth or a lie.

'If we're going to have a fresh start, it's for the best. Anyway, you're not Chloe Black anymore, are you? You're Mrs Chloe Marsden now, so you'd have to change your accounts anyway.' He emphasised the 'Mrs', stamping his ownership on her. She was his now, that's what he was telling her, she belonged to him.

The muscles in Chloe's jaw ached and she made a conscious effort to unclench her teeth. He was being so difficult, and she was struggling to understand his thinking. 'That's not the point. The point is you have taken something away from me that was mine and mine alone.' She huffed out a breath, trying not to get distracted from her line of thinking. 'But what I asked you originally was why I couldn't get you on the phone. Why was your number unavailable?'

'I got a new SIM card.'

'I know that. Remember, I rang Gran on your phone? Because my phone mysteriously went missing?' She glared at him, the accusation clear in her voice. 'So, I rang you on that number. And it told me it was no longer available. So why was that?'

He was still fiddling with the zip, running it up and down, a noise that was seriously annoying her now. 'I had to go and get a new one – it wasn't working properly. Must have been faulty. Apparently, it happens sometimes.' He wasn't looking at her.

He's lying.

But why? And why would he want a new SIM card when he knew it meant she couldn't contact him? Unless he wasn't worried about her at all, in which case… She clasped her head in her hands, trying to work out a logical explanation and there just wasn't one.

He's lying.

She heard him move, felt his hand on hers, his thumb rubbing in little circles.

'Chloe, let's just stop this squabbling about things that don't matter. What matters is who has your possessions and your money and who sent in your resignation. Because that wasn't me. I didn't do any of that.'

She glanced at him from between her fingers and caught a look that made the hairs stand up on the back of her neck.

He's lying.

CHAPTER THIRTY-TWO

Chloe stood, wanting to put a bit of distance between them. She stalked into the kitchen area and poured herself a glass of water, gulping it down. The sound of his footsteps behind her made her turn, her skin prickling.

What else is he lying about?

'You've got to believe me.' He stood in front of her, his body reacting to her every move, as if he might pounce if she tried to get past him. She could feel the tension buzzing off him as adrenaline filled her veins.

Stay calm, she told herself while her mind alerted her to all the potential lies he'd told her.

What do I really know about him?

The answer was not enough.

She leant against the sink and gazed at him over the rim of her glass, deciding that the best thing to do was keep him talking and see if she could get to the truth. 'Well, I don't believe you. Who else could it be?' She saw his hands clench into fists and she steadied herself, ready to kick out if he came any nearer.

His jaw clenched. 'I don't know why you're being like this. I haven't changed. Nothing has changed between us, but look at you! You're behaving like I'm going to beat you up or something. What's going on?' His frown deepened. 'Has somebody said something to you? Have they?'

She slid away from the sink and walked back towards the lounge area, where there was more space and she wouldn't feel quite so threatened. 'Nobody has said anything. But somebody has done quite a few things that have turned my life into a mess. I have no home, no job, no money and no contacts. And where's my phone? I know you took it. You could at least give that back to me.'

He walked into the lounge and she moved, making sure the sofa was between them. He was starting to look angry now, his face reddening, arms folded across his chest as he leant against the wall, watching her. *Cat and mouse*. That's what it felt like. She could see his teeth nibbling at his bottom lip, a habit that she used to find endearing, but now she realised it was evidence of a lie, something he wasn't telling her.

He looked at the floor, the toe of his shoe rubbing at a mark on the tiles. 'I haven't got your phone.'

'But you took it?'

He nodded.

There, see, I was right. And he lied about that, didn't he?

'But why? What was the point? It just made everything difficult. Impossible. If I'd had that, you could've rung me. And my contacts, everyone I know, they're all on there.' She tilted her head to the ceiling and let out a strangled scream before glaring at him. 'For someone who wants to keep me safe, you made me very vulnerable.'

He kicked a little harder at the floor, still not looking at her. 'I can't explain at the moment. But you have to believe me when I say that it's important you can't be traced to here. That's why I had to get rid of your phone.'

A shiver ran down her spine. She hadn't thought about that, the fact that nobody actually knew where she was. Yes, her Gran and Janelle knew she was in Menorca, in a rented house, but that was all. If they thought she was in trouble, they wouldn't be able to find her. Not without help from the police, and even then… She paced up and down, keeping an eye on Dan because she was feeling more insecure with every revelation.

He walked towards her and she backed away, raised a hand. 'No. Don't you come any closer.'

He held out his arms to her. 'There's nothing to be scared of, babe. Honestly.'

'Well, you're going to have to tell me the truth if you want to convince me of that.' Her voice was shaking. 'I shouldn't have come back.'

'Of course you should. You're my wife. We belong together.' His hands dropped to his sides and his expression softened. 'I wish we could rewind to before the wedding. We were so happy, weren't we? So full of hope for the future.'

She glared at him, unable to keep up with his changing persona. *Is it all an act?* Whatever was going on, she was feeling very uncomfortable and lashed out with her words, the only weapon she had. 'Well, whose fault is it that it's ended in this mess?'

'I've only tried to do what's best for you, for us.' His eyes pleaded with her. 'Giving us a fresh start in a place where I know I can get work. Where we'll be safe.'

'That's all great for you, but what about me? You just went ahead and did exactly what you wanted. But this is a step too far.' She slapped her hands on the back of the sofa, needing to get rid of some of her pent-up anger. 'This house and this place and the idyllic dream that you have – it's not real. What I had in Brighton was real, but you've taken that away from me. I don't exist anymore.'

'Oh, Chloe.' He looked genuinely sad, but she didn't trust his expression, didn't trust anything about him, and when he stepped towards her, she backed away again. 'I wish you could see things differently. I wish you could see that I've given you a future where we can thrive, rather than taken something from you. Come on, you've got to admit your gran had you on a short leash, keeping you feeling guilty, running around after her. You didn't have a great life in Brighton. You spent all your time looking after everyone else. Here, there's none of that. You can just be yourself!'

He's mad, she decided, her body so tense now she thought she might snap into little pieces. Some of his points had hit home and her head was fuddled by his arguments. *The baby*, she thought, *this isn't good for the baby.* Her hands gravitated towards her stomach as she backed towards the kitchen and the hallway beyond.

'I can't do this. I need to rest,' she said, reaching the doorway. 'I don't want you to come near me, understand? Keep away.'

He raised his hands in surrender. 'Okay, okay. You'll probably feel better for a bit of a nap.'

She turned, ran up the stairs and slammed the bedroom door behind her, suddenly weary of it all. She stared out of the window, at the grey drizzle, and she wondered what she was going to do now. *I've got my passport, a return ticket, money and my new phone.* Everything she needed to get herself back to the UK. *There, nothing too much to worry about.* She tried to talk herself into a state of calm, but the weight of her worries pressed down on her and she lay on the bed, hands on her stomach, consumed by the thought that he was looking in her bag, taking her means of escape. He'd done it before and would surely do it again.

Nothing much you can do about that now, she told herself, thinking that she'd hide her valuables at the next opportunity. She tossed and turned, trying to get herself comfortable, all the time wondering what Dan was doing. And more to the point, what he was hiding. She shuffled over to his side of the bed, considering where she might find some answers. *In his bedside table? Isn't that where he'd kept the keys?* Maybe there was more that he was keeping in there.

She stopped and listened, could hear his footsteps downstairs, the sound of chopping. He was cooking. Good – that meant he'd be busy for a little while. Time for her to have a look around.

His bedside table held nothing of interest, so she crept over to the wardrobe and looked through pockets, under folded clothes, quietly got a chair to stand on and felt on top, searched underneath. Nothing. She scoured the whole room and was about to give up when she had a thought. *Under the mattress.* It was the only place she hadn't looked, and it had been one of her favourite hiding places when she was a child.

Her hands wriggled under his side of the bed, up and down, then they caught on something. It felt like an envelope and she was about to pull it out when she heard footsteps coming up the stairs. She threw herself back on the bed and feigned sleep, hoping he wouldn't notice the heaving of her chest or her body shaking with each thunderous beat of her heart.

The door opened and she heard his feet come in, then stop. She could hear his breathing; could he hear hers? Far too fast for someone who was supposed to be asleep. She blinked her eyes open.

'Dan?'

'Oh, you're awake. I didn't want to disturb you, but I've made some pasta if you fancy something to eat.'

Hunger gnawed at her insides, and after a moment she slowly pushed herself up to sit on the edge of the bed. A wave of dizziness made her hesitate before standing.

'Can we just rule a line under the past and start again? Please, babe. Can we do that?' His eyes gleamed and she thought he might have been crying.

He sat next to her, took her hand in both of his, and she was reminded again of how big he was, an enormous presence that had once filled her with unconditional love. Now she didn't know how she felt. His thumb caressed the back of her hand, and she longed for everything to be normal. Back to how it was just over a week ago. Her stomach grumbled, and he laughed.

'Come on.' He squeezed her hand, starting to stand. 'Food's going cold and it sounds like you're ready for it.'

He stood and pulled her to her feet, a movement she couldn't have resisted even if she'd wanted to. She could believe everything was normal, couldn't she? *Gran's happy with Janelle looking after her. More than happy.* Chloe was no longer needed, or even wanted, in Brighton. All her ties had been cut. Perhaps she should relax and see what happened, let this thing run its course. Treat it as an extended honeymoon, and let everything settle down. She decided that she wouldn't mention any of her questions over their lunch. She'd wait and see if Dan volunteered any information first.

The smell of garlic and basil got stronger as they headed down the stairs and into the kitchen, where he'd laid the table; a salad and a jug of fresh orange juice sat alongside a steaming bowl of pasta.

'Smells delicious,' she said as she sat down, light-headed with hunger. She poured herself a glass of orange juice and gulped it down, the sugar zinging into her bloodstream. As they ate, she thought that her life had become completely surreal. They chatted about the weather and the food and the chill in the air. Everything except his secrets and lies. Or her worries and fears. She watched him, studied his face, his eyes, noticed the vein pulsing on his forehead again.

He's not as relaxed as he's making out, is he?

She chewed her food, taking her time while she thought about her next move. *The envelope.* What was in the hidden envelope? It would only take a minute to whip it out and sneak it into the bathroom where she could have a proper look.

'I'll clear up, don't you worry about that,' he said when they'd finished. 'How about a coffee? Or is it true that coffee doesn't taste very nice when you're pregnant?'

I'm pregnant. The fact of the matter hadn't really registered yet and she knew she needed to look after herself better, focus on the needs of this new life inside her.

She forced herself to smile, act normal. 'I hadn't noticed any difference to be honest. But I feel a bit grubby after travelling. I'm going to have a shower and freshen up, change out of these clothes.'

He smiled at her. 'Okay. Take your time. Then maybe we could go for a walk this afternoon, now that the rain's cleared. Bit of fresh air would probably be good for both of us.'

She nodded, her focus not on what he was saying but on what he might be hiding.

Upstairs, she closed the door and dashed over to the bed, reaching under the mattress and pulling out the envelope. It was very ordinary, didn't look special in any way, but she clasped it to her chest like it was treasure. She hurried into the bathroom, locked the door and knelt on the floor, shaking out the contents. There was a white envelope with 'Marriage Certificate' printed on the front. She pulled out the crisp document, recognising it as the one they'd signed. A second envelope was more battered, older, and the document inside had been handled a few times, judging by the folds and the dog-eared corners.

When she pulled out the contents, she realised there were two pieces of paper, one folded into the other. She pulled them apart and laid them on the floor, her heart pounding as she started reading. The first one was Dan's birth certificate and it took her a moment to work out what was puzzling her before it clicked. The surname. His mother's maiden name was Watson and that was the name Chloe knew her by as a patient: Alma Watson. She'd assumed his father must be Marsden and Dan had kept his surname after his parents had divorced, but his father's surname was Romano. She studied the second document, and everything became clear. It was a certificate confirming that Dan's surname had been changed to Marsden by deed poll just over six years ago.

The thump of footsteps coming up the stairs made her jump up and turn on the shower before checking that she'd actually locked the door.

Dan had changed his name six years ago. *Why would he do that? And why didn't he tell me?*

The bedroom door opened, footsteps slapping across the tiled floor. 'You all right, Chloe?' He was standing right next to the door.

'Fine,' she shouted, 'I'm fine.' But her thoughts were racing and fine was the last thing she was feeling. She listened, but she didn't hear him go out of the bedroom. He was waiting for her.

CHAPTER THIRTY-THREE

After a quick shower, she opened the bathroom door to see Dan sitting on the bed in front of her. His jaw was hard, his face stern. But that wasn't what caught her attention. What made her heart flutter like a trapped bird was what he was holding in his hands: their passports and her purse.

He's been in my bag! And he was intent on making sure she didn't go anywhere, taking away any choices, any means of escape.

Panic churned in her belly. *I'm trapped.*

She stopped in the doorway, feeling vulnerable, wrapped only in a towel. *Does he know I've got the envelope? That I know his secret?* She'd pushed the envelope on top of the bathroom cabinet, to be retrieved later when she had the opportunity, and she couldn't help glancing over her shoulder, checking that it couldn't be seen. Satisfied that it was hidden, she decided that the best means of defence was attack. She turned and scowled at him.

'Why are you taking things out of my bag?' She pointed to his hands, finger jabbing the air. 'Were those going to mysteriously go missing, like my phone? Hmm?'

He put the valuables on the bed and was silent for a moment. When he looked at her there was fire in his eyes, and she could tell that he was wrestling with his temper. 'For the hundredth time, I'm just doing my best to look after you.' There was a hardness to his voice that made her shiver. 'You can't go running off again. I've got to keep you safe.'

She threw up her hands, frustration building at the back of her neck, filling her head. 'But why am I not safe, Dan? Why? You just haven't given me a sensible answer to that one, have you? All I can see is you becoming more and more controlling and paranoid about non-existent threats. And now, if you'd hidden those things—' she pointed to the pile of stuff on the bed '—I'd be a prisoner here, wouldn't I?'

He glared at her. 'I can't risk you doing something stupid... We were lucky last time, but—'

'Me, do something stupid?' she yelled, unable to contain her anger a moment longer. 'Yes, well, I'm beginning to think that marrying you might have been the most stupid thing I've ever done.'

He winced as if she'd hit him, looked down at his hands, his fingers twirling his wedding ring round his finger. Tension fizzed through the air and her chest heaved with indignation.

When he spoke, his voice was thick with emotion. 'Don't say that, babe. Please don't say that. I love you more than anything. Honestly I do.'

His words tore her in two, making her want to hold him and slap him at the same time. A silent scream echoed inside her head, piercing through her thoughts. *How are we ever going to make this right?* The strength was seeping out of her, the emotional tension draining all the energy from her legs, and she knew that she needed to sit down before she fell over. She shivered and leant against the wall, pulling the towel tighter round her body.

'I don't want to fight,' he murmured. 'I really don't.' His eyes met hers, beseeching. 'Why won't you stop asking questions and let me look after you?'

'I don't need looking after!' she snapped, her hands bunching the towel closer to her chest. 'That's not why I married you. I don't need a bloody security officer!'

His eyes dropped to the pile of possessions on the duvet and she could see his lips moving as if he was working out what to say.

Obviously, he'd come up here to hide her things. Then it occurred to her that he'd probably tried to hide them with the rest of his valuables. In the envelope. Which she'd taken.

An angry silence filled the air, pressing her against the wall. *Christ! He knows.*

His eyes met hers and she couldn't look away, could feel him searching her face for the truth. She'd always been a terrible liar, her face too expressive, and she could feel her resolve starting to crumble under his steady gaze.

'I think you have something of mine,' he said eventually, anger thrumming in his voice.

He stood, and she started to shake, her voice wavering as he stepped closer.

'What are you hiding, Dan? Why did you change your name six years ago? Coming to Spain… that was you running away from something, wasn't it?'

Her wet hair dripped down her back and her teeth started to chatter but she couldn't move, couldn't think about getting dressed until he'd given her an answer.

He stopped, and she noticed the movement of his hands, clenched by his sides. She slid a step along the wall, closer to the doorway of the bathroom.

'Goddammit!'

She jumped, startled by his shout. 'Tell me, Dan. Tell me everything. Otherwise we're finished. This is over.' She moved a step further away, pulled her towel even tighter round her body, her shivering uncontrollable now. 'Because if you don't tell me, it means you don't trust me, and without trust, what have we really got?'

He gazed at her for a long moment then nodded, his lips the thinnest of lines. 'Okay. If that's what you want, I'll tell you.' He went and sat on the bed. She couldn't move. He stared at her while she shivered. 'Why don't you get dressed?'

She scurried past him to the wardrobe and flung on the first clothes she could find, somehow embarrassed by her nakedness and the knowledge that he was watching her. A couple of minutes later, she was dressed and feeling more comfortable, though her teeth still chattered. She pulled a fleece over her sweatshirt, zipped it up to the neck and gave her hair a quick towel dry, all the time wondering if she actually wanted to know what his secret was, whether the knowledge would draw a line under their relationship forever.

He beckoned to her, patting the bed next to him, and she hesitated a moment, deciding instead to pull up the chair that stood in the corner of the room. The hurt in his eyes was clear to see and she almost relented before settling opposite him, telling herself she could move closer when she felt more comfortable. When she knew what he was hiding.

He leant forwards, elbows on his knees, hands clasped together, staring at the floor. She waited for him to speak, all the while thinking this must be something bad because he was struggling to get whatever he needed to say out of his mouth.

'Dan, you're probably overthinking things,' she murmured, the suspense creating a knot in her stomach. 'Like me and my mum. All those years I convinced myself I'd killed her, but when I talked it over with Gran, I realised my perception of the situation was all wrong. I was overwhelmed by guilt and it coloured my view of things.'

Dan huffed. 'Oh, I don't think there's any doubt about what happened with me. No doubt at all.'

'So, tell me.' She sighed into the silence, frustrated by his reticence. 'We can't move on until you do.'

She heard him swallow before he mumbled, 'I killed a man.'

Her eyelids fluttered, and her heart missed a beat. 'Sorry? What did you say?'

He ran his tongue round dry lips. 'I said, I killed a man.'

Her imagination set off at a jog, flicking terrible images through her mind. Blood and guts and scenes of horror. Lifeless, staring eyes. Battered, bleeding flesh.

She leant back and stared at him, but his eyes were downcast, his shoulders slumped.

'It was an accident,' he muttered, hands clasped together so tightly his knuckles were white. 'But I still killed him.'

Her mind latched onto the word 'accident' and it soothed her slightly. Perhaps this wasn't as bad as it sounded. Or perhaps, like her, he'd gathered a blanket of guilt around himself and worn it like a straitjacket.

'What…?' She hardly dared ask but knew she needed details. 'What happened?'

She heard him sniff and she realised he was crying, his shoulders shuddering, and her heart went out to him, her body wanting to wrap itself around him to soothe his pain. It wasn't like he was a cold-hearted killer. *Not dangerous.* And she knew the power of guilt, how it gnawed at you in the night, robbing you of sleep, gobbling up any confidence and self-esteem you might have had.

He killed a man.

The words were on repeat in her brain, going round and round, getting louder and louder. When he did eventually speak, she jumped, the sound of his voice shattering her thoughts like glass.

'He was a guy from rugby. Jason.' He stopped and took a deep breath, wiped his hands over his face. 'More of an acquaintance than a friend, if I'm honest. We'd always rubbed each other up the wrong way, something about him… Cocky, you know? He always had to be centre of attention, playing tricks on people, making them look daft. Most of the other lads took it in their stride, but I just thought he was a tosser.'

Dan's hands found each other again, clasping together as if his life depended on it.

'I didn't see him that often. We didn't play on the same team, but our teams were in the same league, so we'd play them a couple of times a year. He was bloody rough, always getting binned for fouls, bad tackles, you know, hurting people to get them off the field.'

His voice wavered, and he came to a halt, his flow of words blocked by memories.

Without thinking, she went and sat next to him, stroked his arm in encouragement, needing to know what had happened. 'Go on, you'll feel better once you've told me. Then there'll be no more secrets.'

'We'd just played against them and we were all in the pub. I'd managed to avoid him and was at the bar waiting to be served when this girl started talking to me. We were just chatting, having a bit of a joke about how long we were having to wait. Anyway, I got my round of drinks and took them outside. Next thing I know, I'm being shoved in the back, and the four pints of beer I was carrying went flying everywhere.'

She could see a sheen of sweat on his brow as he chewed at his bottom lip. Still he wouldn't look at her.

'And then…' His breath was coming fast now, like he was running. 'And then I swung round, didn't think about it, didn't know I was going to do it, you know, just instinct. And I caught him in the stomach and he went flying. There was a big group of us outside and everybody laughed. But he didn't see the funny side. He got up and his face was bright red. I knew then he was after trouble. Anyway, he started shouting at me, coming right close, his finger stabbing at me, shouting, "You keep away from my girlfriend!" He was right in my face, so close he was spraying me with spittle. So, I started backing off a bit. I didn't know who he was talking about. Then a girl came running out, shouting at him to stop being a stupid bastard – it was the girl I'd been talking to at the bar.'

He turned to look at Chloe then, pain etched on his face. 'Honestly, it was nothing, I wasn't even flirting with her or anything, but he'd got the wrong end of the stick.' He drew in a deep breath, shook his head. 'I tried to tell him, tried to say I just happened to be stood next to her at the bar, nothing more than that. But the more I spoke, the angrier he got. Anyway, he backed me against a wall and I just knew he was going to hit me, so I hit him first. He wasn't expecting it, went hurtling backwards, sort of bounced off the edge of a picnic bench and smacked onto the concrete.' He heaved in a huge breath, letting it out in a long sigh before he spoke again. 'I could tell by the noise when his head hit the floor.' He closed his eyes as if he was still looking at the scene. 'I knew he was dead.'

Chloe let the breath she'd been holding trickle out of her nose, not wanting him to realise how relieved she was. Yes, he might have killed someone, but it wasn't a cold-blooded murder.

'That sounds like an accident to me,' she said, softly.

Dan was looking at the floor, his shoulders drooping.

'Look at me, Dan.' He didn't move, and she saw that his shoulders were shaking. Slowly he turned to her, his eyes red, his cheeks tear-stained, and her heart went out to him. *What a terrible thing to have on your conscience.* 'It was self-defence. You didn't mean for that to happen.'

'Wrap it up however you like.' His voice was laced with regret. 'I punched a guy and he died. In my book, that means I killed him. And I'll always feel guilty that I took his life away.'

'But you didn't mean to kill him, did you?'

He didn't answer for a moment, then his voice was a whisper. 'I hit him so hard. Way, way harder than I needed to. I was so angry with him and it all came out in that punch, all my weight behind it. It wasn't just self-defence, I wanted to hurt him for being such a tosser, ruining the evening.'

They sat in silence for a while, both of them lost in the horror of the situation until Chloe said, 'But you weren't charged with murder. You didn't go to prison.' She said it as a statement, wanting it to be true, but she didn't know, did she? And as soon as the words were out of her mouth, she wondered if that's why he'd run away.

She thought she saw fear in his eyes.

Had he been escaping the justice system?

Is he a fugitive?

CHAPTER THIRTY-FOUR

It was a long moment, a deathly silence, before either of them spoke.

'You're shaking,' Dan said, his arm snaking round her shoulders as he pulled her close to him. 'You need to get warmed up.'

Chloe tensed. It wasn't the cold that was making her shake. It was the idea that she was holed up with a killer who was determined that she should stay. *An accident*, she reminded herself. *But he obviously lost it*, another voice in her head replied. *Excessive force. He said as much himself. What if I make him cross? What if he lashes out…?*

He pulled her closer, but she pushed away, giving him a fleeting smile, unable to catch his eye. 'You're right. How about you make us a cup of tea while I sort out my hair?' She went over to the wardrobe and opened the door, her back to him as she reached for the hairdryer. 'It'll only take a few minutes, then I'll be down.'

She busied herself with her hairbrush, smoothing out the tangles. The bed creaked as he got to his feet and she listened, waiting for his footsteps to head downstairs, hoping that he'd be distracted and leave her valuables on the bed. If she could reclaim them, then wait for her moment before he noticed…

And then what? There was a silence in her head because she didn't have the answer, no plan as yet. But at least if she had her passport, money and phone, she'd have options. Without them she was stuck.

But he didn't move. His voice cut into her thoughts. 'There's more that I need to tell you.'

She stopped for a moment, a weight settling in her stomach as she realised that her opportunity was not going to materialise. Not yet, anyway. She switched off the hairdryer and turned to look at him while she steeled herself for whatever was going to come next.

A frown clouded his face. 'Don't look so worried, babe. Nothing's changed. Honestly. I'm still the person you loved when we got married.'

She chewed her lip, worried now about angering him, causing a flare of temper.

'Can we talk downstairs?' She hugged herself. 'I really do need a hot drink or something to warm me up.'

She turned and walked towards the door, hoping that he'd follow and forget about her stuff on the bed, then she'd sneak up later and put it somewhere safe. She skittered down the stairs before he could reply and was leaning against the kitchen worktop waiting for the kettle to boil when he came down. He looked deflated. A haunted expression in his eyes that made him appear older.

'I should have told you sooner, I know I should. But I didn't think you needed to know about the past. I mean, it's gone, and there's nothing I can do to change it however much I may want to.'

Chloe looked at the floor, his words triggering feelings of guilt about her mother's death. *That's how I feel about Mum's death now, since I talked to Gran.* But Dan was directly responsible for this man's death, whereas she was only responsible by neglect. Did that make their situations any different? She thought so. Especially when it was Dan's anger that had let him down.

That could happen again, couldn't it?

'What about afterwards, Dan? I need to know the whole story. Why did you change your name and run away?'

He sighed and sat at the table while she made the tea and brought it over, sitting opposite him.

'I think I was in shock at the time. I just stood there while his girlfriend ran over to him. Someone else rang for an ambulance.

I felt… numb, weird, like I wasn't really there. My mates tried to get me to leave, but I couldn't. I didn't want to. There was a chance that he was okay, you see. And I was clinging onto that. But once the paramedics came, it was obvious that he was dead.' He sighed again, his voice weary. 'Then the police arrived, and we all got interviewed.'

He took a sip of tea, his eyes on his mug rather than Chloe. *What's he hiding?*

'And were you charged with anything?'

He shook his head slowly, cradling his mug in both hands. 'Nope.'

Do I believe that? Her mind filled with frantic questions. *How long would you get for ABH or GBH or manslaughter? Would he be out of prison by now? Has he really been working in Spain?*

She began to doubt everything he'd ever told her about the past few years and her heart started to race. *It could all be lies, couldn't it?* Then she remembered his baby in the village. So, he had been in Spain; that, at least, had been true. She clung onto the fact, telling herself it was evidence that the rest of it was the truth as well.

His eyes met hers and she wondered if he could tell what she was thinking. Could he see the doubts in her eyes, in her body language? She leant back in her chair, making a conscious effort to look relaxed, waiting for him to carry on.

'There were a lot of people to interview. A lot of drunk people. And there were so many conflicting stories of what had happened. Well, the police decided at the end of it all that it was an accident.'

'So, what? You just walked away?'

A twisted smile flashed across his face, his voice tainted with sarcasm. 'Yep. That's exactly what happened.' He grimaced. 'Except the truth is, you don't just walk away from something like that. It stays with you forever. Eats away at you. And people react in different ways.' His finger traced patterns in the wet ring that his mug had left on the table, eyes downcast. 'I went to see his parents. Apologised. And they were really lovely about it. Accepted that it was an accident. We were both drunk, a misunderstanding gone wrong – that's what his dad said anyway.'

'So, why did you change your name? Why run away?'

You don't do that unless you have something to hide, do you?

He sighed. 'Everyone has an opinion when something like that happens. Social media was buzzing with it. So many hateful comments I stopped all my accounts. But it wasn't just me it affected. Mum had problems too. People threw eggs at the house, stuffed shit through the letterbox, daubed things on the wall. Broke windows. All sorts of horrible things. It was a terrible time.'

'Couldn't the police help?'

He snorted, looked up at her at last. 'Oh, I think the police would have liked to charge me with something really, but the CPS said there wasn't enough evidence. Too many conflicting opinions to make a case in court. Six of one and half a dozen of the other. In their eyes, Jason and I were equally to blame for what happened.' He picked up the teaspoon and spun it in circles, lost in his thoughts for a moment. 'The police said all the right things about the harassment, took reports each time, but nothing happened. Nobody was caught, and we still don't know exactly who was behind it all.' He shrugged. 'Truth is, the whole of his rugby team had it in for me. It could have been any of them. Or all of them working together.'

'So, you moved away?'

'Mum's sister was living in Brighton, so she moved in with her. I was going to tough it out, but then I lost my job. I was an infant teacher at the time, and the governors decided they didn't want a guy who'd been involved in someone's death in a drunken brawl teaching little children.' He laughed, a harsh bark of a sound. 'You can't blame them for that, can you?'

'So, you went to Spain to start again?'

He nodded. 'I'd studied languages at uni, had done work experience in Spain and still had some contacts over there. I went for a holiday to start with, just to work out what I wanted to do. Then my friend Sofia, who was living in a house share with me at the time, said they needed TEFL teachers at the college where she worked, and I realised there was an opportunity.' He shrugged. 'I thought it would all blow over if I moved away.'

'So why come back?'

'Well, you know that part of the story. Mum had the fall and needed looking after. Her sister has dementia and is in care now, so Mum was on her own. I had no choice really. I wasn't going to stay long, though. Just till she was better.' His eyes met Chloe's again. 'Then I met you and my life changed.'

His hand reached for hers across the table. 'I think about Jason every single day and that's the price I pay for that moment of anger.' He shook his head. 'It won't ever happen again. I stopped drinking after that. And I saw a therapist for six months to help me with anger management. I promise you that's a lesson that I have well and truly learnt.'

She understood now why he was so anti-alcohol, and his explanation sounded very genuine. *Can I believe him? Or has he made it up to make me stay here, to give up everything in my old life?*

'I wish you'd told me before. I mean, withholding something that huge… I feel like… I feel like there's a massive part of you that you've kept hidden. Deliberately.' She gazed at him, saw the earnest expression on his face, felt his hand clasping hers – not tightly, but with that familiar gentle grip, his thumb caressing the back of her hand. 'I feel like I married someone I don't really know.'

'But you do, babe. You do know *me*. It's my past you don't know.'

'There's more, though, isn't there? There's still something you're not telling me. The move here. Telling me we can't go back, wanting to keep me safe. Is that to do with Jason's death?'

Dan closed his eyes for a moment. 'I'm… in the process of sorting it out. But if I'd told you about it, then I would have had to tell you that I'd killed someone and then…' He sighed. 'Well, who'd want to marry a killer?' He gazed at her. 'And I didn't want to frighten you.'

'But you did that just by being weird.' She could hear frustration sharpening her words and she wondered if he was playing on her sympathy, taking advantage of the caring side to her nature. She knew she was gullible like that, had been told many a time that she was a sucker for a sob story and needed to wise up. 'If you'd told me all this earlier, there wouldn't have been a problem. Our whole honeymoon has been… It's been a mess because you didn't trust me enough to tell me what was going on.' She glared at him, snatched her hand away from his. 'You still haven't told me everything, have you?'

He held up his hands in surrender. 'Okay, okay. I don't want to fight with you.' His voice was soft, laced with regret. 'I'm really sorry I've messed everything up.' His eyes glistened. 'I just thought you wouldn't want to know me if you knew the truth about my past. I wanted to put that behind me once and for all. Make a proper new start.'

Despite her better judgement, her heart went out to him and she wanted to hold him in her arms, make his pain go away. Give him some hope.

'But we can't, can we?' she found herself saying. 'Tell me what's happened. Come on. Or this relationship is going nowhere.'

She crossed her arms over her chest and waited, her leg jigging up and down under the table as a mass of emotions swirled in her chest. *What do I believe?* She really didn't know. He sounded so genuine, his story believable. She watched him carefully as he spoke, looking for tells that might give her reassurance or cause for concern.

'After it happened, my rugby team kicked me out. Then my friends sort of drifted away. There were all sorts of split loyalties, and it even got to the stage where I couldn't go into any of the local pubs. Not that I was drinking, but if I wanted to meet up with my mates, there was always someone wanting to call me out. So, my social life came to an end. Then there was all the trouble at the house.' Dan ran a hand over his hair. 'It was scary for Mum. That's why we left. But even in Brighton, there were problems. Whoever was doing it was following me. That's why I went to Spain.'

Now she was starting to understand.

'So, you think when you came back to Brighton to look after your mum, they knew somehow and started making life difficult again?'

Dan nodded. 'As soon as I met you, I started getting weird messages, saying I didn't deserve to be happy and I'd sealed my fate. Stuff like that.' His jaw clenched. 'And that's why I wanted us to come here. I thought we'd be safe while I worked out who was doing it. I thought I could protect you.'

Chloe frowned. 'So, these messages… they were threats?' Her heart skipped. He'd been right all along. She really was in danger and she hadn't believed him. *Christ!* It was a moment before she could gather her thoughts enough to speak. 'Who do you think could be doing it? Can you narrow it down?'

He shook his head.

'Well, we should stop messing about.' She tapped the table with her finger as she spoke. 'Let's go to the police.'

Dan laughed. 'It won't work. I tried that before. The police haven't got time to sort out petty crimes.'

'But this isn't petty!'

Dan shrugged. 'There's no evidence.'

'But the threats… we could show them those, couldn't we?'

Dan grimaced. 'No, because they were on my email and social media accounts. And I've deleted them now. I had to get rid of your phone, so you couldn't be traced. I did the same with mine. Nobody knows where we are, so we're safe here. As long as we don't leave a trail, we'll be fine.'

Chloe leant back in her chair, disbelief filling her brain, muffling the world around her. Dan really had been trying to protect her. But that thought was quickly contradicted by another. If he hadn't wanted them to get married so quickly, then she wouldn't have been in danger in the first place. He should have stayed away if his presence in her life put her at risk, not pull her closer. *Selfish*. She could hear her teeth grinding.

Am I still in danger? She remembered the man she thought had been spying on her in Brighton. *But there was nobody there,* she reassured herself, uncertain now if that was true.

They sat in silence, Dan fiddling with the teaspoon, caught up in his own thoughts, Chloe feeling dazed by his revelations.

As long as I'm with Dan, will I always be looking over my shoulder? Living in fear?

And then the voice in her head asked a different question.

Do I believe him?

CHAPTER THIRTY-FIVE

When Dan finally looked at her, Chloe could tell by the tremor of his chin that he was fighting back tears. There was no pretence here; his anguish was very real.

She sighed. 'It's a lot to take in.'

He stayed silent, gazing at her with red-rimmed eyes. His pain was palpable, souring the air in the room. Still, she was unsure whether to believe his version of events and longed for some time on her own, some space to get her thoughts straight. *Do something*, she told herself, unable to sit in the uncomfortable atmosphere any longer.

'I'm so tired,' she said, as she pushed back her chair. 'It's crazy to think it's affecting me already, but I honestly think this pregnancy is hammering my energy levels. I'm just… I'm going to have a bit of a nap, then we can talk some more, okay?'

He nodded, eyes following her every move.

She grabbed the rucksack that she'd taken to Brighton with her and turned, feeling a need to explain her actions. 'I've got some toiletries in here. My teeth feel disgusting.'

He made no move to stop her but watched her go, and she climbed the stairs hardly daring to breathe. She closed the bedroom door and looked at the bed, hoping that her stuff would still be there, but no, that had been wishful thinking; he'd obviously stashed it somewhere. She chewed her lip, considering where he might have hidden everything, aware that she didn't have time to look now. She found her jeans, where she'd left them on the floor earlier, her body sagging with relief when she felt the weight of her phone, still in the back pocket. *Yes!* At least she had a way to check out his story and to message for help should she need it.

The sound of footsteps trudging up the stairs made her push the phone under the bed, snatch up her toiletries bag and dash into the bathroom, just as she heard the bedroom door handle turn.

Quickly, she turned on the tap, fumbled her toothbrush and toothpaste out of the bag and started brushing her teeth, waiting to see what Dan would do. Her heart thundered in her chest. She was so confused, had no idea what to make of his confession or the fact that he genuinely believed they were in danger. It didn't seem real. She stopped brushing for a moment. *Maybe it isn't real?* Even though he'd denied it, Dan could be suffering from mental health issues brought on by the trauma. *Isn't that possible?*

She felt his presence behind her, heat radiating from his body. 'Are you feeling okay?' he said. 'I mean, do I need to get you anything special? For the baby? You know, vitamins or special foods you should be eating?'

She spat out the toothpaste, wiped her mouth on a towel and turned to him, giving him a quick smile. 'Oh, yes. Actually, I have a real craving for something sweet. Those pastries from the village shop. I don't suppose you could go and get me one, could you?'

He grimaced and shook his head. 'I'd love to, but I don't really want to leave you on your own. Maybe we could both go when you've had a sleep?'

A surge of heat flowed through her body and there was an edge to her voice. 'So, you're saying we have to go everywhere together? Is that it?'

I was right, then. I am a prisoner.

He must have seen the horror in her eyes, and after they'd stared at each other in a simmering silence for a few moments, he relented. 'Well, I don't suppose it'll take me long to jog down there and back again. Is there anything you fancy for dinner?'

'Lots of calories. And folic acid. Green vegetables.' She shrugged. 'Whatever you want to cook will be wonderful. I'm sorry, I'm so wiped out, I'm not going to be up to much today.'

'Hey, it's fine. You've had a long journey and I know… well, it's all a bit of a shock, isn't it?' He walked towards her, folded her in his arms, and after a moment she sank into his embrace. She could feel his heart thumping steadily in his chest, the solid mass of his muscles beneath his skin. She felt safe here with him, didn't she? But then, she'd felt safe before she'd met him. Now she was worried, and as her mind went over their conversation, his confession, a little chill of fear settled at the back of her neck.

Am I always going to be afraid now I'm with Dan? Does he bring danger with him?

She closed her eyes and willed her uncertainties to go away. She wanted to be back where they had been just over a week ago, all the excitement of their love, the whirlwind romance, the wedding. She'd never imagined she could feel so happy, so filled with joy.

And now? How do I feel now?

She needed to consider that. Work out what was fact and what was fiction. And once Dan was out of the house, she'd have time to do some research, see if she could find anything online. Once she knew the truth, she could make some decisions about what to do.

'I'm going to lock the door. And don't answer it for anyone, okay?'

She nodded and got into bed, then he bent down and kissed her, a kiss so gentle and tender that it sent a glow around her body. After he'd left the room, she had to remind herself that whatever she was feeling, it was a primitive response to his pheromones and had nothing to do with common sense.

Ironically, it was his gentleness that had attracted her to him. The way he was with his mum, so caring and considerate. And he loved babies. Genuinely loved them. A quality which had a strong magnetic force as far as she was concerned, given her experience in past relationships.

She stroked her belly and wondered if she regretted anything. *How can I regret a child?* And how could she regret the love she still felt for Dan? Despite everything she now knew about him, her heart refused to waver, and for the sake of their child, she wanted to try and make this relationship work. With that thought in her mind, she fell asleep, only waking when Dan brought her a tray of tea and pastries, and she realised that her opportunity to check out his story had gone.

The rest of the day was spent quietly, watching films snuggled on the settee, while the weather turned bad again outside. Neither of them said much, both lost in their own thoughts, his story seeming more melodramatic and unlikely by the hour.

Her mind took her on a twisted journey, meandering through possibilities until she'd lost any thread of logic. She stared at him while he watched the film, trying to work out how comfortable she was going to feel living with a deluded man and a baby. That couldn't be safe, could it?

You have no evidence that he's lying, she told herself. *But he might be*, another voice said. Her head ached with the turmoil of conflicting thoughts and she knew she wouldn't sleep until she'd found out the truth.

Later, when they'd gone to bed and Dan had dropped off to sleep, she slithered her hand under the bed, where she'd stashed her phone earlier, thinking she'd slip downstairs and do some research.

But it wasn't there.

She got out of bed and lay on the floor, her arm sweeping the area where she knew she'd left it. But now there was nothing. She lay her cheek against the cold tiles while she stifled a scream of frustration. *He's taken it!*

'Chloe?' She heard the bedclothes rustle. 'Chloe?'

She wasn't quick enough, and Dan's head appeared over the side of the bed. The silvery moonlight crept through a chink in the shutters, casting an eerie shadow over his features, only one eye visible. An eye that was narrowed and definitely angry.

'For God's sake!' She flinched at the sudden volume of his voice. 'What are you doing?'

She still had one arm under the bed. It was very obvious what she was doing. Heat flared through her body, but words would not come, her imagination devoid of any excuse. She rested her forehead on the tiles, not wanting to look at him, her heart jumping up her throat with each beat.

A sudden burst of light flooded the room and her vulnerability was even more apparent as she lay on the floor in just a T-shirt. The heat of embarrassment was replaced by a tremble of fear. *Don't be stupid*, she told herself. *He's not going to hurt you.* And for a few seconds she hugged that thought as she pulled her arm out from under the bed, not daring to look at him. He was close. She could feel the smouldering presence of him behind her. Then his arms hooked underneath her, and she found herself being lifted and put back on the bed. She squeezed her eyes shut against the brightness of the light.

'Look at me,' he said, sounding like he had his teeth clenched, clearly furious. She felt his breath on her face, but still she couldn't open her eyes. *He lashes out when he's angry.* Her body shook and the bedclothes rustled as he carefully tucked the duvet around her. His hand stroked her hair.

She felt his sigh on her cheek. 'What's going on, babe? Look at me.' His fingers caressed her face. 'Please.'

It was the tone of his voice, the softness of his touch that persuaded her she wasn't in danger. But the idea that she had been,

The Honeymoon   227

that he might have hurt her, refused to go away. She swallowed, and her eyes flickered open. A mistake, she realised, when she saw the accusation in his gaze.

'What were you doing?'

She took a deep breath while her mind sorted out an excuse. 'I couldn't sleep. So, I thought I'd read my book. It's on the Kindle app on my phone, which I thought was on my bedside table. But it wasn't there. So, I thought it must have fallen off… and…' She stuttered to a halt, cheeks burning, the derision in his expression telling her that her story wasn't convincing. She desperately wanted to close her eyes, block out the sight of his anger, which bloomed in red splotches on his cheeks, but she couldn't look away. He had her trapped and she was going to have to face the consequences whether she liked it or not.

His hand scrunched the duvet, lips pressed together as if they'd been sewn shut. It was a long moment before he spoke and then it was with forced patience, a tone that told her not to argue. 'I don't know why you won't listen to me. I've told you. We can't take any risks. I can't have you using any technology, going anywhere that leaves a footprint in cyberspace, because I have no idea what this person is capable of, have no idea what spyware he's got access to, how clever he is at IT. Why can't you understand that?' His face was inches away from hers and she held her breath, a whimper stuck in her throat. 'All your accounts, your devices, are being monitored, along with mine. That's what's been happening. I'm sure of it.'

'But how?' It was obvious from the tone of her voice that she didn't believe him. She cursed the words as soon as they were out of her mouth, but she honestly didn't see how it was possible.

He grunted in frustration and she heard the ripping of cloth; the duvet cover, she presumed. *Don't wind him up*, she cautioned herself, hands pulling the duvet under her chin as if it could offer protection. *Just go along with it. For God's sake, don't make him angry.* The opportunity to do some research had gone for the moment, but that didn't mean it was gone forever. *Just deal with this for now. Get past this moment.*

They stared at each other, his face looming over hers, and she started to shake again. His expression changed then, and he sat back, rubbing his hands over his face. 'I'm sorry, I'm really sorry. I didn't mean to frighten you.'

He closed his eyes and tipped his head back. 'I've made such a hash of it all. You've got to believe me, everything has been about protecting you. But if this thing is going to go away, we have to stay off the grid.' He opened his eyes and looked at her. 'Completely off the grid. And that's both of us, okay?'

She nodded. 'Okay. Okay, I'll do it. Whatever you want.'

He carried on staring at her and she wondered if he could tell that she had no intention of doing what he asked. She had to know for sure if this was real or some weird delusion that only existed in his head.

'You'll have to trust me, babe. Know that I would never do anything to cause you harm.' His eyes narrowed. 'You do know that, don't you?'

She nodded again, too scared to speak, and swallowed her fear that he could see through her lie.

CHAPTER THIRTY-SIX

Chloe slept fitfully. Dan had a protective arm around her – it felt possessive and hot, and every time she moved, he would shift closer, hold her tighter. By the time the soft grey of dawn had started to filter through the shutters, she was wide awake and too tense to even contemplate going back to sleep.

She had a plan.

Her bladder drove her out of bed and she managed to slide out from under his arm without waking him, sitting in the bathroom for a while, relieved to be somewhere cool. What she needed above everything else was clarity. None of this second-guessing. Doing the research had to be her mission, her focus.

'Chloe? You okay?'

His voice at the door startled her and she jumped up, flushed the loo.

'I'm fine,' she called as she washed her hands, worried that he was going to be monitoring her movements from now on. Would she even have a chance to get away on her own? It was something she had to engineer, somehow.

She turned out the bathroom light and climbed back in bed, thinking she might settle now she had an idea of what she needed to do, but her stomach had other ideas, nausea bringing acid up her throat, a precursor to the inevitable morning sickness. She leapt out of bed and ran into the bathroom, just in time.

She didn't hear him come in the room, but felt him crouch beside her. 'Oh, babe, can I get you anything? Some water? Or do you need something to eat?'

She shook her head, wishing he'd just leave, not wanting him to see her like this, so vulnerable and weak. After a few minutes, he left her to it while she retched again, spitting and cursing at how helpless she felt.

When she'd finally emptied her stomach and gone back into the bedroom, he was up and dressed and she could hear him downstairs in the kitchen. Completely awake now, her only thought was food, and she dressed quickly, hurrying down the stairs to join him.

He was beating eggs when she entered the room and gave her a warm smile. 'I thought you'd be hungry.' His smile widened. 'Given that you're eating for two now.' He poured the mixture into a pan, still grinning. 'I can't tell you how excited I am that we're having a baby! I don't think it quite sunk in yesterday, but this morning…' He did a little happy dance. 'I'm going to be a dad!'

'You're already a dad,' she said, quietly, a tinge of bitterness in her voice.

The smile fell from his face. 'Oh, babe. I've told you. I was a sperm donor. That's it. Nothing more, no emotional attachment.'

Her stomach churned and she grimaced, annoyed with herself for ruining his good mood, which could have been a help to her plans.

He stopped what he was doing and gazed at her for a long moment. 'Life would be a lot easier if you could just bring yourself to believe that I'm not a liar.' He turned back to the pan and flipped the omelette, letting it cook for a minute before lifting it onto a plate and taking it to the table. 'That one's yours,' he said without looking at her, pouring the rest of the mixture into the pan for himself.

She stood behind him as he fiddled with the pan, wrapped her arms around him and lay her head on his back. 'I'm sorry, Dan. Let's forget I said that. It was stupid. And…' she hesitated for a second, 'I do believe you. Now you've explained everything to me, it makes a lot of sense.' She sighed. 'I'm glad you're happy about the baby. And I understand that you're just trying to protect me.'

He turned and stooped to kiss her, then gave her a gentle push towards the dining table. 'Eat, Mrs Marsden, before it goes cold.'

She checked the clock on the wall. Seven o'clock. *Perfect.* Now was the time to get the day moving in the right direction.

'That was lovely,' she said, when they'd finished. 'But I have an overwhelming urge for bread. You know those crusty loaves.' She closed her eyes. 'Hmm. Dipped in olive oil with a few sundried tomatoes. I can practically smell it.' She rubbed her stomach. 'I think we have a baby with Mediterranean taste buds.'

'Okay,' Dan said as he cleared the table. 'I'll go and pick up some bread and a few groceries. Got to keep my family happy.'

His smile was infectious, a reminder of how he put her at the centre of his world, something that had never happened before in Chloe's life. Even her mother hadn't been able to do that, not with Lucy and Mark to look after as well. She smiled back, hoping that whatever she found out today would help her to shelve her reservations and be completely committed to their future together.

She stood at the window and watched him walk away from the house, down the track that led to the village, then she scuttled around, making her preparations. She didn't have long. Her plan was to go to Mahón and find an internet café, where she could research to her heart's content without anyone knowing, Dan's warning about cyberspying still fresh in her mind.

For this plan to work, though, she needed money. *Where's he hidden my purse?* She scoured the house, getting more frantic by the minute as her time started to run out, but there was no sign of any of her valuables. Then she remembered the rucksack that he'd slung over a shoulder when he'd left. A weight landed in the pit of her stomach, making her stop still. *He's taken everything with him. Dammit!* It looked like he trusted her about the same extent she trusted him.

Pockets, she thought. *There's always change in pockets.*

She dashed back upstairs, searched the pockets of her jeans and gasped when she felt a folded note. *Twenty euros! Yes!* It was some of the money that her gran had lent her that she'd changed at the airport and forgotten to put in her purse. Her heart did a relieved flip while she ran back downstairs, slipped her feet into her trainers and pulled a waterproof jacket off the coat hook because it looked like it was going to rain. She tied it round her waist for now and pulled on the door handle. But the front door wouldn't budge. *Locked!*

She leant her head against the glass. If he'd locked the front door, were the patio doors locked too? As well as the windows? She screamed, her hands thumping on the door as she let her frustration out. *Use your brain*, she told herself firmly. She pushed herself upright and made a quick tour of the downstairs doors and windows to check that they were all locked. They were, except for a small window in the downstairs utility room at the back of the hall, under the stairs. *Yes!* Without waiting to wonder if she could get through a space that small, she heaved herself up on top of the washing machine and opened the window wide, poking her head out to check out the landing. Fortunately, the garden outside was at a higher level here, and with a bit of heaving and grunting, she wriggled her way through and hauled herself up onto the path that ran round the house.

Her watch told her she had to be quick. It was twenty minutes since Dan had left, and if he'd jogged down to the village, he'd be halfway back by now. She couldn't risk meeting him on the track, so she made her way through the scrubby trees and shrubs to a higher level. If she kept the sea to her right, she knew she would meet up with the road a little way out of the village. And, as an added bonus, she'd be above the treeline instead of having to navigate the forested track.

She knew that Mahon wasn't far away, only six miles if she remembered rightly. An easy walk along the road, and if she jogged, she could be there in an hour or so. She was confident she could do it, given her regular keep-fit routines, and it would mean she'd have all her money for the internet café. Initially, even when the road came into sight, she kept to the scrubland, worried that Dan might find her somehow, but after she'd rounded a couple of bends, and was confident that she was well out of sight, she slipped down onto the road where her pace picked up as she headed off to find the truth.

In the centre of town, she found a tourist information centre and they directed her to the nearest internet café, tucked in a square down by the harbour. With a cold drink and a snack at her elbow, she started her research.

She knew Dan's real name from his birth certificate and she was shocked to see the volume of newspaper reports on the subject. Not just the original incident, but his sacking from the rugby team – it turned out he'd been a semi-professional player, something he'd not told her. His comment had been he used to play a bit of rugby, but according to the reports, he'd been a rising star in the game. Until the incident ruined all that.

There were comments from the dead man's teammates about what a great guy Jason was, what a bright future he'd had in front of him, and she could imagine there would be a strong bond, a real sense of camaraderie, in a team like that. They'd all want to see justice done, even if it was done vigilante-style, and she could understand why Dan was having problems working out who was behind the threats. Then there were articles about him losing his job. As the morning wore on, she saw his whole life unravelling before her eyes. It had been front-page news in his local paper and it was understandable that they'd had to move away.

Suddenly, the computer switched itself off and she realised her time was up. But she'd got what she'd come for, and she sat back in her chair, hands covering her mouth as the tragedy of Dan's life replayed itself in her head.

He's been telling the truth.

Why was she so surprised? So shaken? She chewed at a fingernail. If he was telling the truth and his story was real, which appeared to be the case, it meant that the danger to her was real too. He hadn't been making it up, wasn't delusional or suffering some sort of breakdown. Someone wanted to cause her serious harm.

Without sight of the threats he'd received, without knowing their exact content, she couldn't be sure. But if someone had actually threatened to kill her… The thought sent a chill through her body, goosebumps standing up on her arms. She rubbed at her skin as if she could erase the thought, make it less frightening.

Why didn't he go to the police? That was the puzzle. If the threat was that serious, then surely… Then she remembered what he'd said: the police thought he was a murderer who had escaped justice and weren't sympathetic to his problems.

He didn't want me to know he'd killed a man in case it put me off marrying him. Ironic, given her own secrets, but if that was the case, he'd still chosen to put her in danger.

I love him.

The thought came from nowhere, squeezed her heart, and she knew it to be true, despite everything she now knew about him. It wasn't a rational feeling, but love never was, was it? Love existed in its own reality, a truth that had to be acknowledged rather than explained. Could she let a perceived threat tear their marriage apart before it had even begun? Or could she trust him to sort it out, while they built a new life here?

She leant on the table, her head in her hands. Nothing about the situation was palatable.

If coming here made the threat disappear, why is he locking me in the house?

There was no way she was going to live her life in a prison, only allowed out when he accompanied her. How would that play out when he was working? It would be impossible. No, she couldn't live like that. And it was obvious that Dan didn't trust her to live by his rules. How would that impact their relationship? Not to mention his temper and his violent nightmares.

I can't stay here.

Should I go back to Brighton?

Then she remembered she had nowhere to stay if she did go back, her gran having made it clear that she wanted Chloe to leave her alone for a while. She recalled the feeling that someone was watching her when she'd tried to get in her apartment. *Maybe they followed me back here? Maybe they're out there now, watching, waiting.* She winced as she bit her lip, a bead of blood tasting metallic on her tongue. Her head buzzed, her muscles tensed and she felt afraid. Properly afraid.

CHAPTER THIRTY-SEVEN

With no money left, Chloe couldn't afford a bus back to the villa, but that's where she knew she had to go. Now she was clear about the truth, or most of it, she felt she could have a different conversation with Dan. One that considered their future rather than worrying about what might have happened in the past. She also wanted to go through all the options with him, including going to the police, if he was so worried about her safety that he felt he had to lock her in the house. She had to make him see that it wasn't a workable solution. *In fact*, said the little voice in her head, *why does he think it's an okay thing to do? You haven't thought about that, have you? And what on earth is going to happen when the baby comes along?*

Her thoughts matched the rhythm of her strides. *The baby, my baby, our baby. I'm going to have a baby.*

An unexpected burst of emotion flushed through her, making her eyes prick with tears, and a lump filled her throat. She strode on, knowing that whatever else happened, she was going to do what was best for their child.

Determination lengthened her strides, and when her thoughts started to clear, and she began to notice her surroundings, she realised she'd left the town behind. To her left and below the road, trees stretched out in a shady pine forest, and to her right lay olive groves and fields, with hardly a house to be seen. The air hummed with the sound of insects, busy with the last of the year's wild flowers, which speckled the grass at the edge of the road. Birdsong echoed around the trees and she started to feel calmer about her situation. *It's all solvable*, she told herself as her fear started to fade. *Everything can be sorted. We just need to sit down and have a good heart-to-heart.*

The day was being fickle, the weather turning from grey and misty when she'd set out, to bright blue skies and blazing sun. She hadn't dressed for the heat and sweat inched down her back, trickled off her forehead, beaded on her upper lip. Her waterproof jacket was tied round her waist, creating an uncomfortable, sweaty band. Her mouth was so dry her tongue stuck to the roof of her mouth, but she hadn't thought to get a bottle of water for the journey back.

She frowned, hands on her hips as she stopped and looked up and down the road. *Did I pass a water trough?* She had a vague recollection of something at the side of the road when she'd been walking to town earlier in the day, a freshwater spring siphoned through a metal tap and into a stone bowl beneath. *It might not be too far away.* She studied her surroundings, the quietness folding around her, the sun burning the back of her neck. *Further along, nearer the village*, she decided and knew there was no alternative but to press on.

The road was quiet, with little traffic going in either direction. The heat shimmered off the tarmac and her feet throbbed in her trainers. They were new, bought for the holiday, and were slightly too small. Now they rubbed at the back of her heel and she knew there would be a blister. She stopped and wriggled her foot, trying to get it more comfortable before carrying on. That's when she heard the roar of an engine behind her. She wondered for a moment about hitching a lift, then decided that would be foolish – a woman on her own, it could be asking for trouble. She walked on.

The vehicle was getting closer, travelling fast by the sounds of it. Chloe had noticed that most cars pottered along this road at conservative speeds due to the potholes and lumps and bumps that covered the surface, the remains of slapdash repairs over the years. She frowned and turned, a scream catching in her throat as she realised the car was veering off the road and heading straight towards her. She flung herself backwards and tumbled down the embankment towards the forest, twigs and stones scratching and bruising her flesh, before she came to a halt where the land flattened out, maybe thirty feet below the road.

Her head was spinning, her body so sore she wondered if she was going to be able to get up. And who would find her down here? *My baby!* A protective hand went to her stomach as she lay still, letting the shock of the fall dissipate before she tried to move. She cursed the idiot driver for not looking where he was going. Then her brain made a connection.

Maybe he knew exactly what he was doing.

Perhaps he was trying to kill me?

She held her breath, eyes wide as she replayed the scene in her mind. There was no doubt that the car had headed straight for her. What other explanation could there be? *Oh my God, it's him!* Fear paralysed her, adrenaline pumping round her body, making her heart pound so hard she couldn't think.

A shout made her look up, and a man came skidding down the embankment towards her, bringing rocks and leaves and a landslide of dead vegetation with him. Instinctively, she wrapped her hands over her head and screwed her eyes shut as debris peppered her body. *I'm going to die.* She could hear herself whimpering.

'God, I'm so sorry,' he called, and after a moment, she heard the avalanche quieten.

He apologised?

A potential murderer wouldn't apologise. She'd got it all wrong, she realised, had allowed Dan's paranoia to colour her thoughts. Her fear turned to anger.

She opened her eyes, squinting at him as he picked his way more carefully down the final section of the slope.

'Hey, are you okay?' he said as he got closer. 'I'm so sorry. I was…' He looked at the ground and grimaced. 'I was checking my phone, hit a bump and it sent me flying towards the edge of the road.' He shook his head. 'Phew! I can't tell you how glad I am that you're okay.'

She glared at him, so livid her eyes felt like burning coals.

He frowned. 'You are okay, aren't you?' He walked the last few feet and crouched beside her. 'Can I do anything? Is something broken?' He grabbed his phone out of his pocket. 'Do I need to ring an ambulance? Or is there somebody…?'

'I'm fine,' she snapped. Her voice rasped up her throat, which was coated with dust and dirt. She spat pine needles out of her mouth before looking up at him. 'No thanks to you.'

'God, I'm so very sorry.' His eyes pleaded for forgiveness. 'I was in a rush, you see. Supposed to be meeting my sister and I was late, and she gets really narky if she's kept waiting and I…' He grimaced again, clearly mortified. 'You don't need to know all that. It's not an excuse.'

Being a physiotherapist, it was second nature for Chloe to run through her musculoskeletal system in her mind, assessing for damage. She tried to move, carefully stretching arms and legs, testing to see if everything was working properly. *Just bumps and bruises,* she thought, relieved.

She took a few deep breaths before rolling onto her side and getting onto all fours, before sitting back on her heels. The world span and she swayed for a few moments before everything came to a halt and her eyes were able to focus again.

The realisation that she could have died sent a tremor through her body and she rocked on her heels as another wave of dizziness passed over her. Not only was she shaken, she was also dehydrated, and she wondered how she was going to get back to the house in this state. She held her stomach. *Please be okay.* Tears threatened, and she pressed her lips together, pinched the bridge of her nose to try and keep them at bay. No way was she going to break down in front of this tosser.

'I've got some water in the car if you want to wash the dirt out of your mouth.' He pointed to their left, up the slope. 'I think if we go this way, the embankment is a little easier to climb.'

She nodded, spitting more pine needles on to the ground, her mouth gritty and dry. Water would be a godsend. Something clicked in her mind then, and she realised there was something familiar about him. Yes, she'd definitely seen his face before. Perhaps in one of the cafés in the village? He was obviously a holidaymaker, given his English accent.

She tried to get to her feet, but pain jabbed at the base of her spine, making her cry out and her legs buckled.

He grabbed her arm to stop her falling and she clung onto him while the pain eased off, but her legs were still shaky. She looked up the embankment. That was quite a tumble she'd taken, and it was amazing that she wasn't injured.

'You sure you're okay? Do you want me to call anyone to come and get you?'

She shook her head and straightened her spine, easing out her shoulders, moving her arms and legs to get the blood flowing. She knew she had to keep moving because if she stopped, she would seize up in no time. She gritted her teeth and let go of the man's arm.

'No bones broken, just a bit of bruising. I think I'll be fine.' She puffed out a breath as a twinge of pain stabbed at her hip. 'But if you could help me back to the road, and if I could have a drink of water…'

'No problem, that's the least I can do.' They started making their way up the slope, Chloe having to stop and take a breather every few steps as she fought against the pain of her bruises.

'Tell you what,' he said while he was waiting for her to be ready for the final push, 'can I give you a lift? We're obviously going the same way.'

She looked at him, unsure for a moment, Dan's words about safety and danger echoing in her mind. *If he'd wanted to kill me, he's had his chance,* she thought, deciding that she was sounding as paranoid as Dan now. She chewed her lip. In all honesty, she was in no state to walk anywhere, and with no money or phone, getting a lift was the only way for her to get back to the house. 'That would be great, thank you.' She gave him a proper smile. 'It's not far, is it?'

'No, not far at all. Only take a few minutes. Honestly, I'm so sorry.' He put a hand to his forehead. 'Phew, I think I'm a bit shaken up myself after that.'

A few minutes later, they were back on the road beside his car. Chloe leant over with her hands on her thighs, stretching out her back, glad that she wasn't going to have to walk any further. What she needed was a hot bath and a good, long rest.

He opened the passenger door and she sank into the seat, leant back and closed her eyes. *Bloody hell, that's sore,* she thought, adjusting her position to see if she could ease the throbbing pain in her lower back. She could hear him rooting about in the boot of the car, humming a tuneless song.

'Here you go,' he said a few moments later, handing her a bottle of water, the top already unscrewed for her. He watched as she drank, a little smile on his lips. She took a sip and wiped her mouth, then drank deeper, relishing the coolness of the liquid in the stifling heat of the car.

He shut her door and got in the driver's seat, started the engine. But instead of setting off, he just sat there looking at her while the air con blew a welcome blast of cold air onto her legs. She drank the rest of the bottle and he held out a hand. 'I'll take that.'

Her tongue started to feel peculiar, like it was swelling, getting too big for her mouth, her eyelids so heavy she was struggling to keep them open. She frowned, her heart pounding as she tried to tell him she wasn't feeling well, but her mouth wouldn't form the words and blackness invaded her vision.

CHAPTER THIRTY-EIGHT

Chloe could feel a breeze on her skin and she shivered, her teeth chattering. She felt damp, and realised she was lying in a puddle. Her mind was fuzzy, unable to make sense of anything; she wondered, with a curious detachment, if this was a dream. There was a sound she couldn't place, a gentle chugging, vibrations thrumming through the hard floor that she was lying on. Her mind swung and swayed, her world lurching about, moving up and down and from side to side, like a crazy fairground ride. She could hear other noises now. Splashing and slapping. A spray of water landed on her cheek.

I'm on a boat? Why…? How…?

She forced her eyes to open, but everything was still black. Completely black. It took her a minute to realise she was blindfolded. *What the hell…?*

She frowned, confused. *Am I dreaming?* She tried to swallow but her saliva didn't seem to be working properly and there was something in her mouth. *A gag!* She could taste salt. Her mind was having problems working out what was happening, but it was a long way from normal, a long way from being right. Her heart raced faster.

What happened?

Last thing she remembered, she was sitting in a car and then she'd had a drink of water and then… Her body tensed. The man in the car. An image of his face loomed in her mind, a little smile on his lips. A weird sort of smile. Knowing.

Her senses flickered back to life, ignited by adrenaline. She could smell the sea. It was a small boat by the sounds of it, the slap of the waves clear to her ears now, the throb of the engine shaking through her body.

And then the final piece of knowledge fell into place. The man. She'd thought he'd looked familiar and now she knew why. She'd seen him at the hospital, waiting in the corridor. She had a good memory for faces and she was sure she was right. She'd run out of time to treat him and he'd limped off and she'd felt guilty. Was that the day she'd met Dan? She took herself back and decided that it was, remembered that he'd acted a bit weird at the time. He'd dashed off when she'd offered to organise an appointment, said he had a bus to catch and she'd felt guilty because she'd spent far too much time with Dan and his mum.

Oh my God, he was following Dan, he must have been!

There was no doubt in her mind now that the man in the car was connected to the death of the rugby guy. What was his name? Jason, that was it. The man who'd died was Jason McCarthy. Her body trembled, her mind numb now she understood her predicament. Pins and needles fizzed through her hands, which were tied together with a cable tie, her ankles as well. Her heart was pounding so fast, she thought it might explode in her chest, its beating filling her throat, shaking her whole body.

Oh my God! Dan was right all along. There'd been nothing delusional about his thinking. *If only I'd believed him.* Because, thinking about it now, the only way this man could have found them, given all the precautions that Dan had taken, was if he'd followed her when she was in Brighton.

It's all my fault. I led him here!

She cast her mind back and a memory made her groan. She'd seen him, hadn't she? When she'd been outside her apartment, locked out. There really had been someone next door behind the hedge, watching her. She'd been sure of it at the time, but when she'd looked there was nobody there. *Was that him?* It seemed likely. Then he must have been outside her gran's house, waiting to see what she would do.

Christ, I'm so stupid! Why couldn't I just trust what Dan was saying? Why couldn't I just do as I was told for once?

She grunted with frustration, writhing against her bonds, which dug into her skin, and she realised that escape was impossible. Her body shivered with the cold, fear weaving its tentacles through her mind. There was no happy ending in a situation like this. Tears wet her cheeks and her teeth bit into the gag, which was stuck in place with duct tape.

No, no, no. Stop with the negative thinking. Just stop it!

With all her writhing, the blindfold had lifted a little and she could see a sliver of night sky. Stars, loads of them. She squirmed, moving herself round to get a better idea of what was happening. There he was, standing at the back of the boat, his hand on the rudder. He was looking back the way they'd come, but she was at the wrong angle to see past him and had no idea how far they were from land. She was struggling to breathe, the gag making her choke, and she had to dredge air up through her nose.

Where is he taking me?

That was a stupid question, she decided, and one which really didn't matter. What really mattered was how she was going to escape. She tested her bonds again and knew with certainty that they were secure. But plastic could be cut. If she could only find something to cut it with. She thought about the construction of the boat, wondered if there would be anything sharp to help her. But it was a very small boat, and surely he could see her every move.

I'm going to die.

She whimpered and forced the idea to the back of her mind, where it hovered at the edge of her thoughts, taunting her.

The engine puttered to a halt, the boat rocking as the man came towards her. His shadowy form towered over her before he stepped to one side and sat on the seat behind her, behind her. She could feel his presence, the ominous size of him. Too big for her to have any chance against, that was for sure. Her mind was clearing now, the effects of whatever he'd drugged her with being swept out of her system by a new surge of adrenaline.

Play for time. That was the first thing. She needed to strike up a conversation.

She drummed her feet on the bottom of the boat, gasping and spluttering in an effort to make him remove the gag. That would be a win, for starters, she decided; if she could breathe properly, then surely the frenzy of panic would start to calm, and she'd be able to think. She whipped her head from side to side and the blindfold edged further up her forehead, revealing a bigger slice of sky, which see-sawed as her movements made the boat rock.

A hand on her hair.

She flinched, eyes wide as the blindfold was yanked from her head, chunks of hair ripped from her scalp with it, making her scream against the gag.

'Calm down, Chloe! For fuck's sake, just calm down.' His voice was that of a parent telling off a naughty child. 'You're going to have us both in the water if you carry on like this.'

She rolled her eyes, coughing and choking. Her wrists were bound so tightly together that she'd lost most of the feeling in her hands. She clawed at her mouth, and after watching her for a few moments, he leant down and ripped off the duct tape then untied the gag, letting it fall to the bottom of the boat.

She started screaming and he laughed, his head looming over her.

'There's nobody to hear you out here, you daft bitch. Nobody at all. Go on, knock yourself out.'

Save your energy, she counselled herself. *Dialogue, remember. Make a connection.* But it was difficult with him sat behind her. Somehow, she had to move, or get him to.

'I know who you are,' she said. 'You're a friend of Jason McCarthy, aren't you?'

'Ooh, clever, I like that you worked that out.' There was a sneer in his voice, an edge of bitterness. 'He told you, then? Told you that he's a killer?'

Chloe was quiet for a moment, choosing her words. The last thing she needed was a confrontation with this man. What she had to do was try and get them on the same side. 'I had no idea until yesterday. No idea at all. Can you believe that? I married the man without knowing what he was capable of.'

He got up and stepped around her, sitting at the other end of the boat now, staring at her, his elbows resting on his knees, hands cupping his chin. 'Hmm, interesting. So, you're having second thoughts now, are you? Wishing you hadn't been in a such a rush to tie the knot, eh?'

She nodded. 'You could say that.'

He sighed. 'Such a shame that you got yourself mixed up with him because you seem like a nice girl. From what I've seen anyway. Dutiful, committed and loyal. I admire those qualities in you, I really do.'

There was a strange gleam in his eye, a distant look, almost as if he wasn't really present.

'Don't hurt me. Please don't hurt me.' The words burst out of her and she cringed. *Begging's not going to work with a man like him, is it?*

'It's not you I want to hurt, Chloe. It's that husband of yours. He's the one who needs to feel the pain.' The man's hands bunched into fists, his teeth clenched. 'Losing someone you loved through no fault of your own... the suffering never goes away, you see. He's been able to move on with his life, but me? I'm stuck in the deepest, darkest hell.' He nodded. 'It's a place he needs to experience, because it just doesn't seem fair to me. That he gets to have a future and I don't. He's the killer. He's the one that did wrong, but I'm the one who's suffering.' His hands covered his face for a moment and his shoulders shook.

She could hear his sobs, feel them rocking the boat, his emotion so raw, so visceral she could almost taste it.

He sniffed and after a moment started talking again, his voice loaded with regret. 'Jason wasn't just my friend. We were business partners. Or about to be. He was going to invest fifty grand so we could expand. I'd already signed the lease on new premises, ordered the new equipment. Then when he died...' He shook his head, jaw working from side to side. 'When your husband killed him...' He glared at Chloe and his voice took on a mean edge that made her insides turn to jelly. 'Well, it all went to shit, didn't it? I couldn't afford the commitment on my own, the business went bust. I lost my house, my wife... my daughter. My whole life taken away from me in a fit of temper.' He nodded. 'Now that action must have a consequence, don't you see? I'm only doing to him what he did to me. An eye for an eye.'

Christ! What's he going to do? Kill me to punish Dan? Her eyes widened as the truth of the thought struck home. That's exactly what he was going to do. *Oh my God! Oh my God!*

Her breath came in little pants as she wriggled and writhed, trying to get into a sitting position, but all she managed to do was make the boat sway, startling the man from his sorrow. He glared at her, lips pressed together.

'For fuck's sake, will you stop doing that?' He stepped towards her, his eyes locked on hers for a second before he raised his hand and slapped her face so hard her head bounced against the side of the boat. She cried out, tears springing to her eyes. His face loomed in front of her, inches away, his spittle sprinkling her cheek. 'Just stop it, you stupid bitch. Understand?'

She stilled, and the rocking motion of the boat gradually lessened until it came to a halt. The sea was calm, she realised, the night perfectly clear, and now she could see the moon, almost full.

'Right. Let's get on with this, shall we?'

'No, no, you don't have to do this. There must be another way.' She was tripping over her words, hardly able to get them out fast enough. 'I'm innocent, I've done nothing. If you kill me, then you're as bad as him, aren't you? It'll be on your conscience forever.'

She wracked her brain to find his name, but realised she didn't know it.

'Please, I know it's been hard for you, losing your friend and family, but the future will be even harder with the death of an innocent person on your hands.'

He laughed then, a sound devoid of joy. 'Oh, you've got it so wrong, Chloe. Just because you want to live, it doesn't mean that I do. I'm not sure I want to go on.' He nodded, his eyes glistening in the moonlight. 'Grief consumes you, eats away at you. You can grieve for losing a life you had, just as much as you can grieve for a person. I can never get back what I had. Never. I'm not sure I've much left to live for.'

'Oh, don't say that. There's always hope, always a reason for carrying on.'

She was shaking now, her fear threatening to burst out of her in a fit of sobbing. *Is he going to kill both of us? Is this a murder–suicide thing? One final righteous blaze of glory?* Her heart clenched at the thought, forgetting its rhythm for a moment. Tears trickled down her cheeks as she gulped in air.

He sneered at her. 'What would you know about it, eh?'

'I know about grief. My mum died.'

'Oh yeah?' He shook his head, his expression derisive. 'Let me tell you, all grief isn't equal. It's not. When someone has been taken from you, it's a different thing. Especially if the justice system is fucking useless. He should be in prison now, that husband of yours.' He stabbed the air with his finger, emphasising his words. 'That's the very least that should have happened.'

She nodded, vigorously, her voice loaded with tears. 'I can see why you'd think that. But none of it's my fault, is it? And is it really justice to kill an innocent woman? Is that what your friend would have wanted?' She watched his expression change, a frown creasing his brow, and she knew she'd made him think.

Can I do this? Can I change his mind?

CHAPTER THIRTY-NINE

The man stood up, pulled his phone out of his pocket and pointed it at her. 'I want you to stop talking. Now. Just shut up!' He took a picture, scrolled, then tapped at his screen and put the phone to his ear.

'Dan, is that you?' His eyes never left Chloe's face, the moonlight making them gleam in a way that sent another flush of adrenaline through her bloodstream. 'I just sent you a picture of your lovely bride.'

Chloe's breath started to come faster, her chest tight with panic. *How on earth does he have Dan's number? He changed his SIM card only yesterday. Maybe he's pretending it's Dan to scare me?* But what would be the point of that? It didn't make sense.

Her teeth chattered, and when she saw that little smile creep across the man's lips, she knew that whatever was in his mind, he was enjoying seeing his plans come to fruition.

'I have someone here who'd like to say hello.' He leant forwards and held the phone towards her. 'Chloe, why don't you say something to your wonderful husband.'

'Chloe?' Dan sounded puzzled. 'Chloe, where are you?'

'Dan, it's a friend of Jason McCarthy. His business partner. He's kidnapped me. I'm in a—'

The man snatched the phone away and put it back to his ear. 'Tell you what, let's do this on speakerphone, then we can all have a proper conversation.'

'Liam?' Dan was quiet for a moment. 'Liam Bowden?' He sounded confused, incredulous. 'It's been you all along?'

Liam laughed. 'That's right, Dan. Well done. You remember me, then?'

'Of course I remember you. I remember all of your team.' Dan's voice sounded high-pitched, frantic. 'Don't you hurt her. She's got nothing to do with this. Nothing. This is between you and me.'

'I told you, Dan. I told you what would happen if you married her, didn't I?' Liam nodded, his voice strangely calm. 'But you chose to ignore it.'

'I didn't know it was you sending those messages, and anyway… Look, I know how upset the team was when Jason died, but—'

'Upset?' Liam snarled. 'Upset! You don't know the half of it, you bastard. And Jason was killed. Murdered. By you!'

Chloe tensed as Liam worked himself into even more of a rage. The boat rocked with his movements, his spittle sparkling in the moonlight as he forced the words from his mouth.

'I'm sorry, I'm sorry.' Dan's breath rattled down the phone. 'Look, Liam, we've known each other for years—'

'Oh, shut up, will you!' Liam snapped. 'Don't try your social worker, bereavement counsellor chat with me. I know what happened.'

'You weren't there, Liam.'

'No, but I should have been.' Liam's fist slammed onto the seat. 'If I hadn't been done for drink-driving, it would have been me on the team instead of Jason. If I hadn't been so stupid, none of this would have happened and he'd still be alive.' He put his fist to his forehead. 'I'd have a business and a family and a home and a friend instead of this… this nothingness. But every day that I wake up, I'm tortured by the idea that you haven't been punished for what you did.'

Chloe understood then. Liam blamed himself for his business partner's death, and he had been dealing with his guilt by hounding Dan for all these years. That put a different spin on things and she had to reconsider how she might distract him, change his mind.

Her body convulsed with shivers, which rattled through her teeth. Her wrists throbbed where her bindings had been pulled too tight, her feet and hands numb with the cold.

'Oh, but I have been punished,' she heard Dan say. 'You saw to that. I lost my job, my friends, my place on the team. I lost all of that. I lost the life I had, too. I even moved away to another country, started again.'

'Oh, boohoo!' Liam's face contorted into a mask of hatred that sent a fresh chill through Chloe's body. 'You think that pays for what you did?'

It struck her then that Liam was completely focused on revenge. There was no arguing with him, no way she going to be able to talk her way out of this situation. *Is Dan going to manage to calm him down?* She really didn't think so. *Nobody's coming to help.* That was the bare truth of the matter. If she wanted to live, she had to work out a way to make that happen.

It's up to me.

I need to get my hands free. That was her first priority, but how? Slowly, while Liam was focused on his conversation with Dan, she started to manoeuvre her body, inching herself onto her side, where she had a better view of her surroundings.

The puddle of water she was lying in lapped around her face, making her starkly aware of Liam's plans.

He's going to throw me in.

Surely that's what he was thinking. Chloe was a strong swimmer, so being thrown into the sea was not an instant death sentence, if only she had the use of her hands and feet; but with them tied together, she would struggle to even float. No, the only way she was going to survive would be if she could cut the ties. She scanned what she could see of the bottom of the boat, under the seat behind her, but there were no sharp edges, no tools or bits of equipment that could come to her aid.

'Have you considered my offer?' she heard Dan say. 'I've got the money. I know you can't pay for someone's life, but surely if I give you everything I have, that shows how sorry I am for what happened?'

She stopped and glanced at Liam, who gave a little laugh. 'Can you hear him? Trying to buy me off.' He pointed at her and gave that knowing smile again. 'With your money, I do believe.'

Chloe gasped. So, it *had* been Dan who'd closed her bank account. *He lied to me!* She'd been saving for a deposit on a property and had managed to get over twenty thousand pounds put away. And Dan had taken it to give to Liam. How had he managed that? Then she remembered some forms that she'd signed, Dan pushing them under her nose when they were about to go out, telling her they were for an online bank account to use for household expenses. She hadn't even checked what she was signing, just did what he'd asked, trusting him completely.

Her mind raced. *He did it to keep me safe*, she reassured herself. *That's all he's bothered about.* Then another voice in her head said, *Or is it about keeping himself safe?* It felt like a betrayal of the very worst kind.

She could hardly grasp what was happening, her picture of Dan being coloured by a different brush now, one that was dark with secrets and lies. He could have gone to the police. He could have done that. But he'd chosen to deal with the situation himself, and instead of keeping Chloe from danger, he'd landed her in the middle of it. *You meet your destiny on the path you take to avoid it.* And hadn't that little bit of ancient wisdom been proved right? It had been inevitable that Liam would catch up with Dan again at some point. He'd just had to be patient and vigilant. Surely Dan must have known from the moment he met Chloe that her association with him could have dire consequences. But he'd wanted her, so he'd gone ahead with their relationship, regardless.

I've got to think about me now, she told herself. *Me and my baby. That's all that matters. And we will survive this. We will.*

'So how much is your lovely wife worth, Dan? How much?'

'I've given you my offer. Fifty thousand is what I have.'

So, he'd lied to her about money, told her he had nothing, hadn't earned enough to save while he was working in Spain. It made her wonder when Liam's threats had started. *Was that why Dan was so keen for us to get married? Why it all happened so quickly? Was it all about money?*

Her mind fizzed with confusion. It was easy to think ill of her husband, but the person to blame for it all was Liam. He was the one who'd decided that taking away her life was the only way to find justice for his losses.

Liam gazed at her, their eyes locked, and she could hardly breathe. That little smirk appeared on his face again before he spoke.

'You know what? Fifty thousand would be lovely. Let me send you my bank details. Once it's in my account, I'll ring you back, okay?'

He disconnected and looked at her. 'You know, why shouldn't I have his money? And you don't need yours anymore.'

'But you said…' She stopped herself, knowing that there was no sense trying to reason with the man. 'Look, I know I'm going in the water. But do you think I could sit up? Just lean against this seat for a few minutes? I feel so sick lying down here.' She tried to keep eye contact. 'If it's the last few minutes of my life, then please let me be a bit more comfortable. Please?'

He scowled at her. 'No. You're staying there.'

He fiddled with the phone in his hands for a few moments, then laughed. 'You know what's funny? Dan thinks that the money will be the end of it.' Moonlight glinted in his eyes. 'Stupid man. I don't really want his money. I just want to see him suffer, watch him experience a little bit of what I've been through. But just as important, I need to see justice done.' He nodded. 'What he doesn't know is that I hired this boat in his name, with a credit card that also has his name on it.'

Chloe frowned as he carried on speaking, wondering how that was possible.

He seemed to read her mind. 'Oh yes, amazing what you can get when you know the right people. Those with contacts on the dark web. Your husband will not only have lost his lovely new wife and all his money, he's going to be banged up for murder as well. Which is exactly what should have happened six years ago.'

Chloe could see the flaws in this plan but kept her mouth shut, hoping that Dan had contacted the police, that they were trying to locate Liam's phone at this very moment. The longer it took for Dan to ring back, she reasoned, the more likely it was that help was on its way.

What can I do to keep him distracted? Her mind scurried around, looking for ideas, and she blurted out the first thing that came into her head.

'But you don't look anything like Dan. They'll know it wasn't him.' Arguing was the only thing she could think of, and by the expression on his face, it wasn't the best idea she'd ever had.

'You think I'm stupid, don't you?' he snarled.

'No, no, I don't. I really don't.' She cringed as he stepped towards her, bracing herself for pain.

But he didn't strike out. Instead, he pulled a wallet from his pocket and showed her the card. 'See? And you can do everything on the internet these days.'

'Yes, but…' Her scientific mind flagged up all the reasons the police would not believe that Dan had done this – especially if he was already on the phone to them, a detail which Liam had obviously failed to consider. But also, things like fingerprints, which Liam must have sprinkled liberally about the boat. *Unless he's planning to wipe it down when he's finished with it.* But then there would be phone records to prove Dan's innocence. No, whichever way she thought about it, Liam's plan was not going to work.

'Look, don't you think Dan might be ringing the police right now?'

Liam glared at her.

'You've given him a chance to track you. Or the police anyway. As long as you have the phone, they know where you are.'

'He doesn't value your life very highly then, if he's stupid enough to do something like that.'

'I've got to tell you that our marriage has got off to a very rocky start. He's not the man I thought he was.' She hoped that by playing down her value to Dan, Liam might realise that killing her wasn't worth the risk. 'I only came back to tell him I was leaving him. We both agreed that it wasn't going to work. Too rushed. We've realised that we're not right for each other.'

He scrolled through his phone again then looked at her, eyes narrowed. 'It's not there. He's not transferred the money. Fuck him!' He stood and threw his phone into the sea before turning back to her. 'Shows what he thinks of you, then, doesn't it?'

Her heart skipped a beat. *Dan's willing to risk my life.*

CHAPTER FORTY

Without warning, Liam lurched towards her, his hands grabbing at her clothes, pulling her up. 'I told him what would happen! I told him.' She could hear the rage in his voice, see it in his face, feel it in the roughness of his grasp. His hands clutched her skin through her clothes, making her cry out. 'He's got a hard lesson to learn, when he realises that your death is down to him.' He snorted. 'That'll break him. And maybe he hasn't gone to the police. Maybe I can still get him done for your murder, eh?'

He grunted as his arms hooked under her legs and round her shoulders.

He's going to throw me in!

She writhed and screamed, the boat rocking wildly with the force of her movements. His eyes widened as gravity started to pull him this way and that, making him stagger backwards and forwards. *He's going to drop me*, she thought, hopeful, until with a final savage sway of the boat, his feet went from under him and they were falling backwards.

It seemed to happen in slow motion, her eyes noticing the sky, the Milky Way a brilliant blaze across the darkness, the silver moon, small and high. Then the shock of the cold water, stopping her breathing for a moment until she remembered her lifeguard training, from a holiday job she'd had while she was at uni. The first rule when you fell into cold water was to float on your back until your body got over the shock and your breathing sorted itself out. Otherwise, your lungs would fill with water and you'd drown. Simple as that.

Her clothes dragged her down, her arms and leg stiff and unwieldy in their bindings.

Get to the surface, she urged herself. *Come on, up, up, up!* She could hear her voice shouting in her head while she tried to keep the water out of her mouth and her nose and quell the panic that filled her chest.

Frantically, she scraped her trainers together, trying to loosen them, rid herself of their unwieldy weight. *I'm wasting time, wasting too much time*, she told herself, striking upwards, aiming for the silvery light. Her lungs were bursting, the pressure building in her ears as she fought to get to the surface. She managed to get her legs working like flippers, arms scything through the water, despite her bindings.

I'm not going to die, I'm not going to die, she told herself, in an effort to keep calm. *And neither are you, baby. We're going to get through this.* Quite how that was going to happen, she had no idea, but with Liam in the water as well, he would be distracted, and she'd have a chance.

When she thought she couldn't hold her breath any longer, she burst to the surface, coughing and spluttering as her lungs sucked in air. Adrenaline sharpened her mind, speeding up her thought processes. She scanned the water and spotted Liam grasping the side of the boat. He was trying to heave himself back in, but it was such a small, light boat and he was a big, heavy man, making the manoeuvre much harder than it would seem.

While he was distracted, she headed to the back of the boat where the propeller glistened, Liam's weight pulling it out of the water. It was the only sharp object she could think of to cut her bindings. Liam fell backwards and her heart skittered when the boat slapped back down into the water. *Is it even possible? Might there be a real danger of it slicing into me if he lets go?* But she had to try.

Because if she couldn't cut the ties, and her arms and legs stayed bound, then her hopes of survival were limited to say the least.

Come on, come on, you can do this!

Gasping with the effort, she managed to manoeuvre herself next to the propeller, but it was dipping in and out of the water as Liam tried to get back on the boat. She watched and waited until Liam paused to get his breath before she launched herself towards it, hooking her arms over the top blade and pulling down and back as hard as she could, her feet braced against the boat. Her hands sprang apart, and she gasped with relief, managing to get herself away from the rear of the boat before it crashed back into the water as Liam's grip slipped once again.

She watched for a moment as he made another attempt, calculating whether she could get her feet free, but decided that it was far too dangerous, the risks of being slashed by the blades too great. No, she'd have to manage with just her arms.

The sea was mercifully calm, and she looked around, trying to work out where the nearest land might be, and how far she was from safety. She spotted the horizon, wavy with the outline of the hills. Her heart thudded a little bit harder. *Way too far.* The effort of keeping herself afloat was pulling at her body, threatening to take her under the surface, and just for a moment, numb with the cold and weak with exhaustion, she wondered if that might be the easiest solution. Just let herself slip away from the chaotic mess of her life.

I'm going to die.

The inevitability of it relaxed her shoulders, slowed her arm movements, because what was the point of being so frantic when the end result was going to be the same? *I'll just float for a minute*, she told herself. *And then... I'll let myself go.*

Everything that had happened slipped through her mind, whispering truths that she didn't want to acknowledge. *It's all my fault. What on earth would Mum make of it all? She'd be horrified.*

But then she heard her mum's voice, telling her she loved her. That she just wanted her to be happy. Something she'd said to Chloe so many times over her life, when choices had to be made, backing her decision, whatever it had been.

It's all about guilt, she realised. *About how the three of us have responded to tragedies.* All of them had dealt with it in different ways, but the poisonous emotion was the common denominator, a deadly catalyst, culminating in this final showdown.

You've nothing to feel guilty about, her mum's voice told her, firmly. And she remembered the conversation with her gran, how she'd lived her life based on assumptions about what others thought, trying to make up for imaginary wrongs. She'd let guilt twist her logic and take her life away from her.

'I only want what's best for you.' That's what her mum had said to Chloe before she went on her travels all those years ago. 'You have fun while you can, don't you worry about me.'

Her feet started to sink, and her mouth filled with water. She began to splutter. *Is this it?*

If she had another chance, Chloe thought, she'd make the most of the gift of life that her mother had given her, not let other people trap her in a prison of their own negative emotions. It all seemed so clear now she was at the end. Next time she'd do things differently.

Come on, fight it! Fight it! Her mum's voice was shouting inside her head and she knew she'd be horrified at the thought of Chloe giving up. The easy way out was never the route her mum would have taken, and she'd want Chloe to be the same.

She could see the silvery surface above her and clawed her way up through the water, coughing and spluttering as she broke through, gulping in air. Once she'd got her breath back, she looked around her, assessing the situation. If she could get far enough away from the boat before Liam got himself back in, he wouldn't be able to see her, would he? Not with the lazy rise and fall of the sea, the dips providing hiding places in the dark. There was a chance of escape, and until the sea claimed her, she had to try. If not for herself, then for her baby.

She floated on her back, sculled with her arms for a moment, and watched Liam over the tops of her feet while she allowed her panic about dying to sink from her mind. She'd always felt at home in the water, loved the way it made her weightless, how it felt like flying. This was a mind game now.

I can stay afloat for hours if I can conserve my energy. Maybe the currents would take her to land. Maybe the coastguards would come looking for her. But first, she had to be sure she was safe from Liam.

He couldn't get himself back in the boat, and every time he tried to heave himself in, the little vessel dipped into the sea, filling with a bit more water, slowly sinking lower. Finally, his last effort tipped the balance and the boat disappeared from view. They were left looking at each other, no more than ten feet apart. That was when she saw the life jacket, and in an instant she found herself flailing towards it, just seconds before Liam did the same. He tried to snatch it from her, but she had it firmly in her grasp. He grabbed at her instead, and his weight started pulling them under, the life jacket no match for the weight of the two of them.

She writhed and squirmed, lashed out with her free arm, hand scraping his flesh, his face, scratching and gouging and doing whatever she had to do to get him off her. Her legs kicked, her body bucked. She was like a crocodile doing a death roll, the gift of life hers for the giving or taking.

CHAPTER FORTY-ONE

Later, with no concept of how long she'd been in the water, she began to wonder if she'd used up too much energy too soon. Land was still a long way away, although the outline of the hills was more visible on the skyline. Closer. She couldn't see any lights, but at least she had the life jacket now, keeping her buoyant. Thank goodness there had been one in the bottom of the boat; it must have flipped into the water, either when they'd first fallen out or when Liam had been trying to get back in.

She wasn't going to think about Liam, she decided, as her arms moved in a slow back crawl, bringing her closer to land with every stroke. Her priority was to get herself to safety, and the boat was long gone.

We're okay, baby, we're still okay.

Weariness pulled at her arms with every stroke, but she didn't dwell on it, filling her mind instead with the order: *left, right, left, right.* A slow but steady rhythm. People did amazing things. All the time. They pushed their bodies to the limit and beyond. Look at the guy who ran seven marathons in seven days. Or the one who swam round the UK. People did that. Ordinary people, with extraordinary determination. She could be like that. For the sake of her baby, she'd do anything.

Keeping moving meant she was staying warm. Her stomach muscles quivered with the effort of keeping her legs up, but she ignored their protests, kept lifting her arms. *Left, right, left, right.*

It took her a few moments to realise that there was a new whooshing sound filling her ears and she righted herself for a moment to look. *It might be a boat, somebody looking for me.* The foamy lines of waves breaking on the shore made her heart lurch and she set off with a new determination, lying on her front now, doing a breast stroke with her arms, just to get different muscle groups working. *I can do this! I can!* Her breath fractured into sobs as she realised the ordeal was nearly at an end and she had to stop for a moment, coughing as water filled her mouth.

Not here. Don't stop here, she told herself, turning onto her back again, a safer way to swim, although her arms would no longer go above her head, her muscles like jelly. She floated, sculling with her hands, hoping the current would do the work for her. *Be patient*, she told herself, no idea how deep the water was, where it became shallow enough for her to stand. Her energy was seriously ebbing now that the end was in sight, her legs like lead, sinking lower with every stroke... until they hit the bottom, and she realised with gasps of relief that she could stand.

Her breath sobbed out of her, but with her legs tied together, there was no way she could walk. She had to lie on her stomach and let the waves wash her onto a pebbly beach, where she clawed her way out of the water, legs dragging behind her, until she was high enough up the shore to be certain she was safe.

She lay on her side, curled up in a foetal position, her whole body shaking as she gasped and cried and laughed.

'I'm alive, Mum. Look, I did it,' she whispered into the grey of the pre-dawn. 'I bloody did it.'

Her teeth chattered, and violent shivers jerked through her. Hypothermia wasn't far away, she thought, as the urge to go to sleep tugged at her eyelids. She shook her head and pushed herself up into a sitting position, looking around her, frowning. They had explored a lot of the coastline over the last week, but this place didn't look familiar. There was a small cliff behind her and she knew there was no way she'd be getting up it. What she needed to do, and quick, was to get the bindings off her legs. She scoured the high-water line, noticing that it was speckled with litter. *There must be something I can use to cut through the ties.*

Slowly, she pushed herself backwards, checking under seaweed for anything suitable. Then her hand snagged on something sharp: a tin can. *Yes!* She leant forwards and carefully sawed at the plastic that bound her ankles together until the ties finally snapped. Her legs were free.

With her knees against her chest, she rubbed at her ankles and feet, trying to get the blood flowing again. At the moment, they were completely numb and lifeless, like blocks of wood on the end of her legs, and she knew it would be a while before she could walk anywhere. A violent shiver wracked her body, pain burning through her lifeless limbs as the blood slowly made its way through compressed veins and arteries. It was almost too much to bear, and a tear tracked down her cheek when she realised the impossibility of her situation.

It's not over yet.

She flopped onto the ground, exhausted by her efforts.

Is this it? Is this where I'm going to die?

Her eyelids drooped and she slowly succumbed to sleep.

She was woken by a whirring sound that was getting louder. She forced her eyes open and saw a helicopter coming over the headland towards her.

'Oh my God, oh my God,' she muttered as she scrambled to her feet, lurching and swaying as her limbs refused to respond to her commands, her muscles weak and shaky. It passed overhead, swung round the headland and was gone, all in a matter of seconds. Out of sight, the sound of the propellers slowly faded into the distance and she stared after it, open-mouthed, dismay filling her chest, making it hard to breathe.

They didn't see me. Nobody was coming to her rescue.

She looked up at the cliff that blocked her escape from the beach, and her knees crumpled under her as she stared after the helicopter, willing it to come back, her ears straining to pick up any sound of it. Her eyes widened. *There it is!* She tried to work out if it was real or just wishful thinking, then her head whipped round and it was coming towards her, hovering overhead. She tried to stand, but her legs were no longer working, and she fell back down, shielding her face from the downdraught while she waited. Tears ran down her cheeks and dripped off her chin. *We're safe, baby. We're safe.*

A few moments later, a man was lowered on a winch; he landed a little distance away and unclipped himself before heading in her direction. He spoke to her in Spanish and she shook her head, unable to think of a single Spanish word, her mind numb after her ordeal.

'All okay,' he said, giving her the thumbs up before he clipped her into a harness and she was winched into the helicopter. A crew member wrapped her in silver blankets before the helicopter wheeled around and headed back to Mahón, a journey that lasted only a few minutes.

She didn't remember much about it, was barely aware of being trundled into the emergency department, where she was hooked up to monitors and drips, allowing herself to finally relax and succumb to an exhausted sleep.

It was the sound of Spanish voices that woke her, and her eyes flickered open to see a doctor and nurse at the end of her bed. The doctor held a clipboard, and when she glanced up from her notes, she caught Chloe's eye. '*Hola*,' she said, smiling. 'You're awake!' Her English was perfect, with only a slight accent.

I'm safe, Chloe thought. *It's over.*

'My baby,' she said, her voice a hoarse whisper.

The doctor came and stood beside her. 'I'm pleased to say everything is looking fine. We are treating you for hypothermia and dehydration, but you'll be able to go home by the end of the day. Just another couple of hours to make sure everything has stabilised.

Chloe swallowed, trying to get saliva into her mouth.

'My husband?' she croaked. 'Does he know I'm here? Can I call him?' Then she remembered that she didn't have his number, had no way of contacting him. *What if he doesn't know where I am? But he must, mustn't he?* she reasoned. *Or how would they be searching for me?* Her thoughts scattered like leaves in an autumn gale, making no sense, flashing images into her mind that she didn't want to see.

The doctor put a hand on her shoulder. 'Don't worry. He's here. I sent him to get something to eat, but he should be back soon. Talking of food, you must be starving. Do you think you could manage something? And a hot drink?'

Chloe nodded, not really thinking about anything the doctor had said except that Dan was nearby.

After everything that had happened, she needed to see him, because only then would she really know what direction her future was going to go in. So many questions, so much that she didn't understand. Once she had answers... Her thoughts started to blur, her eyelids refused to stay open, and sleep claimed her again.

CHAPTER FORTY-TWO

Chloe's hand felt warm, pleasantly warm, and she smiled to herself as her dream spun its magic in her mind for a few moments more before fading away. She stirred in the bed, and a hand squeezed hers.

'Chloe? Are you awake?'

Her eyes opened slowly, her vision blurry with sleep, but there was no mistaking the voice. Dan gazed at her, concern in his eyes, worry lines wrinkling his brow.

She tried a smile but couldn't make it work. Something was troubling her. But she couldn't quite remember, couldn't dig the thought out of its hiding place. She ran her tongue round dry lips and edged herself into a sitting position, a headache pounding behind her eyes. She noticed a cannula in her hand, saw the drip by the bed.

'Do you need a drink?' he said, watching her closely. 'There's some water here.'

She took the plastic cup he held out to her, guzzling it down. Her eyelids felt so heavy she could hardly keep them from closing, her muscles so weary it was an effort to hold her head up. She leant back on her pillow, closed her eyes while she thought, uneasy under his scrutiny. There were things she needed to say, questions to ask, so she could understand exactly what had happened to her. She wanted to make sense of it and tuck it away somewhere, so she didn't need to think about it again.

She wiped a hand over her face.

Where to start?

She glanced at Dan and knew that things had changed between them. He even looked different now she understood that he'd lied to her, had willingly put her life at risk. *How can you believe you've fallen in love with someone you don't know?* And that thought led to another question. *Do I still love him?*

His thumb caressed the back of her hand, a movement she'd always liked, but now it annoyed her, and she slid her hand away, held the plastic cup out to him.

'I don't suppose I could have some more, could I?'

'Of course.' He refilled the cup from a jug on her bedside table. 'There you go.'

She sipped at the water while he started to talk.

'I'm so glad you're safe. I was beginning to think…' He leant forwards and looked down at his hands, which were clasped together in front of him on the bed. 'Well, the coastguards had been out, and when they found…' He sighed, and it was a moment before he carried on. 'They found Liam's body.'

She gripped the cup tighter, sending a spurt of water onto the covers.

'And that's when I thought…'

'You thought what?'

'I thought you were dead too.' His voice was thick with emotion. 'Oh, babe, you've no idea what I've been through.'

She gazed at him, astounded. *What you've been through? And I nearly died, because…* She frowned and a flash of conversation replayed in her mind, Liam talking.

'There's something…' She studied his face, looking for the truth. 'Dan, I don't understand why you didn't transfer the money. Liam said he'd let me go if you paid him, so why didn't you?'

Dan stared at her for a moment, mouth open as if he was about to speak, then his eyes slid away. 'I know how it looks…' He swallowed. 'But the police told me not to.'

The silence stretched out between them, her heart pounding as the truth began to crystallise in her mind. She cleared her throat before she spoke. 'So, when did you call the police?'

He sat back in his chair, swept an imaginary bit of something off his jeans, fiddled with his wedding ring. 'When I got back to the house and you weren't there, I thought you'd run off again like last time. I rang your gran, but she didn't know anything, said you hadn't been in touch. So then I got a taxi to the airport to see if I could find you. Asked at all the airlines, but nobody could find a record of you travelling with them.' He sighed. 'I didn't know where to look then. I walked round town, went back to the village, but nobody had seen you. So… I went back to the house.' He looked at her, face flushed, and threw up his hands. 'I was beside myself with worry, but there was nothing else I could do.'

Chloe nodded, chewed at her lip. *He's avoiding my question.* She stared at him, eyes narrowed. 'When exactly did you ring the police? I need to know.'

He shuffled in his seat, crossed his arms over his chest. 'When I got off the phone to Liam.'

A sudden rage erupted inside her, burning up her throat, surging round her body.

'What?' Her chest heaved. 'But I'd been gone for hours by then. And you'd kept telling me I wasn't safe. That he'd made threats to my life! I can't believe it took you so long.'

He reached for her hand, but she snatched it away.

'Chloe, you don't understand. I'd already negotiated terms, made him promise not to do anything.' A sheen of sweat coated his brow. 'I was going to pay him. I thought we'd done a deal a few days ago.'

'Oh yeah?' she sneered. 'So, when did you know that you hadn't?'

'When you were on the boat,' he whispered.

'Let me get this straight.' Chloe felt her head would burst with the enormity of the truth. 'You didn't get the police involved until you knew I was out in the middle of the bloody sea—' her voice was rising, getting louder '—with a lunatic who wanted to punish you by killing me?' The magnitude of what had happened, how close she'd come to death, hit home then. 'Don't you think that was just a bit bloody late?' she hissed, her teeth clamped tight.

'But… I didn't know where you were.' His eyes pleaded with her. 'For all I knew, you'd just gone walkabout.'

'And that meant I wasn't in danger?' She glared at him, incredulous. 'The whole honeymoon had been rearranged, supposedly to keep me out of danger. But I'm beginning to wonder about that. I'm beginning to wonder if money was a part of this whole thing. That you were trying not to pay him, playing a game of cat-and-mouse, thinking you could hide us and then we'd be safe. Playing games with my life.'

'Oh, babe, it wasn't like that, it wasn't.' His hands were pressed together as if in prayer. 'You've got to believe me. Honestly, I did everything I could to make sure we were safe from him. I'd worked out he was unstable, but I didn't think he'd go that far. I really didn't.' He squeezed his eyes shut, his body rocking slightly as he pleaded his case. 'I was trying to make a future for us. I thought if we came here, wound up everything in the UK, then he'd have no idea where we were, and we'd get to keep all our money. Enough for us to make a new start.'

Chloe gasped as his admission hit her. 'Oh my God! It *was* you who closed my bank account, resigned me from my job, terminated the lease on my flat.' Her face burned hot, her pulse whooshing in her ears. 'You did all that?'

He nodded and looked at the floor. She could see the blush spreading up his neck, colouring his cheeks.

It was all barefaced lies. The glimmer of hope that had been burning in her heart was snuffed out. She stared at him, unable to speak.

He chewed his lip as he looked at her. 'I was trying to do what was best for us. That's all. If you'd only done as I'd asked, if you'd stayed in the house, none of this would have happened.' His eyes glinted, his apology over.

Chloe's hands grasped at the blanket that covered her body. 'Oh, it's all my fault!' she shouted, hardly able to believe what he was saying. 'I nearly died because of something you did, and it's all my fault?' Her mouth opened and closed as she struggled to find the words to express her fury.

A nurse bustled over, looking concerned, said something in Spanish. She looked at Chloe while Dan answered.

Chloe pointed at him. 'I want him to go now.' She hoped the nurse understood and turned her back on him, curled herself under the blanket, her shoulders heaving as she struggled to hold back the sobs that threatened to burst out of her. 'Please, I don't want him here.'

The nurse spoke to him in hushed tones, and finally, she heard him get up and leave. Only then did she allow herself to cry until all her tears ran dry.

Alone with her thoughts, she had no idea what the future held, no idea what she was going to do, her anger shredding any plans she might have had, any ideas about happy families. Her life was a horrible, ugly mess, and the man who she'd thought was the love of her life was the cause of it all. He'd made her behave in a way that was alien to her. He'd made her into an animal, fighting for her life and that of her baby.

CHAPTER FORTY-THREE

A year later

Chloe woke up, confused for a moment before remembering that she was staying at her gran's house. Something she'd started to do more often since Jonah was born; the odd night here and there, giving her the chance of a break. Her tiny second-floor apartment near the hospital was not ideal with a baby – she'd rushed into renting it as soon as she'd got back from Menorca. At the time she'd had nowhere else to stay and there wasn't much else on offer. Still, it would be handy for work when she returned in a few months' time, and Jonah would go to the crèche, which was just a few hundred yards down the road.

She glanced at her phone to check the time. That's when she saw the date: it was her wedding anniversary and a day when she'd have to make a decision that she'd been avoiding. She sighed and listened, could hear the snuffles, the little mewls that told her Jonah was awake and would be wanting his feed soon.

She flopped onto her back, memories of the events that brought her to this place, this day, flowing like water into her mind, filling it with images she didn't want to see.

There was uncertainty still. There were questions she couldn't answer, because she only knew the outcome of one set of events, couldn't possibly know what might have happened if she'd made different decisions. She could see the scene so clearly, could even feel the panic that had filled her chest at the time, experience the flush of adrenaline that had sharpened her senses, allowing her a chance of survival. But the calculation was brutal. There was only one life jacket and only one of them was going to have a chance. It was her or Liam.

She had chosen her life over his. A natural reaction, and one that she couldn't regret.

Jonah's cries brought her mind back to the present. Nobody knew what had happened out there, nobody. She got to be the judge and jury of her actions, and the verdict was impossible to tie down. *He told me he wanted to die*, she reminded herself as she picked up her child and nursed him at her breast, let his tiny hands grasp her finger.

Jonah opened his eyes and gazed at her, a look that never failed to fill her heart with love and make her smile. How could she have done anything different?

A knock at the door made her jump and she turned to see it open, Janelle's face peering round. 'Thought you might be awake. I've got a cup of tea here.'

'Oh, you're a lifesaver,' Chloe said, smiling.

It's funny how things work out, she thought. If she hadn't married Dan, Janelle wouldn't have come into her life, and now she was like a mother, who helped her with all the worries of being a new mum.

Janelle sat next to her and gazed at Jonah. 'Oh, he's such a gorgeous lad. And I hadn't realised until your gran showed me some photos yesterday how like your mum he looks.'

Chloe took a sip of her tea and studied her son. She could only see Dan in him and wondered if everyone saw what they wanted to see in people. It was fair to say her gran was besotted with her great-grandchild; his arrival had given her a new lease of life, and her anger at Chloe had thankfully dissipated. Their relationship had a warmth to it again, the bad feeling between them forgiven and forgotten as Jonah made them look to the future rather than wallow in the tragedies of the past.

Today's the day.

The thought made her tense. She was meeting Dan later and she'd promised him a decision on what happened next.

'What time are you going out?' Janelle asked. 'I don't mind coming with you if that would be easier. I can always take this little fella while you and Dan have a chat.'

Chloe sighed and put her tea down, moving Jonah to the other breast. 'Thanks, Jan, but I've got to do this on my own.' She gazed at her son and realised that she would never be on her own now, a thought that filled her with warmth. Whatever decision she made, it was about the future of this little boy as much as it was about her.

Janelle got up to leave. 'We're off shopping today, and no doubt your gran's going to be dragging me into the baby shop. Is there anything you need?'

Chloe laughed. 'A few more bibs maybe, but that's about it. Honestly, this child has more clothes than he could possibly wear.'

Janelle stood. 'I'll try and control her, but you know what she's like. Loves this little fella, she does.' She looked thoughtful. 'So much better, isn't she? Since he came along. It's like she's got a reason to keep going now.'

Chloe smiled. 'Brilliant, isn't it? She's been struggling since Mum died, but she's been able to put that behind her now she's got Jonah to focus on.'

Janelle sighed. 'She's always a bit sad after you've been staying, you know. I'm sure she'd be happy to see more of you, if that's what you wanted. But it's your life, just remember that. You've got to do what's right for you and Jonah.'

Chloe nodded. 'I'm not sure I've even made a decision yet.'

'You'll know.' Janelle rubbed her shoulder. 'I'm sure you'll know. It's been a while now, hasn't it? You can't just tread water, you have to move forwards now. Do what's right for your family.'

Chloe watched Janelle walk out of the room, looked down at her son and knew that she was right.

*

It was a beautiful day, the sea sparkling, the air still and warm for the time of year. Chloe sat on a bench on the promenade, looking out to sea, oblivious to the people passing by as she waited for Dan, her decision flickering between a yes and a no. He'd been in Brighton for the past year, back living with his mum. When she'd first got home, Chloe had decided that she didn't want anything to do with him, but over time, as she chatted to Janelle and her gran, she realised that life wasn't black and white and the decision had to be more carefully considered. They were married after all. And they had a child growing in her belly, which changed her perspective.

Dan had done a lot of things wrong, but for all the right reasons. It had taken her a while to work that one out.

She had also done things that had been wrong. And in a way, her actions had been more culpable than his. It had taken her a long time to admit this, because it was always easier to blame someone else, wasn't it? Human nature.

Her decision couldn't be about who was to blame for things that had happened in the past. It had to be about what was best for her and their child in the future.

She watched Dan walk up the promenade towards her, an imposing figure, a goliath of a man, who cherished her above everything.

As he got closer, her heart started to race.

Am I ready to move on? Ready to let go of the horror of our honeymoon?

'Hey,' Dan said, a gentle smile on his face. He pulled a bunch of red roses from behind his back. 'Yeah, yeah, a cliché. Not that I think you'll be swayed by some flowers, but I love you, Chloe.' He sat beside her and took her hand. 'I love you now as much as I did on our wedding day. I know I can't make up for what happened, but I really want us to be a family. I want us to try. Can you forgive me? Please, can we try again?'

Jonah's face broke into a big smile at the sound of his father's voice and Dan leant over the pushchair, stroking a finger against his son's cheek. 'Hey little 'un.' He turned and smiled at Chloe. 'Can I take him out?'

She nodded, her heart beating so hard she was feeling a bit dizzy. 'Yes,' she said, taking the roses, their heady scent filling the air. Dan picked up their baby and cradled him gently in his arms, his eyes alight with love.

Everyone makes mistakes, she thought, *but we shouldn't have to pay for them forever.* If she was able to forgive herself for her mother's death, then surely she should try and forgive Dan? He'd been nothing but a gentleman since their honeymoon. He'd been patient. He'd let her be moody, let her rant, accepted his share of the blame. And now she had to accept her share too. If they were to move forward, she had to trust him.

'Dan, the other question…' She started to speak before she even knew what she was going to say. Her eyes stung with sudden tears. 'My answer is yes.'

He swallowed, his eyes glistening as he leant forwards to kiss her, and she let herself respond, clear in her mind that this was the right thing to do. For the sake of Jonah, she was willing to give their marriage another try.

CHAPTER FORTY-FOUR

Six weeks later

Chloe lay Jonah in his cot and covered him with his blanket, relieved that he'd fallen asleep at last. He had a cold, and a fractious night had been followed by an equally fractious morning. On top of caring for Jonah, Chloe was having to look after her gran at the moment, who was recovering from pneumonia and had become quite frail. Janelle had been called back to Ireland to look after her own mother, who'd had a stroke, so she was no longer available to help.

The strain of the extra responsibility was starting to take its toll on Chloe; it was a constant juggling act that left her feeling she wasn't looking after either of them properly. Thankfully, Dan almost passed her gran's house on the way to work, so he'd agreed to pop in on his way to and from work when he could.

Today it had all caught up with her though and she was beside herself with tiredness. She walked into the living room and grimaced. It was a tiny room, cluttered with all their stuff and in need of a good tidy up, but there was no way she had the energy to tackle it today. The apartment was definitely not working now there were three of them living there, and she knew that moving was inevitable. But it all depended on money, and that related to whether she was going back to work or not, a question that was rarely far from her mind.

Another six weeks and she'd have to return. *Too soon*, she thought, panic rising in her chest.

Marie, her boss, was pressing her for an answer. Dan was pressing her to stay at home... if that's what she wanted. He was always very careful to add that, but she knew his preference. It would be so much better if she was looking after their son, wouldn't it? Bringing him up in the way they wanted. Yes, his words were never far from her mind. And he was determined they should buy a house rather than carry on renting. Nothing but the best for his family, he kept saying, taking her out to view properties that raised her hopes, gave her dreams that she knew in her heart were unachievable.

It hadn't been easy for Dan to find a job, and while he was unemployed, they'd had to dip into their savings to make ends meet. Finally, he'd been offered a role through a charity for disadvantaged youths, where he'd been volunteering as an activities coach. It was only for six months, a pilot project, but if he could show there were real benefits to the work he was doing with the youngsters, then the organisation could apply for funding for a longer-term position. Unfortunately, his short-term contract meant that banks were unwilling to consider his income for a mortgage application and her income on its own wasn't enough. To make the dream possible, both of them would need permanent jobs.

'How about we ask your gran for a loan?' Dan had suggested a few weeks before, when they were have having a run through their finances, trying to work out a way forward that didn't involve Chloe going back to work. Dan wanted to be able to do this for her, give her the time at home with Jonah and she knew it was his attempt to make up for the horrors he'd put her through. Those experiences still felt fresh, making her more distant than she used to be, always on alert. It was a subconscious thing, something she had no control over and she hoped, in time, that she would be able to accept what had happened and put it behind her.

She'd stared at him, open-mouthed. 'What? No… I couldn't. No way could I ask her for money.' The very suggestion appalled her, the comments from Lucy never far from her mind. There was no way she'd be asking her gran for money, because that would just prove her sister right.

He'd shaken his head, frustrated. 'But it's what families do, babe. They support each other. Especially in this day and age. I'd ask Mum, but she's renting and I know she hasn't got anything to spare. But your gran, well…' He'd shrugged. 'It's got to be worth a try. I mean, we've exhausted every other avenue. It's our only hope.'

'No,' she'd said, firmly. 'No way am I asking her for money. Honestly, it would ruin our relationship and we've just got it back on track.'

'Please, Chloe. Think of Jonah. Think of that house we saw yesterday. That lovely village, perfect school. Everything we've dreamed about. And your gran could make it possible.'

Chloe had stood up, hands on her hips. 'No. No. No,' she snapped. 'And that's the end of it.' She'd left the room, hoping that the conversation was over.

The ringing of her phone brought her mind back to the present and she snatched it up from the sofa, making sure the noise hadn't disturbed Jonah before dashing to their bedroom, where her voice was least likely to wake him.

It was Dan, the chatter of people loud in the background. She pressed a finger to her ear, trying to work out what he was saying.

'Dan, I can't really hear you.'

He went quiet for a minute. 'That better?' There was a clunk, a door shutting perhaps, and then silence.

'Yes, fine.' She sat on the bed, yearning to lie down and go to sleep.

'I'm sorry, but I've got to stay for a staff meeting tonight. I forgot all about it. So I can't do your gran's tea. I'm sorry – I know I said I would, but—'

Chloe groaned. This was the last thing she wanted to hear. 'Do you have to be there?'

'It's some anti-bullying thing, new measures, so yes, I've got to be there I'm afraid.'

Chloe's shoulders slumped.

'I can pick you up on my way home,' he continued, 'so you won't have to worry about that and we can get a takeaway if you like.'

Silence. He was obviously waiting for an answer, but Chloe was so disheartened she couldn't speak.

He sighed. 'I'm sorry, babe. I know it'll mess up Jonah's routine a bit, but there's honestly no way I can do it tonight.'

She heard shouting in the background.

'Christ! I've got to go. There's a bit of a situation kicking off. See you later, babe.'

Silence. He'd gone.

She flopped backwards and lay on the bed, looking at the ceiling. Today of all days. Why did these things always crop up at the worst moment?

I'm not ready to go back to work.

The thought flashed into her mind, a certainty that she hadn't allowed herself to consider before. How would she ever do a full day's work when she felt like this? Even getting off the bed, now that she was lying down, seemed like too much of an effort. And how could she leave Jonah for all those hours? It would be like ripping off part of her body.

We can't manage if I don't work, another voice told her, and she felt the hot trickle of tears as they rolled down her face. She was paralysed with despair and exhaustion and it wasn't long before she was asleep.

Jonah's cries jolted her awake, the apartment gloomy now in the late-afternoon light. She checked her phone and saw it was almost four o'clock, time to give Jonah a quick feed, then they'd have to think about getting round to her gran's. It was a bit of a hike from the apartment, with no easy bus route, so she had no choice but to walk it, given Dan had the car and there was no spare money for a taxi.

'Nice bit of fresh air,' she said to Jonah as she bundled him into his padded outfit and tucked him in the buggy, and it was indeed a lovely crisp evening. She plodded through the streets until she reached the familiar row of Georgian terraced houses where her gran lived, the road busy with people returning from work, lights on in most of the properties.

She frowned as she turned up the path to her gran's house. It was dark, no lights, not even the flicker of the TV. A chill of unease settled on the back of her neck, and when she pushed open the front door and flicked on the light, her heart jumped up her throat, her mouth open in a silent scream as she saw the crumpled form of her gran sprawled at the foot of the stairs.

The phone was already in Chloe's hand, emergency number dialled when she crouched by her gran's side, taking in the lifeless eyes, the peculiar angle of her neck. There was no question that she was dead.

CHAPTER FORTY-FIVE

Two weeks later

The funeral was delayed to give Lucy time to get back from her trekking holiday in Nepal. It had taken a while before she could be contacted and Chloe had no intention of angering her by holding the service without her. Anyway, it had been her gran's instructions that her funeral should be held on a date when her three grandchildren and Janelle could all be there, because she wanted the solicitor to read the will after the funeral tea. She'd got it all laid out in writing and, as her sole executor, the solicitor followed her wishes to the letter.

It was a simple burial service, followed by an equally simple funeral tea, an awkward event, given that Lucy and Mark weren't talking to Chloe. They were even angrier with her after the will had been read and left straight afterwards, without saying a word.

It turned out that Chloe's gran was a wealthy woman, not only owning a house worth £1.7 million but having stocks and shares worth another couple of million as well. Together with cash reserves, her estate came to almost £5 million. Chloe had been astounded, having no idea the inheritance would be so large, and her gran had been true to her word, sharing it equally between her three grandchildren, with a small legacy for Janelle as a thank you for her companionship and care.

The cash element was to be distributed as soon as probate had been granted and taxes paid and on its own, this would allow

Chloe and Dan to buy their dream house, with still more money to come when the sale of the Brighton property was completed.

'It's karma,' Dan said, when they settled in their living room that evening. 'I know you were getting on better with your gran, but she was pretty mean to you for years, wasn't she? In the end, you've been rewarded for all the time you spent looking after her.'

Chloe sighed and shuffled in her seat, uncomfortable with the idea, her sadness still an ache in her heart. 'I know, but I understand why. And things have been different since Jonah came along. She loves… loved him to bits. You know that. He was her world and it's sad that he doesn't have anyone on my side of the family now.'

Dan slung an arm round her shoulders and pulled her close. 'Well, I think we deserve this after what we've been through, don't you? A little bit of good fortune. You don't have to work now. We can buy the house you've got your heart set on, and I can have a bit of space to think about where I want to go next in terms of career. Maybe invest some money in setting up a language school.' He shrugged. 'The pressure's off, so I'd say we must have done something right.'

Chloe snuggled against him, her eyes lingering on Jonah, who was asleep on her lap. Yes, it was sad that Gran had died, but perhaps she should look at things differently, think of the joy that her gran's gift would give them, thank her for it and enjoy the possibilities it could bring.

Funnily enough, the minute the thought popped into her head, she sensed that she was tempting fate.

That night, she woke with a start. A loud noise in the bedroom. Dan was having a nightmare, shouting at somebody again, as he paced the floor. She could see his silvery form, the moonlight streaming through a gap in the curtains. With her heart racing, she climbed out of bed, and crept over to the door so she could get out of his way should she need to. This was the first nightmare he'd had since Menorca and she'd forgotten how scary it was.

'Stupid woman!' he shouted. 'Why are you being so mean about money? Just a short-term loan so we can get a mortgage. I know you've got plenty. I know you do.' He walked forwards, his arms in front of him, moving as if he was pushing someone. 'You don't deserve her. You never did.'

Chloe was frozen in place. *Who does he think he's talking to?*

An icy hand wrapped around her heart.

He's dreaming, she told herself. *It's not real.*

But she knew.

CHAPTER FORTY-SIX

Dan was so excited at work, he'd found it hard to concentrate. Who knew the old lady was so rich? Well, he'd had an inkling, having done a bit of research and found out that Chloe's grandfather had been a stock-broker, something she'd never mentioned. Surely a stock-broker would have had some money stashed away, he'd thought at the time, and look how right he'd been. This was just what they needed. Hopefully, once they had that lovely house and he had a proper career, Chloe would be able to forgive him for everything he'd put her through. Although she'd agreed to take him back, things hadn't been the same and sometimes he wondered about her commitment. He thought she might be having second thoughts, caught a look on her face that he didn't like and it scared him.

She still doesn't trust me.

He couldn't blame her for that. An image flashed into his mind, making him shake his head to get rid of it.

It was an accident. She lost her balance, he told himself as he parked the car outside the apartment block.

He should have felt sorry. Should have felt remorse, but it was exactly the same as when he'd hit Jason. He felt relieved that a problem had been solved, a bully had gone away and now he and Chloe could have the life they'd dreamed about.

He smiled to himself as he walked up the stairs to their apartment, anticipation swirling in his belly. He'd put in an offer for the house Chloe had set her heart on and it had been accepted.

He couldn't wait to tell her. She was going to be so delighted. Perhaps now she would find it in her heart to forget the past and their relationship would get back to where it had been before their honeymoon.

He put the key in the lock. Or at least he tried to, but it wouldn't go in. He peered at the keyhole, checked his keyring to make sure he'd got the right key, then tried again. Still it wouldn't work. He frowned. *Bloody stupid thing.* He'd have to have a look at that later, but he had no patience to mess about now. He rang the doorbell, and waited for Chloe to come and open the door. A few minutes later, he was still standing there, waiting. He leant on the doorbell for a little while, thinking she must be asleep and hadn't heard him, but still there was no answer. He frowned. *What is going on?*

He bent and peered at the lock and that's when he noticed the scratches on the wood, saw how shiny the metal was. *It's new. She's changed the lock.* He leant against the wall, confused. He ran a hand through his hair, annoyance tightening his jaw as he thought. *Perhaps she went out and lost her keys, decided to get a new lock fitted?* That made sense, he decided, but it would have been handy if she'd told him. The shine had gone off his day now. He was tired and hungry and just wanted to sit on the sofa with his son and relax.

It was odd for Chloe to not be at home, though.

Perhaps something's happened to Jonah! That thought terrified him. His son was the most important person in his life, if he was being honest. That little boy had stolen his heart and if anything happened to him… He could feel himself welling up and pinched the bridge of his nose. He couldn't get the thought out of his head, unable to see another reason why they wouldn't be at home. There was no point speculating, he decided with a sniff, that wasn't getting him anywhere.

He pulled his phone out of his pocket and rang Chloe, only to hear an announcement that her number was no longer in operation. His mouth hung open, his thoughts in turmoil for a moment.

Perhaps she was mugged, lost her handbag?

He nodded to himself. The idea horrified him, but it was the only possible answer. *So where is she?* If she'd had the locks changed, then why wouldn't she be at home? He decided she'd be at one of two places: at his mum's or at her gran's old house. But then he realised there were other places she might be. The hospital. Or the police station.

He sighed and rang his mum, but there was no answer. His mouth twisted in annoyance. He tried the hospital, but neither Chloe nor Jonah had been admitted. He wasn't going to ring the police station yet. That would be a last resort.

He thought for a moment, tapping his phone against his chin, and it dawned on him that a familiar pattern was emerging.

No, that can't be right. She wouldn't. Not when all our problems have been solved. His heart pounded in his chest, as he looked at his phone, scrolled to his banking app and checked the balance of their joint account. Zero. Everything had gone. Yes, he had his own account, but he couldn't use that because he was up to his limit on his overdraft. He had no money, just debts.

What the hell is she playing at?

He cast his mind back to the morning, wondered if there had been any signs that something was amiss. But no, he was sure everything had been normal. She'd kissed him goodbye with a smile, said she'd see him later. His head was throbbing with confusion now.

He stormed down the stairs, into the car and screeched away from the kerb. He knew where she'd be – her gran's house. Janelle was over for a few days to help clear it out and the two of them were very close these days. If Chloe was mad at him for some reason, then she'd be pouring her heart out to Janelle, he was sure of it.

Ten minutes later he pulled up outside the house, and yanked the handbrake on before getting out and slamming the door. There had to be a logical explanation, he told himself, but he was damned if he could think what it might be. His fists clenched and unclenched at his sides and he started to feel a little scared. He knew what he was capable of when he got worked up like this and he couldn't let that happen again.

The front door was open and he barged inside, careful not to look at the rusty-coloured stain on the skirting board at the bottom of the stairs.

'Chloe! Chloe!' he called as he stalked into the kitchen.

Janelle was standing by the kettle, about to make a cup of tea and she turned, a hand on her chest, looking a bit shocked. 'Christ, you scared the life out of me,' she said. 'What's got into you?'

'I'm looking for Chloe.'

Janelle shook her head. 'I haven't seen her today. In fact, I was going to pop round later. I've got a pile of stuff she needs to look through, see if she wants to keep any of it.'

Dan realised that his wife and son weren't there and the reality of the situation hit home. He leant against the worktop, head hanging between his shoulders. 'They've gone,' he mumbled. He looked up at Janelle. 'I don't know what's happening.'

Janelle's mouth dropped open and she covered it with her hands. She looked as flummoxed as he was. 'What do you mean, gone? Gone where?'

Dan sighed and walked over to the table, slumped into a chair, his head in his hands. 'She's left me.' The truth of it felt like a massive weight pushing on his back, crushing him. 'I don't know why. Everything was about to get so much better. I just… I don't understand.'

'Oh Dan… I don't know what to say.' Janelle came and sat opposite, putting two mugs of tea on the table. 'She's taken her gran's death quite hard, hasn't she? Grief does strange things to people.' She was silent for a moment. 'Maybe she just needs a bit of space.'

Dan jerked up his head. 'Space? I always gave her plenty of space. We had so much to look forward to now, with her gran's money to give us a boost.'

Janelle sipped her tea.

'She changed the locks on the flat. What's that about?'

Janelle didn't answer.

'She's emptied our account. I've literally no money.'

Janelle raised an eyebrow, but still didn't answer.

'Why is she being so vindictive? How could she do this to me?'

Janelle put her mug down and gave him a hard stare. 'Look Dan, it's probably not for me to say this but…I seem to remember you did the same thing to her.'

'What? But that was… that was different.'

Janelle was about to reply when a loud knocking at the door made them both turn.

'Who's that?' Dan scowled, Janelle's words wheedling into his mind, because she was right. And that meant… well, he wasn't sure he wanted to even consider the possibility.

'I have no idea,' Janelle said, obviously puzzled.

Dan got up, agitated. 'I've got to go. I've got to find her and make her see sense.'

He stormed down the hallway and flung open the door, to find two men standing on the step. There was something official in their demeanour, like they had a right to be there.

'Mr Daniel Marsden?' the one on the right asked.

He nodded, impatient. 'I'm sorry, I'm in a bit of a rush. Maybe some other time.' He made to push past them when the man on the right put a hand on his chest to stop him.

'I'm DS Singh and this is DC Bates.'

Dan's heart leapt into his mouth. *Oh no. Don't say there's been an accident.* He stopped. They held up their identification and DS Singh continued talking. 'We want to talk to you about the death of Jean Armitage.'

The words floated around Dan's head for a moment before he understood their meaning. Jean Armitage was Chloe's gran. 'What? Why?' His heart thrashed in his chest and he could feel beads of sweat sprouting on his forehead as he looked at his car across the road. His means of escape. 'I'm sorry, but like I said, I'm in a hurry.'

'We have new evidence that suggests she may have been murdered.'

He looked from one officer to the other, unsure what to say. *How? How can this be happening? Nobody knew. Nobody.*

'What? That's ridiculous. I've no idea what you're talking about.' His response was a moment too late. His pulse raced and his eyes latched onto his car. *Can I make a run for it?* He discounted the idea as soon as it came. No, he was going to have to bluff this one out. He'd done it before. He could do it again. 'She fell down the stairs.' He gritted his teeth. 'It was an accident. Nothing to do with me.'

The officers exchanged a glance before DS Singh replied.

'A witness has come forward with new information. We're re-examining the post-mortem results and will have to also consider exhuming the body to run some additional tests that weren't carried out during the standard post mortem. Checking for an assailant's DNA.'

DS Singh's eyes locked onto Dan, who felt the blood drain from his face.

DNA. Under her fingernails. He swallowed and knew that this was it; there was no way out for him now. He could bluster as much as he wanted, but the evidence would be there.

He remembered the day it happened. How the old woman's nails had scratched his arm as she'd tried to stop herself from falling. Chloe had noticed the scratch marks and he'd fobbed her off with an excuse at the time. It had been believable given the type of kids he worked with.

His chest felt tight. He couldn't breathe.

She's done this. Chloe. She knows.

He pushed DS Singh out of his way and the man went sprawling to the ground, while Dan made a run for it. A moment too late. He didn't see the delivery van coming down the road, until he bounced over the bonnet and lay writhing on the road.

EPILOGUE

Seven Months Later

Chloe scanned the living room, pleased with how it was shaping up. It was moving in day at last and she was excited about her beautiful new home. They'd been living with Janelle for the last seven months in her mother's house in Galway, on the west coast of Ireland and although it had been a handy bolt-hole, she was more than ready to have her own space again. With the first part of her legacy, she'd had plenty of money to make a permanent move to Ireland, as well as buy the house of her dreams and furnish it just how she wanted it.

She sat on her new sofa in the living room, a wall of glass giving her a view of the Atlantic, the restless sea reminding her of what she'd survived.

'Cup of tea?' Janelle said, as she walked into the room. 'Jonah's still asleep in his buggy. Only took twenty minutes to walk up here, so you're not far away.' She winked at Chloe. 'Can't get rid of us just yet.'

Chloe laughed. 'Cup of tea would be lovely, thanks. If you can find the kettle.'

'Grace just rang to see if you needed anything,' Janelle continued. 'So I said to bring the kids and come over. She'll be great for helping to unpack and she said she'd bring something for lunch.'

Chloe smiled. 'Brilliant. The more the merrier.' Janelle's daughter and her husband were lovely people, who Chloe regarded as friends. No, more than that. She felt that she'd been absorbed into their family since she'd been living in Ireland, with Janelle as a surrogate mother.

Eventually, she'd get a part-time job, although she had no need to work. To have no worries about money was a rare and precious gift, one that her gran had wanted to bestow on her, even if that gift had come sooner than anticipated. In reality, her gran's health had been failing fast, and who would want to die slowly? Her death had been quick, more or less instant. She wouldn't have known anything about it and for that Chloe was grateful. It didn't stop her feeling angry towards Dan, though. He took the life of someone who was precious to her and that was something she could never forgive.

When she'd realised that Dan had killed her gran, she knew she couldn't stay with him. More than that, though, he needed to be punished. She went for a shock and awe approach, so furious she wanted to lash out and hurt him as much as she possibly could. Ultimately, she'd wanted justice for her gran.

As soon as he'd gone to work that morning, she knew what she was going to do. She'd been awake all night working out the details. Her first job was to speak to Janelle and ask for her help. Then she went to talk to the police, told them everything she knew. Thankfully, they believed her and when they went through the file, they realised there was some evidence to suggest there might have been suspicious circumstances. There had been bruising on her gran's chest which they'd put down to the fall, but when they looked closer, the bruises could have been made by fingers. Given Dan's record, and the feeling that he'd escaped justice in the past, they were always going to be on her side.

What goes around, comes around, she thought as she watched the sea.

It was nothing less than he deserved and her plan had worked perfectly, giving her the satisfaction that right was on her side.

Once he was out of hospital, he was convicted of manslaughter, which he admitted to, as a way to avoid a potential murder charge. He would be out in five years and she hoped he wouldn't come looking for her and Jonah. He'd never find her, though, she'd made sure of that. She didn't exist under her previous names and Janelle lived in her mother's house, under a name he didn't know. Chloe had written to him in prison and told him that she'd left the country, posted the letter from France and suggested that's where she was planning to live. She'd left it vague enough for him to realise it would be hopeless to try and track her down.

If the worst happened and he did find her... well, she knew what she was capable of now. He didn't know that she'd killed a man with her bare hands, deliberately kept him pushed under the water until he stopped thrashing, until his hands stopped grasping for the surface.

I'm a killer.

The thought didn't worry her like she'd imagined it might. There was no guilt. In fact, she felt secure in the knowledge that she had it in her to take a life. To protect herself and Jonah, she knew she'd do it again. If Dan found her, she'd be ready.

A LETTER FROM RONA

I want to say a huge thank you for choosing to read *The Honeymoon*. If you did enjoy it, and want to keep up-to-date with all my latest releases, just sign up at the following link. Your email address will never be shared and you can unsubscribe at any time.

www.bookouture.com/rona-halsall

The inspiration for this story came when I was thinking about negative emotions and how some are so much more destructive than others. Guilt is something we all experience at one time or another and I do believe that the burden of guilt is impossible for some people to shrug off. I decided to explore this powerful emotion from different perspectives, in a setting that most of us could relate to, giving the characters dilemmas that any of us may have to face. How would we behave? And how would we live with the consequences?

I hope you loved *The Honeymoon*, and if you did, I would be very grateful if you could write a review. I'd love to hear what you think, and it makes such a difference helping new readers to discover one of my books for the first time.

I love hearing from my readers – you can get in touch on my Facebook page, through Twitter or Goodreads.

Thanks,
Rona Halsall

 @RonaHalsallAuthor
 @RonaHalsallAuth

ACKNOWLEDGEMENTS

Firstly, I would like to thank you, the reader, for choosing my book. I hope you have enjoyed the reading experience as much as I enjoyed the writing.

As always, I have to thank my wonderful agent, Hayley Steed of Madeleine Milburn Literary, TV and Film Agency, for her constant enthusiasm and support and her super speedy responses to all my stupid questions.

Massive thanks have to go to everyone at Bookouture who has had an input to the book – and there's lots of you. In particular, my fantastic editor, Isobel Akenhead, for seeing the potential of the story, when it was only half-formed in my mind and I was making it up as I went along over lunch! This one really has been a joint effort, and I love the way it has shaped up. Amazing clarity, as always, and genius little plot tweaks! And then there's Noelle Holten and Kim Nash, who are Bookouture's publicity magicians and seem to work wonders with only twenty-four hours in the day. Love you guys, for all your wizardry and motivational kicks up the bum.

Talking about motivation and support, I'd be nowhere without the back-up given by my fellow Bookouture authors – thanks for the pep talks, answers to research questions and the laughs; the author's lounge has got to be my favourite place to procrastinate! And then there's the Savvy Authors – what a generous, lovely bunch you are, and especially Tracy Buchanan, who set up the Snug, made it the best place to be and taught me so much about the nuts and bolts of being a published author. Quite an education!

Closer to home, I have to give a shout-out to my friend and first reader of early drafts, Kerry-Ann Mitchell, whose perceptive comments have helped to make this a better book. Also, her mum, Gill Mitchell, and book club friend, Sandra Henderson, for reading and giving feedback on early drafts. In fact, I need to thank all my book club buddies – Clare, Sue, Christine, Voirrey, Gemma and Jenny (not forgetting our recently departed friend, Helen) – for their unfettered enthusiasm for my books and their joy at the fact I'm now a published author.

I have to thank my family for understanding that they should not try and talk to me on certain days and at certain times. And none of this would be possible without my husband, David, who has been ignored for long periods of time during the writing of this book, but has been unfailingly enthusiastic and tolerant.

Finally, there's the dogs, Freddie and Molly, who drag me out when I don't feel like it, take me for walks on beautiful beaches and gorgeous glens and give me space to think.